Someone Like Zita

Susan Day

Someone Like Zita

Susan Day

Someone Like Zita
Copyright © Susan Day 2023
All rights reserved. The moral rights
of the author have been asserted.
Cover artwork © 1889 books

Also by Susan Day
:
Who your Friends are
Hollin Clough
The Roads they Travelled
Watershed
Back
Lostlings

www.1889books.co.uk
ISBN: 978-1-915045-18-8

Chapter One

She has not slept all night. She has not dared to sleep, for fear of not leaving in time. She has no alarm clock because her mother has always woken her, and anyway, an alarm clock would wake her parents as well as herself. She cannot go downstairs to look at the clock on the mantelpiece because they would hear her and Mum would get out of bed whatever time it was, and come downstairs in her dressing gown and ask what was going on, why was she up so early, was she ill, would she like a cup of tea? And she would escort her back to bed, and come into her room, and maybe notice the rucksack, and then what?

So she has not slept all night, but has sat on her bed, in the dark, lights off because sometimes Daddy gets up in the night and he would see the light under her door and open it to see why was she still awake, or why is she wasting electricity by not turning off her light. So she has sat in the dark, quietly. At least, it was dark at first, as she sat there, dressed except for her shoes, but her eyes have become accustomed to it and the street light makes the curtains glow orange, so she has very carefully opened the curtains – they have been her bedroom curtains since Daddy decorated her room when she was fourteen – and by the orange light she can make out most of the things in the room. Although she knows them all so well that there is no need to look; she could enumerate her possessions in her sleep if necessary.

There is her bed. It might be a poor bed with a thin and worn mattress but it is the only bed she has ever slept in, if you don't count going to a seaside boarding house two or three times as a child, and two nights in hospital having her tonsils out when she was six. The covers, however, are lavish and new: Egyptian cotton sheets and pillow cases, carefully laundered in the twin-tub every Monday morning, two wool blankets, a quilted eiderdown of different shades of pink and, folded at the end of the bed, a candlewick bedspread, white with a design of leaves and flowers in green and purple. Her pillow is thin though, barely thick enough to raise her head at all, but that is because at the age of fourteen she had been anxious about getting a double chin and had taken to sleeping with no pillow at all. This thin, limp excuse for a proper pillow is the compromise she and her mother reached back then – and it must have worked, because there is no sign on her of a double chin.

There is a dressing table, which has served her also as a desk through her school years. She could look up from her maths homework, or her geography revision and contemplate her reflection in the triple mirror, her limp dark brown hair that would neither hold a curl nor fall straight, her dark eyebrows that – she thought – made her whole face shadowy, her smile that showed a crooked front tooth that slightly crossed over the one beside it. Daddy, on several occasions, opening her door and finding her studying herself, not her books, threatened to take her mirrors away and for weeks she came home from school every day worried that he might have done it. But he never did, and maybe never intended to. She can see herself now, dimly in the glass, her face pale against the bedhead, her knees drawn up, her arms circling her legs. Not smiling now.

Underneath her bedsprings is the rucksack. She had to wait for a time when her mother was out shopping and her father was at work to go up to the attic and bring down the rucksack. That is two days ago, and she has worried ever since that her mother might come in and clean under her bed and find it, and ask questions, and discover everything. And stop her.

The attic is where her brother used to sleep before he left. When he went – almost eight years ago now – when it was clear that he wasn't going to come back she asked if she could have the attic room, which was bigger than hers, and more private, being at the top of a steep staircase. But no, it wasn't allowed. Why not? Well, he might come back after all. And it was hard work for Mummy to take the vacuum upstairs, never mind the clean sheets and the clean clothes and such. Her mother said she didn't mind that so much, but she would worry if Sally-Ann was so far away from her. What if she was ill in the night?

'I'm not going to be ill,' said Sally-Ann.

'But you don't want your mother to be worrying, do you?'

She knows – or thinks she knows – why they didn't want her up there. For her mother, it was the idea that her brother might yet come home. He might yet, whatever he had said to the contrary, be persuaded to leave his wife and their maybe baby and come back where he belonged. For her father, it was the equally unfounded and even more superstitious idea that if she, Sally-Ann, moved up to the attic, then she would also end up leaving home, and not in the good, socially acceptable, properly approved way of being given away, in a church, in a virginal long dress, by her father, to some respectable young man who would be thereafter responsible for her continuing socially acceptable place in the world. These were not, back then, thoughts she could put into words so she had sulked more than usual, and that was when her mother persuaded her father to use a week of his fortnight's holiday, when the works closed down, to redecorate her bedroom. Even during the painting and the papering she was not allowed to sleep in the attic, where there was a perfectly serviceable bed, but slept on her own mattress on the floor of her parents' room, lying there awake until they came to bed, pretending to be asleep while listening to them getting undressed and dressed again in nightclothes, settling down for the night, the springs boinging as her mother – who was the heavier – got into bed. Then the slower breathing as they relaxed into sleep and later, when her father rolled unconsciously onto his back, the snores that woke her mother and made her dig him in the ribs and tell him to 'Turn over for goodness sake. You'll wake our Sally-Ann.'

Her best friend Marion, who lived across the road and was in the same class at school, pretended to be shocked at the thought of her sharing her parents' bedroom, because what if they wanted to *do it*? 'I don't think,' Sally said, 'that there's anything like that. They're quite old you know. And my mother is quite fat.' 'So?' said Marion.

She must have closed her eyes, or even dozed off for a few minutes, because now and then her head drops forward on to her knees and she wakes without knowing she was asleep. She squints to look at her watch – it is a little gold one, very ladylike, that was her present last birthday from her parents. Until then she did not have a watch of her own but borrowed her mother's little Timex when she needed one, which was not that often. After all, in the library, there was the clock above the door, as big as the one at the railway station, ticking importantly; at home there was the alarm clock on the kitchen dresser, that her mother took upstairs every night and brought down every morning, and in the front room the eight-day clock on the mantelpiece that was wound on Sunday nights. And although she has worn her watch as was expected of her, she does not like it; it is too delicate for her, it makes her wrist look ridiculously masculine by contrast, it makes her want to sit on her hands to hide them. She would leave it behind if she could, but she reminds herself that there is a complicated journey ahead. She takes it off, and puts it on again, and squints at it in the orange darkness. It is not time to move yet, the sky has not begun to get lighter.

The rucksack will not be light either. She is worried that she will not get it down the stairs without it bumping noisily. She has wanted to do a practice run, but there was never a time when her mother was sufficiently far away to not notice. Just packing it has been an undercover operation, since she shares her mother's wardrobe space and has had to make covert visits to their bedroom to extract her clothes. She is not sure, even now, that she has packed the right things, or enough of them, or too many. Three dresses, one of them her best dress – is that too many? Or not enough? What will she be doing to need dresses? But you never know. Better to err on the cautious side. Her winter coat is at the bottom, taking up a lot of room, but she has thought it through – you never know how cold it might be, especially if, as she fears but thinks possible, there might come a time when she cannot find a bed for the night. She is not at all sure, if that happens, where she might go, but she knows enough to know that at some time she will need her winter coat.

Acquiring all the necessary bits and pieces – that has taken some thinking about too. She couldn't pack her toothbrush because its absence would be noticed, so she had to buy a new one. Likewise soap, a flannel, shampoo, a towel. Two big packets of Tampax because who knows whether she can buy them there, and if she could, what they are called. She has put in some paper and envelopes so that she can write to her parents, and to Marion, and a notebook so that she can record where she's been. Her Youth Hostel membership – not delivered to her home but to her place of work – and her pink card, one year only passport are in the most secure looking of the pockets, and her money she is intending to keep close by her, in her shoulder bag. Oh, the worry and the wondering and the planning, the lists she has made, and hidden, and finally disposed of at work where no one would suspect. And the excitement too, the secret, the deception. The letter.

'Dear Mum and Daddy,' says the letter. 'Please don't worry about me, I have gone to visit a friend. I will send you a postcard from the coast and see you again soon. Love from Sally-Ann.' It is on her dressing table, in an envelope, under a magazine so that it cannot be seen by her mother coming unexpectedly into the room. She will leave it visibly at the top of the stairs; it will slow her mother down a bit before she comes to the kitchen and finds the back door unlocked.

They will think she has gone to see Marion, who is, as far as they know, her only friend, and is working for the summer as a hairdresser at Pontin's Holiday camp in Great Yarmouth. They will wonder why she hasn't told them of her plans, they might even try to contact Marion through her mother, but they won't worry too much, not yet. She is after all, of age, almost, a grown woman, as her father repeatedly tells her, when he gets exasperated, when she is what he calls 'a noddy numbskull.'

The room is now perceptibly lighter. Then the street light switches itself off and the room is dark for a few moments. It is time to go.

She pulls out, as silently as she can, the rucksack from under the bed. She opens her door as soundlessly as possible. She puts the letter on the landing floor. She grasps the rucksack to her chest and, barefooted, descends the stairs. They are steep – but she has been up and down them a dozen times a day since she was a tiny child; she could do it in the dark, in her sleep, in her dreams. Her shoes are by the back door, she slips them on. She turns the key in the lock, she opens the door, hurrying now, trembling, and closes it behind her as gently as she can with shaking fingers. Still hugging the rucksack she goes into the yard, out into the back gennel, along to the road. The road is empty. Not even a milkman is about. Once round the corner she stops and puts the rucksack on a wall so that she can get her arms through the straps. It is heavier than she thought it would be and she staggers a little as she moves outwards.

She is away.

Chapter Two

The mother's name is Senga. Senga McHarg Grey. She comes, originally, from Dumbarton, a small bleak town on the north bank of the River Clyde and for the last twenty-nine years she has lived in England, never once going back to Scotland to see her folks, though she writes them a letter every month, and occasionally receives one back from one of her sisters. She is a big woman, taller than her husband, and heavier; heavier with flesh, and heavier with sorrow. The sorrow she tries to hide, dissemble and deny.

Her days, apart from Sundays, always begin the same way. At ten to six the alarm clock stutters and rings. Willie Grey, her husband, swears mildly, turns on his back and goes back to sleep, soon to begin snoring. Senga shrugs on her dressing gown and goes downstairs, there to brew a pot of tea and take a cup up to Willie. Then back down again to cook him a bacon and egg breakfast and get him out of the door soon after seven so that he will get to work by half past. Then she will sit down with the Daily Mirror and drink her own first cup of tea and make fresh pot before going to wake Sally-Ann. On Sundays, though, Willie gets up first and brings her a cup of tea in bed, then sets off, usually, to go fishing.

This morning, being a Wednesday, she is out of bed at ten to six, out of the bedroom and is just about to start down the stairs when she notices the envelope on the floor. Picks it up and sees her daughter's handwriting on the envelope – 'To Mum and Daddy.' She doesn't know why, but instead of opening the letter she opens the door of Sally-Ann's room, sees the empty bed, unslept in but rumpled with having been sat on, sees her dressing gown on the back of the door, her dressing-table cleared of hairbrushes and make-up – not that Sally-Ann was much of a one for make-up – feels the definite absence of her. She's gone.

If she'd thought, if she'd had time to think, she would not have reacted as she did. She should have gone downstairs, made the tea, got over the shock, then brought him his tea and told him calmly that Sally-Ann must have got up early and gone out, maybe to have a day out with a friend, it being her day off from the library. But it is too late. She has cried out in shock and alarm, and she hears Willie come out of his sleep and say, 'What? What's that?'

'Nothing, nothing,' says Senga quickly. 'I'll bring your tea.'

But he is out of bed now and standing in the doorway scratching his armpits, a skinny dog of a man with a small tattoo on his chest.

Senga hurries down the stairs and hums a tune – out of tune – to show him there is nothing to get upset about. While the kettle boils she opens the letter and reads it. It reassures her – to the extent that it might enable her to reassure Willie – that there is a reasonable explanation. Sally-Ann has gone for a day out. Where? To the coast, she says in her note. Brid probably, or Scarborough. Maybe Skegness. She'll be back tonight because hasn't she got to go to work tomorrow?

'Well,' he says, 'if that's all it is, why are you screeching out fit to wake the dead, never mind a man who's just having the last of his sleep?'

'Sorry, Willie,' she says. 'It was only the shock. I mean the surprise. She should have told us last night.'

'Seems to me,' he says, 'she hasn't spoken to us for weeks, not to say anything sensible. I've been thinking she's been acting odd.'

'Not at all,' says Senga. 'I've not noticed anything of that sort.'

'Sneaking out at night to post letters,' he says. 'I've seen her.'

'And why should she not write letters? It'll be only to Marion. Where's the harm in that?'

'Marion,' he says. 'We're supposed to believe that, are we?'

She puts his plate down in front of him and points to the time on the clock and leaves the room to go back upstairs. Sally-Ann's toothbrush is still in the bathroom, a sure sign that she will be back home by bedtime. There is nothing to get upset about. She hears Willie leave the house and feels her usual sense of relief at being on her own, in charge, free to do what she needs to do without having to explain or justify. She will get on with her day; Sally-Ann will be home by bedtime.

Sally-Ann walks away from her house without looking back. She has a superstitious feeling that if she looks behind her she will see her father running down the street after her, her mother behind him, flapping her tea towel. If she keeps her eyes steady and looking ahead, then that's where she will go. Don't look back, she repeats to herself, silently, never look back.

She skirts the edge of the Kelvin flats, passes the Infirmary and sets out east, towards the motorway and the sun. She practised this bit of the journey, on foot, the week before, on her day off, in the rain and was surprised how little time it took her. Now with the rucksack, she knows she is walking slower, and her shoes are not the best for walking, they slip off the back of her feet and she can feel the uneven paving through them; but they are the best she has and there is no going back to change them. Her old school pumps are way down in her rucksack; when she has the opportunity to stop she will put them on instead. And today it is not raining; there is a pearly haze across the sun, but no sign of cloud; it is in fact, she notices suddenly, a beautiful summer morning.

When, half an hour later, she reaches the big road that links the city to the new motorway she takes off her rucksack and stands beside it, choosing a corner where she can easily be seen and, daringly, nonchalantly, extends her arm into the road, thumb up. She has practised this as well, with Marion last summer, before she ever thought of doing what she is doing now, and more recently on her own, so as to be prepared, to leave nothing to chance. And sure enough, by the time her mother is breaking her father's egg into the frying pan, their daughter is in the cab of a lorry 'only as far as the turnoff to Chesterfield' and telling the driver that she is off to London to stay with her cousin and – to explain the rucksack – to have a camping holiday. Not that he is in the least interested; he is more interested in telling her about test cricket. He doesn't even ask her name.

Senga dresses, goes downstairs and washes up the breakfast things, sweeps the floor and tidies round. These actions are to show herself the world is still as it was – yesterday's paper still has to be picked up from where Willie has left it last night, today's paper has to be put on the table ready for him coming home. A bit of shopping has to be done, potatoes peeled for the evening meal – she decides not to cook for Sally-Ann because the waste of it if she's not back till late could make her father more angry. He's worried, that's all, she knows, and trying to hide his worry makes him bad-tempered. At least, that's how it seems to work.

She goes to Sally-Ann's room; it looks tidier than usual, no discarded clothes on the floor for her to pick up, no magazines on the bed. She looks in the drawers of the dressing table; they do look emptier than they should, looks like all her underwear has gone. She goes to her own bedroom, to the wardrobe that the three of them share. At Sally-Ann's end there are a few garments hanging – a thin jacket, a pleated skirt, a blouse she once bought and never wore – but there are more things missing than present. Dresses, a couple of skirts that should be there, and – wait a minute – her winter coat is gone. It is the middle of June. Why would she take her warm winter coat, a very sensible navy blue coat which Senga knows she bought under pressure from her and resists wearing unless it's absolutely necessary, why would she take it on a day trip to the seaside in the middle of June? She is despairing, because how will she tell her father what she suspects? What she knows. She sits down on her bed, exhausted suddenly by the drama, and angry, now that no one is there to see, angry with her daughter, angry with her son, with Willie, with anyone who has had anything to do with all of this. So angry that she twists herself sideways and beats her head, once, against the headboard of the bed.

In the afternoon, having cried on the bed for what could have been hours, having nibbled sadly at a piece of Ryvita, having called the library to make sure she wasn't there, having checked the wardrobe again and the drawers, and the end of the bed where Sally-Ann kept her shoes, each time feeling a small hope that she might be wrong, it might be all right, if not today, then tomorrow, Senga decides to make a visit to Marion's mother. Not that Marion's mother is a particular friend – Senga doesn't have particular friends – but she is someone who has been a neighbour for many years, and who is civil enough to nod politely when they meet in the street, and, moreover, someone who might have some idea about what to do about a missing daughter, or, through something Marion might have said, even know where Sally-Ann could be.

So Senga tidies herself up as best she can after half a day spent weeping and crosses the road to knock on Doris Ward's door.

Doris looks surprised to see her. 'Can I help you?'

'Sorry to bother you,' says Senga. 'I just –' And tears form in her eyes and she has to stop and brush them out of her eyes with the back of her hand.

'Come inside,' says Doris but Senga shakes her head. She has not been in any neighbour's house in all the years she's lived here and doesn't intend to start now.

'It's our Sally-Ann,' she says. 'She's gone somewhere, we don't know where, she's just gone, in the night, her bed's no been slept in. I was just wondering if Marion would know anything.'

'Marion's in Great Yarmouth.'

'Oh, I know, I know fine, but I thought she might know if – if there was a boy involved, or anything. Sally-Ann writes to her, that I do know. I don't know what – does your Marion no phone you and tell you what she's up to?'

'Well, yes,' says Doris. 'She phones once a week, usually on a Monday evening, and she always says to say hello to your Sally if I see her, and I always pass it on when I do see her, but I don't know any more than that. But, Mrs Grey, don't get so upset, you know what these girls are like, they're thoughtless, they don't think enough about their parents, she'll be back won't she. Probably back before bedtime.'

'She's gone and taken her winter coat with her,' says Senga. 'Why would she do that?'

Doris shakes her head because Senga is right; there is no obvious explanation for the winter coat being gone. 'What I'll do,' she says, 'I'll phone and leave a message for Marion to phone me, and if she's got anything – any information at all – I'll call across and let you know tomorrow. Will that help?'

'Thank you,' says Senga. 'Thank you for being such a –'

'It's no trouble,' says Doris. 'Are you sure you won't come in? You look as if you could do with a cup of tea.'

'Oh no. Thank you, but no. I'll need to be getting back inside to put the potatoes on.'

Which is a clear lie because it is hardly past three in the afternoon and Doris Ward knows exactly what time – quarter to six – Mr Grey will return home. But then, everyone knows they are a funny family.

Thoughtless, says Senga to herself. Thoughtless. But to do this? How could she no think about Douglas, how could she no remember her brother and what he did and – how could she do this?

The mother and father eat their pork chop and potatoes in silence. Then Willie, before she's had time to put the kettle on, says, 'Right. I'm away down the police station.'

She hesitates, but then says, 'I'll go with you, will I?'

He nods. 'Bring that letter with you.'

They walk together through the soft summer evening to the local station at Hammerton Road, not speaking.

'I've come to report a missing person,' says Willie Grey to the desk sergeant.

He sighs, the man at the desk, and picks up his pen. 'Name?'

'Mine or hers?' Authority brings out the worst in Willie.

'Let's have your name first shall we?'

They do the names, the address, then explain that Sally-Ann Grey, their only daughter, has gone, last seen the evening before, therefore left the house between the hours of nine forty-five yesterday, or thereabouts, and five fifty this morning.

'Any note?'

They show him the note.

'How old is your daughter?'

'Twenty. Nearly twenty-one.'

The man leans over the desk. 'Sir. Madam. Your daughter is of age. Nearly. She has done nothing wrong. She has left you a note telling you that she will contact you. My advice is to wait a day or two. She'll be back by Sunday, I'm willing to bet.'

'But it's not like her,' says Senga. Except for telling him her own name and address it's the first time she's spoken. 'She's not a flighty girl.'

'Even the quiet ones have boyfriends,' says the policeman. 'I can't put out an alert for a grown woman who's told her parents she's going away for a day or two.'

'But,' says Senga – and she hasn't even told Willie this, so far – 'the thing is, officer, she's taken her winter coat.'

He pauses, the policeman, and seems to think about this. 'Even so, Mrs Grey, it's not a crime. In the eyes of the law –'

'I don't give a tuppenny cuss for the eyes of the law,' says Willie. 'She's my daughter and I want her back home. I want her on a list as a missing person and I want the police to bring her back.'

'She's on a list, Mr Grey. If she gets in any trouble we'll soon find out about it. And I'd be grateful to you if you would let us know when she returns, so that I can take her *off* our list. I'm hoping that will be Monday morning at the latest.'

Chapter Three

Sally-Ann reaches London safely by the middle of Wednesday afternoon, in only three lifts. First the lorry to Chesterfield, delivering some steel tubing to a factory; then another as far as Luton, an older man this time, with photos of his children propped against the windscreen, delivering chocolate from York to some warehouse. He makes a brief stop at the services at Leicester and buys her a cup of tea in spite of her protests and her attempts to pay. 'You're all right,' he says. 'It's worth it for the company.' They sit in the lorry drivers' area, Sally feeling conspicuous among all the men, but sipping her tea gratefully.

'What's your name then?' he asks.

'Zita,' she says.

'Pretty name,' he says.' My girls, they're called Zoe – that's another Z – and Petra. Nice to have something a bit out of the ordinary, isn't it.'

Sally – Zita – could say plenty about the name her parents gave her but decides she might mistakenly tell him her real name so stays off the subject. She already has a vision of a police car following her, stopping whichever vehicle she is in and dragging her back home. She knows it's ridiculous but she can still see it clearly, can still hear the voices of the policemen as they accuse her of wasting their time and upsetting her parents. She asks him instead about chocolate, and how many KitKats he can fit into his lorry, and whether he lives in York – he does – and says she has been there on a school trip, a few years ago, and walked round the old walls and gone into the minster.

'That's what all the visitors see,' he says, 'but there's always more to a city than the fancy bits. It's not the real thing, the historic bits – I mean, it's real, but it's not where real people live and work. You need at least a week to see a city, more if it's London.'

'I suppose so,' says Sally-Zita, in the knowledge that she is staying only one night in London, and her sights are set on Paris and Rome. London – she has all her life ahead of her to see *London* – London can wait.

He drops her at the junction for Luton and wishes her a good holiday with her friend, and gives her one of his complementary KitKats, which she accepts gratefully even though she has been brought up never to accept gifts of any sort from strangers – by which her mother means from anyone who was not herself or her father. She sits on the grass verge and eats the chocolate – she is starving – and marvels at where she is. Not as far as London, but surely she has passed through the Midlands, surely this is the South. The cars and lorries are the same, the road looks the same as it did running past Sheffield, but something must be different. This is the South, where she has never been before. She has never been to London before. She has been to Scarborough and Bridlington, Filey and Whitby. She has been to Barnsley and Chesterfield to look in the markets with her mother. York with the school, Blackpool on a coach trip. That's about it.

Her next lift is in a brand new car driven by an elderly man – he seems to her to be older than her father – who is delivering it to a showroom in North London. He gets out and puts her rucksack in the boot, carefully so as not to scratch the new paintwork.

'We're not supposed to pick up hitchhikers,' he says. 'Possibility of damage you see. But I do if I can. I hitch back home myself you see – you'll have seen people like me with the red number plates, trying to get home.'

Sally-Zita couldn't honestly say she had seen them but she nodded politely.

'The company give me a train fare, but if I can get back some other way I can put that in my pocket. So I will pick up a hitcher when I see one in the hope that someone will see me and think to help me on my way home. Do as you would be done by, do you see. Going far are you?'

Just to London, she says, to meet a friend, hoping he doesn't ask her which part of London.

'Cheaper than the train, eh? Save your money for having a good time.'

That's true, though she does not feel short of money. She has been working for five years at the library; her wage has risen to more than nine pounds a week and her outgoings are small. She has been giving her mother two pounds a week for her keep and she is well aware that she gets more for her money than she should. Her mother seems unable to stop herself from buying her little extras – tights and shampoo, things like that. She packs up a lunch for her every day, she buys magazines which she claims are for herself but her daughter knows very well that they are primarily for her. It has its downside – Senga will accompany her on clothes shopping expeditions and try to pay for items that *she* likes. This has resulted in a curiously lop-sided wardrobe – expensive and frumpy along with the cheap and cheerful that Sally-Zita buys when she's with Marion or on her own. Today, for instance, she is wearing a skirt that is longer than is fashionable and a brown mohair cardigan over a shinily tawdry blouse.

Her driver takes her as far as Golders Green and advises her to get the bus into the city from there.

First, she goes into a Lyons for a cup of tea and a cheese sandwich and as she sits there, almost falling asleep at the table, the clatter of dishes and the up and down of voices reminds her of going into Tuckwoods in Sheffield and she feels that though London might be different – it seems there is more variety in the people on the streets – it isn't foreign. She enquires of the woman at the next table which bus to get and armed with the information finds her way to the bus stop and waits with shoppers and schoolchildren – for, it is past four o'clock by now. She finally arrives at her destination, the youth hostel that looked to her the nearest to Victoria Station.

It is quiet, being midweek and not quite vacation time. She lies down on her bunk and goes to sleep, wakes up hours later to find it's dark outside and someone has just switched on the light.

'Sorry,' says the woman, without sounding sorry. 'I thought there was no one here.' She is taking off a huge rucksack and looking around at the room.

Sally-Zita sits up, ducking her head to avoid the edge of the bunk above her. 'What time is it?'

'Past ten,' says the woman – what sort of accent is that? 'Everything's shut out there.'

'Oh,' says Zita-Sally, 'I thought I might get something to eat.'

'Not a chance,' she says. 'What's your name?'

'Zita.'

'I'm Dora. I've got a banana you can have.' She takes it from a side pocket, a little the worse for being squashed and hands it over without waiting for a reply.

Second time in one day, thinks Zita, and peels it without another thought of what her mother would say.

Dora is as short as Zita is tall, and stocky, like a weight lifter or something. She is from Rhodesia, she says, but has been in Europe for over a year now. 'Everywhere,' she says. 'Greece, Italy, Turkey. First time in England though.'

'Oh,' says Zita, not knowing what the proper response is: Do you like it? How are you finding it? How long are you staying? 'What do you think of it so far?' she finally says, and laughs a little to show that she knows it's a catchphrase from the telly.

'Too many blacks,' says Dora. She pronounces it 'blecks.' 'I didn't know there were so many blecks in England.'

'Are there?'

'Where are you from?'

'Sheffield.'

'North, right? You don't have blecks up there?'

'Well yes,' says Zita. 'Some.'

'At home,' says Dora, 'they're – well I don't know, let's say we don't care for them. I mean, if you should run one down, out in the country, say, you don't stop to see how he's doing. You wait till you get to the town and then you might go and report it to the police.'

'What would they do?'

'Nothing. But you've reported it, right. So it's OK'

'Oh,' says Zita. She thinks that her father might have some opinions in line with the Rhodesians but that he would be more careful about stating them out loud to people he had only just met.

She spends the morning of next day – Thursday – wandering around London, relieved that Dora was gone early. In truth, Zita had been awake when Dora got out of bed and went to the bathroom but she pretended to be asleep in the hope that they wouldn't have to start another conversation that would make her feel inadequate and ignorant. Dora said she was going to Stonehenge for the summer solstice, and seemed to expect that Zita would understand what that was all about. Then she was going down to Cornwall to see Tintagel.

'Oh,' said Zita.

'Haven't you been there?'

'I've never been to Cornwall,' she said. 'It's a long way from home.'

'Seems to me,' said Dora, 'you've never been anywhere.' And as this was true Zita made no reply, but she didn't see why she should be criticised for something that was hardly her fault.

She eats her breakfast at a Golden Egg and then she takes a little walk around the nearby streets. It is nice to be walking without the rucksack; it is interesting to hear the voices and see the fashions – skirts are shorter here – and pick out which people are tourists like herself, dawdling about, looking upwards and bumping into proper residents, who hurry from one place to another, knowing where they are, not looking around them, they've seen it all before. She buys a postcard, borrows a pen from the shopkeeper and addresses it, with a brief message; then finds a post office and buys a stamp – the last English stamp, she thinks. She finds a park – it is Green Park and she has walked along beside the garden wall of Buckingham Palace without knowing it. She wanders past the lake where ducklings paddle after their mothers, and on the grass couples stretch out in the sun – shouldn't they be at work? she wonders. She looks around her – this is London – and then goes back to retrieve her rucksack from the hostel and enquire for the best way to get to the Dover road. The warden has obviously been asked this sort of question every week if not every day. He has bus timetables, and draws her a little map and wishes her a good journey. He shows no curiosity about where she is going.

Chapter Four

On Thursday, on the dot of nine o'clock, Senga calls in to see Beryl at Sally-Ann's work place. She is planning to tell them that her daughter is ill – a nasty summer flu – and will be off work for at least a week. It's the local library, only round the corner, the staff there have known Senga for years, ever since Douglas was a little boy and she used to park him by the picture books while she chose a Mills and Boon for herself. Sally-Ann has worked there since she left school; it was Senga who spoke to Beryl and got her daughter the job. The public are not allowed in until ten, but seeing who it is, and supposing she has come to explain her daughter's lateness, Beryl, the senior, opens the door and lets her inside.

Senga has never been a good liar. Faced with a kindly and well-known face she begins to sob and the hot tears stream once more down her face. Beryl ushers her into the staff room and closes the door behind them.

'Come on now,' she says. 'It can't be as bad as all that, can it. Calm down, tell me what's wrong.'

Senga bats the tears out of her eyes for perhaps the fiftieth time in only a little more than twenty-four hours. 'I'm sorry,' she says. 'Sally-Ann's gone away. She's run away.'

'Well,' says Beryl, sitting down suddenly. 'I never expected you to say that, not for a minute. Not Sally-Ann. Sit down, Mrs Grey, let me fetch you a cup of tea; you look as if you need something.'

She pours a cup of dark amber tea from the pot that stands on a hot plate in the corner, made by the caretaker and topped up at intervals. Sally-Ann always says she won't touch it, it's usually so stewed.

'Now, Mrs Grey, tell me from the beginning.'

'You must be busy,' says Senga, remembering her manners but also longing to tell Beryl the whole story.

'Jane can manage without me for the time being. And I need to know, for our employee records you know.'

With that encouragement Senga does not hesitate but – whatever Willie might say about broadcasting their private business – tells Beryl the whole story, including the detail which to her is the most crucial. 'And she's even taken her winter coat. I don't think she'll ever be coming back.'

'Well, maybe, maybe not,' says Beryl. 'Just think – if she's gone to the seaside – well, just think, it can get very cold in the evening. She maybe only wanted it just in case the weather changes. She can be a sensible girl, your Sally-Ann, she's obviously thought it all through. But did you really have no idea that she had this in her mind?'

'She never said a word.'

'But did she behave just as usual? "I didnae notice anything different about her. Her father, he says she was looking shifty, but I think he's only noticed that after she's gone, if you get my meaning. She seemed just the same to me. Was she no the same at work?'

'Well,' says Beryl, 'I can't say that there's been anything to notice. And you know, she's only been here part of the time, what with her being moved down town to the reference library to cover that sick leave. But I thought she was enjoying that – in fact I know she was, it seemed to put a smile on her face, those days when she said goodbye to us here knowing she'd be down there for the next two days. I suppose it was a change of scene for her. And of course she was expanding her experience. Did she talk about it at home?'

'She said it was a change. She made us laugh about Miss Bunting and her funny ways –'

'Oh yes,' agrees Beryl.

'– she said she's been helping a boy with some maps –'

The two women look each other in the eye, then apparently decide not to say whatever it was that has crossed their two minds.

In the afternoon, as Senga is rolling out pastry for a meat pie, there is a tap on the back door. It is Doris Ward calling as she promised. Senga opens the door and Doris walks in, for all the world as if she's been invited. Senga covers her pastry with a damp cloth and ushers Doris into the front room and waves a hand for her to sit down, which she does, on Willie's chair, but only perched on the edge, as if she's not stopping.

'Thank you for coming,' says Senga. It goes through her mind to wonder if she should offer tea but she is too nervous to do it.

'Not at all,' says Doris. She is perfectly at ease, but then she would be, she's an Avon lady, she must knock on doors all the time and enter people's front rooms and sit on their chairs and look appraisingly at their curtains and notice whether they've got a fitted carpet yet and how big their television screen is compared to her own. 'I spoke to Marion,' she says.

'I hope she's well,' says Senga, out of politeness.

'Thank you,' says Doris. 'She's fine thank you. She hasn't seen your Sally all summer, as you know, but they have been writing letters.' She stops, waits for Senga to say something.

'I know they have. She misses your Marion, that I do know. They were always best friends, so they were, but now —'

'Our Marion's engaged to be married,' says Doris briskly. 'It's bound to change the way things are.'

'Oh I know, but —'

'Now, there's not much I can tell you, but it seems that your Sally —' (Sally-*Ann*, thinks Senga, her name is Sally-*Ann*.) '— has been dropping hints about going away. Not in any detail, mind, but she's said in her letters, she's said, for example, that if Marion comes home for a visit that she might miss her —'

'But she hasn't said where she's going?'

'Marion didn't say. Sally might have asked her not to tell, mightn't she? The other thing she said is that there's this boy that Sally seems keen on.'

'Oh,' says Senga. 'She's never mentioned — well, only a lad who comes into the library to look at maps —'

'Called Terry?'

'She never said his name to us. I thought when she said, it was just a wee boy, you know, looking up something for his homework maybe. It's only this morning, when I was down at the library — I had to tell them you see — it was only then I started to wonder. And — I don't know if this is making sense — but putting it together, taking her clothes, not telling us where she's off to, not even telling us she's going till she's gone — I wondered, is it something to do with this boyfriend.'

'Marion says he's not a boyfriend,' says Doris. 'She says Sally's keen on him but he's already got a girlfriend. So whether he's anything to do with all this —? And Sally hasn't been one for having boyfriends, has she?'

'She's no a looker,' says her mother, 'but she has a nice nature. People like our Sally-Ann.'

'Of course they do,' says Doris. 'She's a nice girl and I sure she'll get herself a nice husband one day. Looks aren't everything. But still, I'm sorry she's gone off and made you worried; she's naughty to do that. And you say she took all her clothes? So, she'll be carrying a suitcase. Someone will have noticed her – at the train station maybe?'

Senga dabs her eyes but notices at the same time that she is hardly crying at all. Maybe she's used to it already, maybe she just has no tears left. 'Would you like a cup of tea?' she says.

'Thank you,' says Doris, formally, 'but no thank you, not today. I need to get back, I've had a big parcel today so I've got customers to deliver to.' She stands up.

'Thank you,' says Senga. 'Tell Marion thank you, and ask her please, if she hears anything to let us know.'

'Of course,' says Doris, and leaves by the back door, the way she came in.

Suitcase, thinks Senga. How could she not have thought of that? The family suitcase, not used for many a year, for they haven't had the heart for a holiday since the business with Douglas, should be on top of the wardrobe. She drags a chair across the floor and reaches up; sure enough, she can feel it's still there, behind the ornamental front. My stars, she thinks, it'll be fair dusty. So what did she use to carry her things in?

*

The young man was called Terry and he was not the usual sort of person who patronised the reference library. The usual sort were male it's true, but mostly older; they came in with cardboard folders under their arms and having requested and received the material they were looking for they made no further demands on the staff but sat well apart from each other, making notes about the coins of Hadrian's reign or the weather records of the South Atlantic or the number of dotterel sighted in North Yorkshire the previous summer. Terry though, came in one lunchtime, approached the high counter as if he was unsure of what he actually wanted, but confident that the two women – Sally-Ann and Miss Bunting – would be delighted to help him.

He was about the age of Sally-Ann but very much more forward in his approach. He pushed back the fair hair that flopped over his eyes; he smiled broadly as if he was already acquainted, he leaned confidentially on the counter and confessed that he had never been in a library before and he didn't have a ticket.

'This is not the lending library,' Miss Bunting told him. 'If you want to borrow books you need to join the library – downstairs. They will deal with you, as long as you are resident locally.'

'They sent me up here,' he said, still smiling. 'I don't want to take the books away. I don't even want books. I want to look at some maps. Please.'

'Are your hands clean?' said Miss Bunting. Certainly his clothes were not; he was wearing jeans and a check shirt, and steel-capped boots. Like a small boy he held out his hands to be inspected, palms up, then down. His nails were rimmed with black but the palms looked recently scrubbed.

'I suppose you'll do,' she said grudgingly. 'Miss Grey here will see if she can help you.' She whispered to Sally-Ann, 'I'll be in the staff room if there's any trouble.'

Of course there was no trouble. Sally-Ann fetched out the atlas that he wanted and left him to look at them while she tidied some books that the entomologist had been looking through. Then the cricket man finished with his 1935 Wisden and departed and she was on her own with the young man. He beckoned her over to him.

'Have a sit down,' he suggested. 'If the old lady comes back you can say you're helping me.'

'What are you looking for?' she asked.

He leaned back and brushed the hair off his face. His face shone, she thought, as if he was a child at Christmas.

'I'm going on a trip,' he said. 'I'm going to go abroad. I'm going to see the world.'

'You're going round the world?'

'Maybe. I don't know where I'll end up. Except I know I'll come back here in the end. My girlfriend's here you see.' Sally-Ann understood that he said this so that she did not get the wrong idea about him, that he was chatting her up, or that he was any sort of threat or opportunity to her. Neither of those things, in fact, had yet crossed her mind.

She looked at he page he was on. 'So you're going to Europe?'

'First stop, France,' he said. 'Unless it's Belgium. But I'll just be going where the lifts take me.'

'Hitch-hiking,' she said.

'Ever done it?'

'Me and my friend Marion went to Whitby and back one day.'

'It's easier,' he said, 'if you're a girl. Or two girls. I've done it plenty of times but it can be right slow sometimes.'

'Isn't your girlfriend going with you?'

He shook his head. 'She's a student. She's going to be a physiotherapist. I know it's the vacation – that's what they call it – soon, but she says she's got some sort of essay or something to write, and some placement or other she's got to do. Basically though, she's not interested. She's been to Europe before, she's seen Paris and Rome, she's done all those things with her parents. And she doesn't like hitching.'

'Why not?'

'Don't know. I think because I get on well with the drivers and have a laugh, you know, and she feels left out. And her mother doesn't like her to do it.'

'But she doesn't mind you going away without her?'

'We've been together two years nearly,' he says. 'I'm going to marry her when I get back from this and she's finished her course. This is just something I have to get out of my system before I settle down.' He turned to her. 'You're a girl. Do you think it's an OK thing to do? Would you let your boyfriend go away for three months?'

'I haven't got a boyfriend,' said Sally-Ann, 'so I don't know what I'd would think about it. But better to do it before you get married I would think – better than getting itchy feet afterwards.'

'That's what I think,' he said. 'And Rosalind thinks the same, really.'

Rosalind, thought Sally-Ann. It was not the sort of name of anyone she had ever known.

He told her he worked in a garage 'just off the Parkway' servicing cars and putting new tyres on, new bulbs in the headlights, that sort of thing.

'Will they keep your job for you?'

'Well,' he said, 'I wouldn't think so, would you? But I don't want to do that all my life. I'll find something else if I have to.'

He lived 'on the Arbourthorne,' he told her, with his mum and dad and a number of brothers 'younger than me, all of them a right pain in the backside.'

She told him she lived near Kelvin flats and did not mention her brother. He told her his name was Terry. Terry Brown.

'That's funny,' she said. 'Cos my surname is Grey.'

'What's your first name?'

She hesitated but only for a second. 'Zita,' she said.

Chapter Five

After posting the postcard as she walks towards the Dover Youth Hostel, Zita purchases another, along with a packet of crisps and a bar of chocolate. She has hitched down in two lifts, feeling like an expert by now, although conversation has been hard work, mainly because she cannot get out of her head things that Dora said the night before. It's all muddled up now – should you accept lifts from black people or not? Do foreigners speak English – most of them, some or none of them? Are the Italians nicer than the Spanish or the other way around? And what does Dora mean by 'nice' anyway? Can you really live on only bread? Should she plan to go further even than France and maybe Italy?

'Go to Iraq,' said Dora. 'The ruins they've got there, you've never seen anything like it. And go to Israel, you can get work and lodging on a kibbutz, it's good, good community.'

'Haven't they just had a war?' said Zita.

'They won the war,' said Dora airily.

'Were you there?'

'No,' she said. 'I would have stayed of course, I wanted to stay, I wanted to join their army – they have girls in their army you know – but I was a foreign national, wasn't I? so I thought I'd better leave.'

'Where did you go next?'

'Turkey. They've got ruins too – do you like history?'

'I suppose so,' said Zita, hazily remembering lessons about cavemen and Vikings. 'It must be interesting.'

'What are you going for?' said Dora. 'You don't know geography, you don't know history. You don't speak a language –'

'You said everyone speaks English.'

'A bit of English, I said. And this person you're going with – does he speak a language?'

'I don't know,' said Zita, though she was pretty sure he would have told her if he did.

'Known him long?' said Dora.

'A few weeks.'

'If I'd had a boyfriend only a few weeks,' said Dora, 'I wouldn't be relying on him as much as you seem to do.'

'He's not my boyfriend,' said Zita. 'He's a friend. He's got a girlfriend.'

'And she knows about you, does she?'

'I don't know. I've never met her. He tells me all about her. He says he loves her.'

'I wouldn't trust him,' said Dora, 'as far as I could throw my panties.'

'I think I'll try to get to sleep,' said Zita.

At the Dover Youth Hostel she writes the second card to her parents. 'Dear Mum and Daddy, I hope you are well. I am fine.' She stops, wondering what to say. How much to give away. 'The weather has been nice so far. Love from Sally.'

She cannot be Zita to her parents. Even calling herself plain Sally causes her mother to twitch her lips and her father on occasions to remonstrate. 'You only do it to upset your mother. What's wrong with the name we gave you?'

Then her mother would say, 'It doesnae matter, Willie. Leave it alone now.' But it clearly did matter.

She has decided she will post it on the other side of the Channel. They will see the postmark – her father will notice it and he'll break the news to her mother – and they'll know she's in France without her actually having to tell them.

Again the hostel is quiet at first. Zita sits in the kitchen, alone, and composes a letter of resignation to Beryl. Later in the evening a group of boys and girls arrive, laughing and relaxed with each other, she can tell, even though she can't understand what they are saying. German, she thinks they are speaking, though she has never heard a word of it before except in the old black and white war films on TV on winter Sunday afternoons. Zita sits quietly in the kitchen, studying her French phrase book, while the group mill around, heating tins of soup and making coffee. They have a loaf of sliced bread which engenders much conversation, none of it complimentary she can tell. One of the girls comes over and, in English, offers her coffee and once again she is filled with conflict. Don't take sweets from strangers, which was almost the first prohibition she ever heard from her mother, but was the first of many. Don't ask for anything from anyone – not even a glass of water from Marion's mother's tap. Don't cause anyone any sort of trouble – better to go without than to cause trouble. Don't go thinking you deserve anything from anyone except your family. Don't put yourself forward. Say no thank you.

'Yes, please,' says Zita. The coffee is not at all like Camp coffee which comes as a liquid in a bottle and which they have in the cupboard at home, though they rarely drink it.

The German speakers – they are actually from Switzerland – have just arrived on the ferry and are planning to go to Wales to walk up some mountains.

'But you have mountains in Switzerland?' says Zita.

'For a change,' says the girl. 'And also, we go to the seaside, which we do not have in Switzerland. Where are you going?'

'France,' says Zita.

'Alone?'

'I'm meeting a friend on the ferry,' she says. Terry on the ferry – it rhymes, she thinks, and suddenly it feels impossible that it will happen. How *did* it happen anyway, how did she get here? She looked at the maps with him, she went to the café with him, she listened to his plans. She said, 'I wish I could do that,' and he said, 'You can come with me if you want.' Just like that. Now, far from home – nearer to France than to home – she cannot believe it will happen. She will miss the ferry, or he will, or Rosalind will be there and make a fuss, or Rosalind will have changed her mind and decided to go with him, or Terry will have changed his mind about having her company and will look at her pityingly and say, Sorry Zita, You didn't think I meant it did you? Or maybe to avoid her he has already gone, arrived there early, bought a ticket, gone. He could be already in France. She thinks she will never sleep tonight, what with the coffee and the crowding anxieties.

But when she wakes up next morning she finds that she did sleep, and well. The police have not been sent after her – or if they have they have failed to find her. Her father is not banging on the door demanding that she be handed over to him, never to be allowed out of the house again. She has made it to the edge of England, all by herself, and if it turns out that Terry has stood her up, then who cares? She will go to France by herself. Yes, that's what she'll do, even if she comes straight back. She will not go home without having left England and set foot in another country. She swings her legs out of the bed and takes her clothes into the bathroom to get dressed. There are showers – no baths – but she has never had a shower before and feels unable to work it. She sniffs her armpits and applies deodorant – her mother bought that for her too

– dresses in a pair of cord jeans and a clean blouse, and checks out of the hostel before the Swiss girls have stirred.

The day seems to have been made expressly for her alone. Blue sky, white clouds, a breeze off the sea. She has a Mars bar for breakfast – 'Helps you work rest and play' – though she doesn't feel as if she's doing any of those things. 'Helps you escape from your boring life?'

She shoulders her rucksack – it doesn't get any lighter – and makes her way to the ferry. There it is. She has never been on a boat before, unless you count a speedboat ride round Scarborough Harbour, which was all over in five minutes. 'Like *doing it*.' Marion said. 'You know, good fun while it lasts, but it doesn't last long.' Marion has *done it* with her boyfriend Brian and she doesn't care who knows, as long as her parents don't find out. (Zita has never *done it*, never had the chance, and doesn't even know if she wants to – she's quite squeamish enough about Tampax thank you very much, never mind anything involving another person.) She reminds herself to send Marion a postcard from France; Marion has never been abroad, at least that's one thing she'll get to do before her.

By nine o'clock she has bought her ticket. One way. She and Terry have discussed this – a return ticket would commit them to coming back the same way, even possibly by a certain date.

'You never know where a lift will take you,' he said. 'You don't know where you'll end up. You have to be free.'

'What would be a good idea,' said Zita – they were sitting in the reference library while Miss Bunting went for her lunch – 'would be to put the price of the ticket home somewhere safe so that you don't spend it.'

'You're not really the adventurous type, are you?' He said it with some affection in his voice.

'I've never had an adventure,' she said, slowly, 'but I think maybe I could get a bit adventurous.' She did not look at him but concentrated on the map; they were looking at the south of France, at Nice and Marseilles and St Tropez, where there would be film stars and yachts and people drinking wine outdoors.

'Tell you what,' he said, 'I've done as much planning as I can stand. Let's you and me go for a cup of tea.'

'Haven't you got to get back to work.'

'They won't mind,' he said. 'There's not much waiting and I can always stay a bit longer tonight. Come on, I'll treat you.'

So when Miss Bunting returned from her lunch and it was Sally-Ann's turn to go, they stepped out into the fine drizzle and he steered her towards Tuckwoods. It was an old-style place, with waitresses, not self-service.

'My Nannan loves it here,' he said. He ordered tea and toasted teacakes; Sally-Ann wondered when she would be able to eat the ham sandwich that was supposed to be her lunch. Then he told her more about Rosalind, more than she really cared to know, but all the same she was happy to be there with him, with his bright eyes and his loud laugh and his complete confidence in himself, whatever he was doing.

So, she has bought her ticket and gone on board. She stands at the rail, looking down at the quay, watching the passengers, looking for Terry.

There's a big noisy party, half a dozen people at least, and there's Terry in the middle of it, with his arm round a girl. That must be Rosalind, dainty, pretty, fair-haired, dressed in a sky-blue summer dress and clinging onto him while other people – that must be her parents, the respectable couple – laugh loudly at their own comments. The two young teenagers, they could be Rosalind's sister and brother, and the redheaded girl could be a friend. Imagine, thinks Zita, if my parents had came to see me off, but no, it can't even be imagined.

A loud noise from some sort of hooter on the boat sends latecomers scurrying up the walkway, and Terry pulls Rosalind close to him and they kiss. When they part she is wiping her eyes and her mother hands her a tissue. Terry heaves up his rucksack on to one shoulder, kisses Ros again, on the cheek this time, and hurries towards the boat. Rosalind calls something after him and Terry waves a hand to show he has heard, but Zita cannot make out what she said.

So, he's on the boat. She will not go looking for him; she will leave it to chance whether he looks for her or not. She will not take it for granted that he will be expecting to see her, never mind pleased. She will wait until they happen to be in the same place. For now, she picks up her rucksack and makes her way to the other side of the boat – she has no more interest in watching Rosalind's family party, she will look out to sea, she will look in the direction she is going.

The boat fills up, the engines change their pitch, suddenly the whole thing is moving. Zita for some time watches the waves, the grey sea, the white gulls, and then takes out her letter to Beryl and finishes it off. Finds her small packet of envelopes and seals the letter inside. Writes the address of the library. She will post it in France. The thought makes her smile.

'You came then?' Terry has been watching her, standing a few yards away, leaning against a railing. 'I didn't think you would. Not when it came to it.'

'I said I would,' she says. 'Didn't you want me to?'

He shrugs. 'I didn't think you meant it. Who you writing to? Boyfriend?'

'Don't be daft,' she says.

'Who then?'

'Don't be nosy,' she says. 'Just handing in my notice.'

'Why didn't you do that weeks ago?'

'My mum and dad would have found out.'

'Why should they? How would they?'

'I don't know,' she says, 'but I wasn't going to risk it.'

'I never thought you would be here,' he says. 'Journey OK?'

'Fine,' she says. Something has changed between them. Three days ago they were in the reference library making their final plans; today there is a brittleness about him, as if he regrets what he has done, as if she has overstepped something and they are not friends any more. She takes out her phrase book again and tries to concentrate on it. He looks out over the English Channel.

'Sorry,' he says, after a while. 'I'm just a bit funny about leaving Ros.'

'I saw you,' she says. 'Down on the dock there. All those people come to say goodbye to you.'

'Never got a proper goodbye from Ros,' he says. 'Stayed at her mum and dad's last night, not so much as a goodnight kiss did I get. They are that thrilled to see the back of me, I don't care what she says.'

'Why would they be?'

'Just not good enough for their daughter. Got no qualifications. Live in a small house – that's what her mum said to her – "I suppose he lives in a small house." If I'd been there I'd have told her – yes it's a small house and do you know what else? – it belongs to the council.'

'What's wrong with that? My parents would love a council house. Better than renting off a landlord.'

'They didn't find out then? That you were leaving? You didn't tell them?'

'I sent them a postcard,' she said. 'Posted it yesterday, and I've got another one to post when we get to France. Then I'll do one a week at least. I don't want to upset them. Not too much.'

He sits down beside her, leaning against the rail, the wash of the bow wave behind them.

'My mum and dad are all right about it,' he says. 'I told you before, didn't I? Me dad said he wished he'd done something like that. He didn't even get abroad during the war, didn't even have to join up. Reserved occupation, see. Coal miner in those days.'

'My dad hates abroad,' she says. 'He went to Africa in the war, and Italy. Says he'll never go abroad again, not if you paid him.'

'Glad I never had to do national service. This is much better. Free as a bird.'

'My brother did it.'

'You never said you had a brother.'

'We don't see him any more.'

'Why not?'

'He lives a long way away.' She looks around hoping to change the subject. 'We could go and get a cup of tea.'

Neither of them, it turns out, has ever been on a proper boat before. It is interesting, all wooden stairways and odd corners. There are English people, and French people, as they expected, and also people speaking languages that are certainly not English and probably not French. You can buy tea and buns and sandwiches at a hatch on a dark hidden deck, but they buy only tea, deciding to wait until they arrive in France, so their first food will be French.

'I don't fancy snails,' she says.

'There'll be other things.'

'I know. And the French for snails is escargots –' she pronounces it with a 't' '– so we can avoid them, knowing that.'

'What's the French for bacon butty?'

She flicks to the food and drink section of the phrase book. 'They don't seem to have bacon. Just ham. Jambon, they call it.'

'If I'd known that,' says Terry, 'I wouldn't have come. No bacon, and ham that sounds like jam. Shall we turn round and go home?'

When she looks at him she can see that his eyes are sad and although he is making a joke, there is a part of him that means it; he wants to be back with Ros, away from her parents, kissing and cuddling and whatever else they do.

'You never know,' she says, and she sounds to herself like a mother cajoling a child, 'they might have something even nicer than bacon.' And she digs him in the ribs with her elbow; it is the first time she has ever touched him.

They go back on deck to watch France approaching. There is a harbour, there are fishing boats, another ferry, people waiting on the quayside, behind it: the town. Abroad, she thinks. I'm abroad.

'Well,' says Terry. 'This is it. *La Belle France*: isn't that what they say? We've made it.'

Zita cannot speak. I'm here, she thinks, this is me, here. In France. She looks at Terry and sees that he has forgotten Ros entirely for the time being.

'Say something,' he says. 'What do you think of it?'

'I love it,' she whispers.

Chapter Six

The postcard arrives on Saturday by the second post. It is not a picture of Bridlington, or Skegness, or any seaside place at all; it is a photograph taken from high up on a sunny day, coloured of course, of a street scene, buildings covered in advertisements, a road with black taxis and a red bus, a statue.

Senga turns it over. At the top is printed in small letters: Piccadilly Circus, London. Under it, Sally-Ann has written, neatly as always, 'Dear Mum and Daddy. I am all right, please don't worry about me. I will write to you every week. Love from Sally.'

'It's not the coast,' she says. 'She said she'd send us a card from the coast.'

'Give it here,' says Willie. He looks at the picture first, then reads the message, out loud, then the address too. He turns it over to look at the picture again. 'That's right,' he says, 'Piccadilly, London. I've been there.' He turns back and studies the postmark, leans back in his chair as if he has won a hand at cards. 'Not posted in London though. Posted in Dover.'

'That's on the coast, is it no?'

'It is,' he says. 'It's where the ferries go from, across to France. To the Continent.'

Senga sits down as if stunned but Willie gets to his feet with a new rush of energy. 'Right then. Let's see what the police have got to say about this.'

When he has gone, Senga clears the table and tidies the kitchen, mechanically, as if she is a puppet on strings. Having done that she feels a need to go and tell Beryl; let's see if Beryl can make me feel better about this, she thinks. But when she gets to the library she finds no Beryl – it's her Saturday off – and Jane is in charge and busy with an influx of children all trying at once to change their books. Here come the tears again, she thinks, I really must stop this. As if telling Beryl is going to make it any different. As if I haven't just got to get used to this. Like I got used to Douglas. It comes back to her that the card was signed from

Sally. Not Sally-Ann. That old argument again, she thinks. You get given your name – it's a *given* name isn't it – and that's it, for ever. Get married if you must, or if you can, and change your surname but your given name is yours for good, like it or not. And there were plenty worse names than Sally-Ann.

Senga McHarg believed that her name must be the ugliest name in the world. It sounded – even her friends said – like someone being sick. Her sisters were called Betty and Maggie and Jeannie and claimed they didn't know what she was talking about. Her mother asserted that Senga was a fine Scottish name and that she was called after an old aunt who might leave her something in her will. Clearly, as it turned out, this was untrue. Her father said that there was nothing wrong with McHarg, it had done his family well enough for long enough and anyway she would change it when she got married, and why had he got four daughters and no sons to carry on the proud name of McHarg.

'What about Uncle Tom's boys?' his daughters would say, affronted at not being properly valued, and he would say, Aye, they were McHargs right enough, but it wasnae the same.

Senga ran away from home to be with Willie Grey. She met him at Girvan, where both their families were having a wee couple of days at the seaside during Glasgow Fair Week. Having talked to him by the penny arcade she agreed to meet him in the evening, and when her parents went to the pub, leaving the girls in the boarding house, she swore she would kill her sisters if they told on her, and spent the night with him, sitting on the sand and talking, mostly about the injustice of belonging to their respective families and how much they wanted to leave home. The sand was warm to begin with but became cold as the evening wore on. Willie untied a deckchair from the stack in the lee of the prom and somehow – they were both skinny – they fitted themselves into it and fell asleep.

Of course she was found out. Some time in the early hours Betty and Maggie put their heads together and decided they would get into worse trouble if they didn't tell than if they did, and Betty, who was the favourite, crept to the double bed where her parents were sleeping and shook her father and told him that Senga hadn't been there all night. Grumbling and mumbling he got up and went out to look for them. He heard them before he saw them, awake with the dawn, wandering arm in arm along the front, singing, 'Strolling with my girlie when the dew is pearly early –'

It was a pleasant sound but it cut no ice with Mr McHarg, father of daughters, and Senga was, after a few words had been said, few but strong, taken by the arm and firmly led back to the boarding house, there to upset the whole family by being the cause of going home a day early. 'I'll give you pearly early my girl,' he said, 'and think yourself lucky it's no a good hiding.' What he did not know, however, was that Senga had, secreted in her knickers, the address of Willie Grey, an address in Motherwell; and secreted in her head, the resolution that wherever it was, however far, she would one day go there.

It did not take long before she did go. Her mother was embarrassed by her behaviour and warned all the girls not to tell anybody, not their friends, not their aunties – especially not their aunties – what Senga had done. But – somehow or other – word got out and soon it was all round their bit of Dumbarton, that Senga McHarg had spent the night with a man in Girvan, yes, *all night*, and it would be lucky for her if she didnae have a wean to show for it. And although Senga swore to her mother, and her father, and her sisters that it was nothing like that, all they had done was sit on the beach and talk to each other, the gossip and the suppositions grew and grew. Soon it was a grown man she was with, a married man, then it was that he was coming to get her and take her to the big city and put her on the streets. And then when she had had enough of it all and walked out of her work one winter's day and went home and packed a bag and emptied her sisters' money boxes, and took herself to the train station and bought a single to Glasgow – then it was proved to everyone that everything people said was true.

It was a poor house, that door she knocked on, boldly; poorer than her own. Nobody answered and she sat on the step until a woman turned up, carrying a string bag of potatoes in one hand and hauling a toddler by the other. Willie would be home any time now, she said, and Senga sat back down on the step. It was the winter of 1938.

*

Zita and Terry in France are like a pair of small children at their first funfair, moving from place to place, wide-eyed, comprehending little. The most mundane experience – buying a loaf of bread, say – is a remarkable event. The shop looks different, the very bread is a different shape and is called something unpronounceable. There are no breadcakes, no Mother's Pride or Hovis, no doughnuts either Terry points out, no cakes at all.

'Cakes are in a different shop,' says Zita.' I've seen them, they don't look like our cakes though. Very small.'

'So is this it?' says Terry, clutching the baguette while Zita counts out coins. 'No butter?'

Zita shrugs. Everywhere they look people are carrying a loaf of something called bread which looks like nothing they are familiar with, sometimes pulling bits off and eating it, right there in the street, and never a sign of marge, let alone butter.

'Or Marmite,' says Terry.

*

The days pass, and the weeks, and the postcards keep on coming, not every week as she promised, the number of days between them growing, so that Senga – and Willie too – never know when to expect one, and their evenings are fidgety with anxiety that they cannot mention to each other. And when a card does eventually come through the front door, it seems to bring only discord between them. For Willie would have gone to work before it came, and Senga could not possibly have left it unread until he came home.

'You've read it I suppose.'

'I couldnae help it Willie, lying that side up as it was. But here, take it, you read it.'

And he would take it and sit looking at the picture, and then turn it over as if he was hoping for the news that she was on her way home, which made Senga sorry for him so that she might say something like, 'Nothing new' or 'Same as usual.' 'I can read,' he would say. 'Leave me alone, woman.' And he would sit with it in his hand, as if he'd forgotten it was there, until she interrupted him with his evening cup of tea, and then he would put the card carefully on the mantelpiece, where it would stay until the next one came, then without telling Willie, Senga puts the older one carefully into a box in Sally-Ann's bedroom. It is an excuse to go into her bedroom, to straighten the bed covers which do not need straightening, to look out of the window at the street outside and the houses across the road, to look in the dressing-table mirror that Sally-Ann had looked in every day as she brushed her hair, to run a duster over her little bookshelf and over the lid of her old toybox.

Then she would go downstairs and get on with something useful – cleaning, washing, ironing, cooking. She is a good housewife, Senga. On any day of the year the Queen of England could knock on the door and she would not be ashamed to invite her in; although, in fact, no one ever comes. The windows and the furniture and the brass doorknobs are polished and the rugs beaten, and the gas oven cleaned every time it is used. She is careful with the grocery bill and economically uses up leftovers (often by eating them herself at midday) but, for all that, her cooking is excellent, if old-fashioned. There is always a cake – plain – in the tin, and scones in another, or shortbread; on Saturdays there is always a suet pudding – which she and Willie call a clootie dumpling – and on Sundays a fruit pie to follow the roast. The remains of the roast goes into broth. She has taken pride in all of this. She knows that her marriage to Willie does not always please either of them – they had been too young for a start and then the war had messed everything up – but she also knows that he can have no complaints about how well she looks after him. He gets the best of everything, coming first even before the children; if there is only one egg, or one slice of cake left then Willie would have it – but of course, if you shop every day, says Senga, there will always be enough for everyone. And she acknowledges too that Willie is a good man, in a providing sort of way. He smokes – they both do – but hardly drinks and hands over her housekeeping without a murmur, often asking if she has enough. And she always does, and because she is careful, there is always a bit of surplus to put away, or to spend on the children when they were little, or to save secretly for Sally-Ann's future wedding.

Chapter Seven

They travel down through France, going, as Terry said, where the lifts take them. Rouen, somewhere on the way to Paris, Orleans – a night in a hostel, a morning walking through the town, buying bread, looking for a road that would take them somewhere else. Tours, where they sleep on a bench beside a petanque court. Carcassonne, where they are taken, kindly, by a driver going well out of his way so that they should see it. When they reach the south they turn eastwards along the coast. It is hot, they sleep on the beach. They meet people from other countries, Swedes, Germans, Australians, the days and the places and the people blur into one another. Zita stops using her notebook to write down where they have been; it doesn't seem to matter any more.

They are careful with each other; neither of them wants to take liberties, or provoke the wrong sort of ideas in the other. They keep their conversations light – what schools they each went to, the jobs they did, but not much about their families, or their feelings, or their hopes.

Terry is not as comfortable for money as Zita is; he has been spending since he started work, taking girls out, going out with mates, while Zita has been staying at home, or else playing gooseberry in the company of Marion and Brian.

'We can get work though,' he says. 'Mate of mine told me you can pick grapes. For making the wine you know.'

But although they see crops in the fields, they are not crops of grapes.

In Montpellier, Terry happens to look into Zita's passport, left carelessly to one side as she repacks her rucksack.

'Oh,' she hears him say, surprised.

'What?'

'Sally-Ann, is it? Or have you stolen this passport?'

She knows him well enough by now to be straightforward about it. 'Sally-Ann's what my parents call me. It's my name. I hate it, so I don't use it.'

'Why Zita?'

'I don't know. It just came to me. When you asked me my name, in the library.'

'You must have been thinking about it before. You must have had it in your head, what you'd like to be called.'

'Maybe,' she says. 'I don't remember. It seems a long time ago now.'

'Long ago and far away,' he says. 'But why would you change? People don't change their names.'

'They do,' she says. 'Sometimes. Look at – I don't know – Cliff Richard. That's not his real name.'

'That's different,' says Terry. 'That's called a stage name. I bet his mum don't call him Cliff.'

'My mum don't call me Zita,' says Zita. 'Not yet.'

'Think she will?'

'She'll have to one day. I won't answer to anything else.'

'That's my girl,' says Terry, and she has to turn away, blushing, and tells herself sternly that he doesn't mean it, not in that way, and he never will.

Zita and Terry, Terry and Zita – people think they are a couple, but they assure everyone that they are just friends. 'He's got a girlfriend,' she says. 'Her name's Rosalind. They're engaged.'

'She doesn't mind?' someone would say, and Zita once or twice found herself thinking the words, silently and fiercely in her head, "*I* mind, I couldn't tell you how much *I* mind," before she made herself concentrate firmly on something else.

In August, in Avignon, she has her birthday – her twenty-first – and they splash out on a proper meal, just the two of them, in the cheapest restaurant they can find. But it is a restaurant, not a café or a tea shop; Zita is afraid they will not accept them as customers, looking as they do, even after washing and changing in the Youth Hostel, but she need not have worried. It appears that even people who are not posh are allowed in.

Terry tells her about places he has taken Ros, and about presents he has bought her.

'She's used to going to those classy places,' he says. 'Her dad's pretty well-off, she's used to nice things.'

'So,' says Zita, thinking that listening to Terry talk about Rosalind is not how she wanted her birthday to be, but unable to stop herself, 'will she expect you to make a lot of money? When you are married I mean?'

'I can make money,' says Terry. 'There'll be opportunities.'

'Like what?'

'Don't know yet. But when they come along I'll be ready, don't you worry about me.'

*

Senga, on Sally-Ann's birthday, finds herself unable to settle to anything. She tells herself it is foolish but there is a tiny hope in her that she will see her today, she will come home, she will walk through the door. Senga has baked a cake, just in case, but she knew fine, even as she weighed out the flour and the butter, that she was being foolish, and that she would not be able to ice and decorate it for fear of Willie saying that she was a weak and deluded woman who could not grasp the reality that their daughter was no longer living with them. He will not hear her name mentioned these days; he refuses to speculate as to whether she would ever come home; he only looks silently at the postcards – and they don't arrive regularly every week, not at all – and makes no comment; he suffers in silence, and Senga suffers just to look at him.

Of course Sally-Ann does not come. A birthday card arrives in the post, from Marion, judging by the postmark and Senga puts it in Sally-Ann's bedroom along with other pieces of mail that have arrived for her – an official letter from the library, one from the bank, one that looks to be an invitation, probably from an old school friend, getting married maybe, or just having a party. Marion's twenty-first had been in May and there had been a proper party over the road there: aunts and uncles and cousins as well as friends from when they were at school, and her friends from the salon. And Marion had come over the next day, in the afternoon, when the hangover had worn off a bit, and showed Senga her presents – bits of jewellery and make-up, records and clothes – and Senga had thought then that she needed to make sure Sally-Ann's, when it came, could match up to Marion's. But no, she couldn't. She couldn't have even if her daughter had been still at home. It would have been just the three of them, only one or two presents, maybe a card or two from her aunties in Scotland if they remembered. Was that, wonders Senga, the real reason why she had gone away? Was that a stupid idea?

*

They hitch out of Avignon and it takes them three lifts to get to Arles. They clamber out of the 2CV into the dusty evening heat of a suburban street, and as the car disappears round a corner Terry causes Zita to jump by a loud scream. 'Nooooo!'

'What?'

He is patting his pockets, unfastening his rucksack. 'My jacket!' He points at the corner where the car had turned.

'What?' Though it is clear what he means. 'You don't need it,' she says. 'It's really warm.'

'Wallet,' he says. His voice croaks. 'Money.'

She is silent. They search his rucksack anyway, just to feel they are doing something. His passport is safely there but his money, all of it, was in his wallet, and his wallet was in his jacket pocket, and his jacket had been taken off and draped behind him over the back of the rudimentary canvas seat of the little grey car.

'You didn't see the number? The registration?'

'Course not.'

'What was his name?'

'Don't know.'

'Does he live here?'

'Don't think so. Even if he does –'

'We should go to the police.'

'What would we tell them?'

'In case he hands it in –'

'Fat chance.'

'We'll go anyway,' she says. 'Just in case. Anyway, I've still got money. We'll be all right.'

They pick up their rucksacks and move to what they hope is the centre of the town. They locate a small police station; they manage to explain what has happened. The man – not a *gendarme*, they discover, not even an *agent de police*, but a desk clerk – writes down their details, asks where they will be staying, advises them that there is a small café nearby, in the *place*, where they might get a cheap room. By the time they find it, the patron is stacking the outside chairs and tables; Terry helps him while Zita goes into speak to Madame.

Well, not speaking exactly, not in French, but managing all the same to explain that they need a bed, not just for tonight, but for as long as it will take for more money to be sent to Terry from England.

'He can work,' she says, pointing out of the door to where Terry is even now sweeping up the day's cigarette ends. '*Et moi*,' she adds, wondering what sort of work she might be able to do; cooking and other housework having been always activities she has taken for granted her mother would carry out; rooms have been cleaned and meals made as if by magic and even her father has never encouraged her to help her mother around the house.

'*Vous êtes mariés, vous deux?*'

Zita understands but has no words to explain; even in English she would not know what to say. She waves her hand in a way she hopes will convey the right meaning, though she does not know what the right meaning could be.

'*Il n'y a qu'une chambre,*' says Madame. '*Deux lits quand meme.*'

One room, two beds. '*Ça va,*' says Zita, looking modestly at the floor and hoping it is the right thing to say.

Her next postcard to her parents says: "Dear Mum and Daddy, I am working in a café to earn some money. My French is improving. From Sally."

*

Zita will find the postcards years later. To her, after all this time, the journey down through France has blurred and softened and become adulterated with the many more trips she has taken in her life. The cards are in a shoe box, in the order, so far as she can see, that they were delivered. Pictures of castles and cathedrals, one of oxen pulling a hay cart, which is certainly something she never saw in real life in France, views across fields towards distant hills, and on the back of each one a variation of the same message – 'Dear Mum and Daddy, I am in Carcassonne, it is very old.' Or – 'Dear Mum and Daddy, this place has a famous bridge, love from Avignon.' Never the word 'we.' Never a mention that she was with anybody, not Terry, nor the other people who wandered in and out of their lives. And once she arrived in Arles, she will notice, she no longer signed her name with love.

One posted from Arles, of women dressed in some sort of regional costume, funny black hats and white *fichus* – to think that one shabby little postcard, could bring back a whole conversation, the heat of the room under the roof, the smell of coffee rising from downstairs, mixed with the smell of meat stew which was what they were mostly given to eat by the *patronne*, a moody woman who laughed only once, when Zita referred to her as *Madame la cafetiere*. Seven days a week she and Terry worked, she clearing tables, washing up and sometimes being allowed to chop vegetables, though she never did it to Madame's satisfaction. Terry swept the floors, and the pavement outside, carried the chairs and tables in and out, dealt with the awning and the umbrellas, was sent to shops to get supplies, and taken by Monsieur to farms to get meat and cheese and chickens. The couple were getting too old, that was their trouble, too old to do heavy lifting or to work a fourteen hour day. Their daughter had gone to Marseille to work and had married someone there – in the winter, Madame said, they would close the café and pay her a visit.

It was one of the best times. She remembers the café in Arles well because they were there for a whole month, herself and Terry sharing the room – though not a bed – and working for nothing more than their food and lodging while Terry waited for his father to send him some money. When the café was closed – which was not often – and the clearing up was done, they sat there on their respective beds, Zita still studying her phrase book and her notebook where she wrote down words she saw around her. She tried to teach some French words to Terry, but he was not a willing learner.

'Forget it,' he said. 'I can say yes and no, and beer, and I can point and shake my head. What else do I need while I've got you with me? Anyway, we'll be moving on soon.'

He would spend an evening writing to Ros, with her photograph beside him on the pillow. He wrote at least twice a week. From across the small distance between their two beds Zita could see his cramped sloping handwriting – 'Holds his pen too tight,' she thought – and wondered what he found to say to her. Ros wrote back to him but not as often. The reason was, he said, that she was busy studying, but Zita wondered whether really she was busy with some other boyfriend.

It was here that things changed between them. Now they were no longer on the move, now there were no other young travellers to meet in the hostels, now that they shared, however chastely, the same sleeping place – they began to talk more confidentially. They would lie on their beds at the end of the day, Terry in his shorts and Zita in her nightie and knickers and talk about home. Other things as well, like their futures, and the strange ways French people behaved, but very largely about home. He told her about his brothers: Lol – short for Lawrence – Barry and Darren – and how his mother really wanted a girl and would have gone on trying for one but his dad had put his foot down. She told him a little about Douglas.

'He's a lot older than me. Seven years older. So I never played with him or anything, really, and then he got his call-up and went into the army so we didn't see much of him. He went to Cyprus I think, and Germany – I never got the chance to talk to him about it – and then when he came back they had this big falling out –'

'Who did?'

'My dad, I think – mostly. From what my mum has said – not to me, but I've heard her talking to Daddy – if it wasn't for him it would never have happened, or else it would have been have been made up by now.'

'What was it about, then?'

'I don't know. They would never tell me. They must have had a big row but what it was about I don't know, I wasn't there. I just remember coming home one day – it were a Saturday, I'd been over in Marion's house and I came home for my tea – and I saw Dougie going down the street with two bags and I shouted him but he never turned round and when I went in my mother were crying and Daddy were listening to the football results and they wouldn't say anything.'

'He went where?'

'Nobody would tell me. My Mum were too upset – if I said anything about him she just cried – I couldn't ask her, I hated her crying anyway, I was only fourteen, I didn't know that grown-ups cried. And my Dad wouldn't hear his name. He didn't seem upset, just angry, as if Dougie had done a crime. I didn't dare say anything in front of him.'

'And you've never seen him since?'

'I look out for him, you know, when I'm in town. But I don't even know if I would recognise him now. And I don't know if he would want to know me. I think he's in Sheffield still – I don't know why I think that – he might have moved away. I try not to think about him, but I do. If my parents are out I go up to Dougie's old bedroom and sit there. I've never told anyone that before, except only Marion.'

Terry would tell her all sorts of things, about his family, about Rosalind and her family, about his feelings for her, and for other people. He had become completely unguarded in his conversations with her, how he loved Ros, how they were engaged, secretly because she didn't want to tell her parents yet – not while they were supporting her while she trained.

'How do you know?' she says.

'Know what?'

'That you love her.'

'It's just – you just do. You just know it.'

'And how do you know she loves you?'

'I just know. It's called being in love. When it happens to you, you'll know.'

Zita tries – and succeeds – in not saying what comes into mind. Instead she says, 'So if she doesn't get a job in Sheffield, would you move to where she is?'

'Of course I would,' he says. 'I can get a job anywhere, me. But it won't be necessary. Because she won't be working after her training's done – we'll get married and she'll start having babies. I don't believe in women working when they've got children at home. My Mum never has.'

'Mine hasn't either. But doesn't Ros want to have a job? You know, a career?'

'She can do it later, when the kids have grown up.'

'And she wants to have a baby?'

'We want four, like my family. Of course she wants a baby. Women always want babies.'

'I don't,' said Zita.

'You do,' he said, quite affectionately. 'You just don't know it yet.'

As well as letters from Ros he had letters from his mother with extra scrawls and pictures added by the brothers, a brief note from his Dad, and rambling accounts of daily doings from his Nannan. Madame, who picked up the mail every morning from the post office, was quick to notice.

'*Et ta mère*,' she said to Zita. '*Elle va bien?*'

'*Oui. Merci.*'

'*Elle ne t'écrit pas, bien sur.*'

Zita pretended not to hear. No, she didn't receive letters from England. A letter from her home would say what? Come home at once, from her father; or, we are so worried about you, from her mother. Knowing this, she was sometimes sorry, sorry for them and for herself that it looked to Madame as if she had no family to care for her. It was just as well, she thought, that Terry was relentlessly cheerful. He shared his letters from his family with her, so that she knew what the weather was doing in Sheffield, how the Blades' last match had gone, how Darren was getting on at the comprehensive. Ros sent letters as well – not as often as he would have liked – which he did not allow Zita to read, although he could not stop himself from reading out selected bits. 'Her friends asked her to go to the disco but she didn't go because she doesn't want to dance with anyone but me. The weather's been cold in Sheffield. She's got a practical assessment to do next week so she can't write very much. Got to prepare.'

Receiving a letter made him briefly joyous but once he had read it he seemed disappointed. It seemed to Zita that Rosalind's letters were not, for him, enough like love-letters. When he wasn't in the room she sneaked a look at one he had left on his pillow. Just a dry little account of where she had been – lectures, the hospital, the student bar – and what the weather had been like. A mention of going shopping and a reference to something she could have gone to with her friends but turned down on account of him. Not a word of love or romance until the end: With love, Ros. That was it. Zita wondered how accurately she was portraying her life. Anyway, she thought, it's me he's with now. You could even say we're living together.

A very chaste living together. When he is out of the room she sits on his bed, touches his pillow, imagines there being an evening when he says, Come over here beside me; when he would put his arm round her, kiss her on the lips, pull her close to him – at that point her imagination stops. The taking off of clothes she cannot imagine, either his or hers; she always gets dressed and undressed under the bed covers, he gets changed in the bathroom. Of course she has seen his body, a flat hard torso, almost hairless, a strong looking pair of legs that have played a lot of football in the street and in the park back home; has seen him running into the sea in only his shorts while she sat on the sand, fully dressed. That's how it is here, him stretched out on his bed in a tattered pair of shorts, and herself fully clothed, her body some kind of secret, hidden from even her own self.

By the end of September, the tourists disappeared and the café closed for the winter. '*C'est trop*,' said Madame. '*On va le vendre. Vous voulez l'acheter, vous deux?*' She laughed for the second time, presumably at her own joke of Zita running a catering establishment.

They moved on to St Tropez, as the next card in the shoe box verified. 'It is very nice here but very expensive so I am going to Nice. Don't worry about me.'

She recalls that there was a small group of them in St Tropez, she and Terry and some Irish people, all leaning on the wall of the harbour, eating bread, looking out at yachts they had never dreamed existed, and then back at the umbrellas of the cafes and bars where tanned and well-dressed middle-aged people looked back at them through their sunglasses, as though they were spoiling the view. Which they were.

They did move on to Nice, but found that it was also expensive. They sat in a bus shelter out of the rain, five of them, complaining about how boring it was to have no money.

'Where does that boat go?' said someone.

On investigation it went to Corsica. 'It's an island,' said someone.

'I've never been to an island,' said Zita.

'Except,' said the someone who knew everything, 'that you were born on one. You're English – you've been surrounded by sea all your life.'

'Yeah,' said Terry, 'but you don't get to see much of the sea from Sheffield.'

'Oh, Sheffield.' It was dismissed, just like that.

'What's wrong with Sheffield?' said Zita, not arguing but truly wanting to know.

'The grimy north,' said the other.

'It's not –' said Zita but Terry intervened. 'Why don't we get our stuff, Zee, and go on the ferry to Corsica? If we don't like it we can come back again.'

So they went, the two of them, to Corsica, where it was not raining.

'You wouldn't know would you, that it was an island,' said Zita. 'It's just like any place next to the sea.'

'What did you expect?'

'I suppose,' she said, 'I suppose I was thinking it would be a little island, tiny, that you could see all of it in one go.'

'Oh,' he said. 'I think you'd call that a rock.'

They walked round a little town, looked at a castle on a headland, exclaimed at the colour of the sea. Found that there was no such thing as a youth hostel, nor indeed anything that spoke of accommodation. 'If we go back now,' said Terry, 'back to the port, we'll probably be in time for the ferry back.'

So they did, and re-registered at the hostel, and wondered where to go next.

It was well into October by now and they walked along the Promenade des Anglais on another damp and chilly day with a wind off the sea which, said Terry, you would think would be a warm wind, coming from the south, but was in fact just as nasty as a South Yorkshire wind.

'In fact,' he said, 'I'd forgotten what bad weather is like, but I can safely say I don't like it. What say we move on, Zee?'

'Where to?'

'Naples?' he suggested. 'Well south of here. Then, what about Greece? They say it's cheap there and you can sleep on the beach.'

'I don't know,' says Zita.

'Don't know what?'

'Going further. I don't want to go any further.'

'I'm fed up with France,' he says. 'Feels like we've been here for ever. Not much different from being at home. I want to go somewhere that's *not* like home. Don't you? What do you want?'

He was exasperated, she could tell. It was the first time she had disagreed with him about a plan, and she couldn't have explained it to anyone, not even herself, but it was as if she was a dog that had reached the end of her leash, or one of her father's fish, hook through its lip, being reeled steadily back in.

'I don't know,' she said. 'I wonder if I ought to go home. It's all right for you, you get news from home, but I don't know anything.'

'What are you worried about?'

'Nothing. I mean, I don't know. Anything could have happened. They don't know where I am, they can't get any news to me and it's four months now.'

'It's not anything I've done, is it?'

'Of course not.'

'Because, next to Ros, and my Mum and Dad of course, and Lol, you're my best mate. I mean, go home if you have to, but don't ever lose touch will you.'

So he wasn't going to come with her. 'No, I won't. I'll write to you ,shall I?'

She found that she was wiping a tear from each eye and then he put an arm round her shoulders in a brotherly sort of way and said, 'Cos we'll always be mates won't we, you and me.'

'Yes,' she said.

Zita and Terry go their separate ways. They stand by the side of the road saying their goodbyes. Zita promises to go and see his mother, and also to meet up with Rosalind and reassure her that she is not forgotten. He promises to write and tell her where he is heading for so that she can send him her news.

'I won't have any news,' she says.

'I want to know it all,' he says. 'What your Mum and Dad have said, where you're working, whether you've tracked your brother down. Tell me what you've had for your tea. Tell me what you've watched on the telly. I want to know it all. Write to me every week, promise me.'

'All right,' she says. 'I'll write to you about all the boring stuff, you'll soon get tired of it.'

'Tell me all about the English winter,' he says, 'and I'll tell you all about the sunshine and you'll get so jealous you'll come back and join me.'

Then he turns to her and hugs her; she feels the length of his body against hers. It might last minutes or only seconds; she only knows that it is the greatest happiness she has ever felt and that she is crying so much she has to pull away in order to blow her nose. He picks up his rucksack and crosses the road so that he is on the eastbound side and Zita stays where she is and waits for a car to take her westward. Unexpectedly, he is the first to have a car stop for him. She watches him load his rucksack onto the back seat of a small red Renault, wave to her and climb into the passenger seat. He is gone. She has hardly been without him for more than an hour in all the time they've been away; his absence is a huge and heavy stone in her diaphragm, her throat feels as if she might be getting a bad case of tonsillitis and she says out loud, to no one, 'I do love him. I do.' Then a car stops and she begins the journey home.

The quality of the lift, though it doesn't cheer her, will at least be something to tell Terry about. The driver is quite an old man, maybe older than her father, French of course; the car sweeps quietly along the coast road, Zita leans back on her leather seat and composes herself. Don't look back, never look back.

Her French is serviceable by now, though spiked with mistakes. She can tell him that she is English, that she is on her way home after four months in France; she can tell him where she's been and what she has seen, enough to make him shocked that she has had no guide book and so missed out many of the most important sights. He tells her, and she is able to understand, that he will not be able to take her as far as the west coast; he will be turning north, going to Haute-Savoie, has she heard of Haute-Savoie? He is going to visit his son, who runs a hotel – *bien sur*, who owns a hotel – in the mountains, *ou on fait du ski, vous comprenez?* He can leave her when he turns away from the coast, or, if she wishes, she can accompany him, maybe as far as Grenoble, and take that route home. If she is not pressed.

No, she is not pressed.

Chapter Eight

Sally-Ann's postcard arrives before her parents have even started expecting one. It says, 'Dear Mum and Daddy, I am on my way home so I hope to see you next week. Sally.'

'There,' says Willie. 'I hope she's got that out of her system once and for all. Let's hope we can get back to normal now.'

'Let's hope so,' agrees Senga, but privately she fears that her daughter will have changed too much. She knows, as Willie should also know, that there are certain things that cannot be forgiven or forgotten, and running away is one of them. And normal – what is normal? Suppose Sally-Ann has gone and got married, like she and Willie did, like Douglas said he was going to. Suppose – even worse – she is not married but pregnant. Suppose she brings someone with her, some foreigner. Senga lies awake at night wondering whether she can arrange it so that Sally-Ann can arrive while Willie is at work, so that she will know what the situation is and can take steps. Though what steps? And she has no way of contacting her daughter or knowing when she will walk through the door. Next week – next week from when the postcard was sent, or next week from when they received it? She dozes on and off through the nights and gets up early. She cleans the house thoroughly, the way people do in Scotland before Hogmanay so as to be ready for the New Year; she makes sure the milkman and the paper shop are paid up to date. She bakes. She wears herself out, Willie says: look at her, fit to drop. And still she cannot get a proper night's sleep.

She lies awake and thinks of him saying that. He does care for her, she knows, it's just that he can only show it by complaining. He loved Douglas – surely he did – but how would Douglas have known, when he always picked on him so harshly. Caring for people scares him – Senga knows that, but knows too that she must never let on that she knows. How could she say to Sally-Ann: You're the most important thing in his life, he only criticises because he loves you. How could she have said to Dougie: I know he's wrong, but it's only because he wants you to be happy. And how could she herself go against him, whatever he did, when he was the only person she could count on?

Senga never has seen her own parents again. She turned up at Willie's parents' home and the next day they ran away and got married. They made their way to Sheffield – it being a steel town like Motherwell – and they got jobs. She wrote to her parents saying that she was sorry for the trouble she had caused them and she hoped everyone at home was well. She enclosed a postal order for some of her sisters' money and promised to send more when she could. She did not tell them – not yet – that she thought she was pregnant. Her parents did not reply, but she hardly expected it, given that they both found reading and writing quite a hard thing to do. Her sister Maggie sent a little note, saying nothing much, but charged with the message that she could expect nothing more from her family. 'You have a new family now,' she wrote.

In later years her sisters softened but even so, Senga has never gone home. First there was the war and travel was next to impossible. Willie had joined up, pretty much within days of Douglas being born, and Senga was on her own, with a baby, in one rented room with the use of a gas ring on the landing, in a town where she knew no one. In her letters home she claimed to be managing fine – the baby was a bonny one and a good sleeper, the people she lived with were kind and Willie would surely be home before long. These were lies, and having told them for the most part of her life she knows that she cannot trust anything Sally-Ann writes. Serves me right, she says to herself.

She calls in to the library. Since the first discovery that Sally-Ann was gone she has only had brief encounters with Beryl: a smile and a nod from the other side of the street if they happen to be at the shops at the same time – nothing more. Senga has felt embarrassed at crying in front of Beryl, and, the longer it is since they spoke, the harder it has been to go into the library at all. In fact, she tells herself, she has no heart for reading anything, never mind stories; she will pick up a magazine and leaf through it, that's all, and afterwards remember nothing of what she had read. But she feels bound to tell Beryl the good news – if that's what it is.

'I'm pleased,' says Beryl kindly. 'You must be very excited. And she'll have so much to tell you.'

'Do you think,' says Senga, 'I mean, is there any chance she might get her old job back?'

There is a pause while Beryl thinks what to say. 'Well, the post has been filled of course. She would have to see if there was a vacancy anywhere in the service and apply for it, like anyone else.'

'But I mean, would they consider her even, after doing what she did?'

'If it was me...' says Beryl. 'I mean, if I was interviewing her – well, obviously, I couldn't ignore the way she left so suddenly, but she was a good enough worker, I know that. It would depend on so many things – who else was applying, who is doing the interviewing, what explanations she could offer. Do you see what I mean?'

'Of course,' says Senga humbly. 'I'll tell her when I see her.'

'I hope I'll see her, too,' says Beryl. 'Tell her to call in and say hello.'

All of which, thinks Senga, is nice enough, but no real help.

*

Zita's French improves on the journey. Monsieur Felix is a gentle corrector of her mistakes and they have many hours of conversation ahead of them as he turns the car to the north and heads towards the mountains. He tells her about his sons – both in the family's hotel business – and his grandchildren who are all *mignons*, and his home in the hills behind Nice. Did she find Nice *agréable*? The temps were *mauvais*, she tells him and he agrees. She was with friends in Nice? One friend, she says, but he has gone on to Italy. 'Ah,' he says '*Vous vous manqué de votre petit copain.*'

'*Pas petit,*' she says. '*Copain seulement.*' And she pretends she has something in her eye that needs to be mopped with a handkerchief.

He amuses himself for a while by testing her vocabulary. '*Comment ça se dit?*' They go through handkerchief, shoes, rucksack, car, road, trees and she earnestly tries to remember them, in case he should examine her later.

He buys her lunch in a pleasant restaurant – she is not, he tells her, dressed smartly enough to go into the best place, he would not want her to feel *mal à l'aise*. He chooses for her – a simple fish dish, he says in English – but it is nothing like any fish she has ever eaten, and she can tell that it is even superior to the cooking of Madame in Arles, which had previously been her gold standard. She tries to tell him so.

'Ah,' he says, in English, 'there is what we call high cooking, you understand, and there is *la cuisine familial,* good peasant cooking. Your Madame in Arles, she will make good flavours, of the house, you understand? But not refined. You see?'

She nods. '*Ma mère aussi,*' she says. '*Elle fait bien la cuisine, mais –*' she gestures at her plate.

'English cooking,' he says, 'it is not – up to many.'

She laughs. 'Up to much, we say.'

He twinkles at her over the napkin he has tucked into his collar – *so French* – and she is suddenly so overcome with the feeling of the goodness of people that she feels the lump in her throat again and has to take a sip of wine.

'*Tu aimes le vin?*' It is the first time he has addressed her as '*tu.*'

'*Oui, je l'aime. J'aime toute la France.*'

'*Mais, tu aimes l'Angleterre aussi?*'

'I don't know. I haven't seen much of it.'

'What should they know of England, who only England know?'

She is puzzled. '*Qu'est-ce que ca veut dire?*'

'It is poetry,' he tells her. 'Kipling. Oh, I know your poets as well as you do.'

'Better than me,' she says. 'We didn't do poetry at school. Not much anyway.'

'When you are home again,' he says, 'go to the bookshop and buy some poetry. Learn it in the heart. It will nourish you in times that are difficult.'

He insists that she has a pastry to follow her meal, while he drinks his coffee and brandy and smokes a cigarette.

'You have heard of F. Scott Fitzgerald?'

'Of course.' She has put his books back on the library shelves, but never read them.

'My father,' he says, 'my father owned the hotel where they stayed on the Cote d'Azur. You have read Tender is the Night?'

She has to admit she has not, nor does she know which poem the title is taken from. He says she is ignorant, which in her language is an insult – a bad insult implying a gross lack of social skill, and he sees from her face he has upset her.

'*Ca veux dire, en français, seulement que tu n'avais pas connu – seulement ça. Ce n'est pas une faute. Je m'excuse.*'

She nods, understanding, and he pays the bill and they get back into the car.

On the outskirts of Grenoble he pulls into a petrol station. 'Here,' he says, 'my road goes north-west, and yours, I think, goes north-east. Unless,' he says, and puts his hand on her knee, 'unless you would wish to come with me into the mountains.'

She looks at his hand and after a few seconds he removes it. 'You have the need to go home,' he says. 'I understand. But next time you come to France –' the words produce a joyful feeling in her – 'call me, or call my son if you will like to work in the hotel trade. He is always looking for staff who speak a language not their own.'

She waves to him as he drives away. She stands by the road once more in the early evening light. She shivers and remembers her winter coat, still unused, at the bottom of her rucksack. Time to get it out.

*

On Saturday, Senga hears a knock on the front door. It can't be Sally-Ann, who knows that they always use the back door, but even so her heart is beating hard as she unlocks it and pulls back the rug that stops the draught. There's a girl on the doorstep, a blonde pretty girl wearing brown leather knee boots and a very short skirt.

'Yes?'

'Does Zita live here?' says the girl.

'Who?'

'Zita?' her voice sounds less sure this time. 'Or Zee? Sometimes she gets called Zee.'

'No,' says Senga. 'You must have the wrong address. There's no one in this street called anything like that.' And she shuts the door and finds she is shaking.

'Who was that?' says Willie, coming through from the yard.

'No one,' she says. 'She got the wrong house. Looking for someone called Zita.'

He shrugs and turns away, but then turns back to say, 'You don't think she was someone that knows our Sally-Ann, do you?'

'No, no, not at all,' says Senga. 'She was a very smart young lady, very nicely dressed. Fashionable, you know. Well spoken. Not from round here.'

'You should have asked her.'

'Asked her what?'

'Well, something at least. You could have thought of something.'

'If it happens again,' she says, 'I'll call you shall I? You can do the talking.'

Chapter Nine

It is several more days before Sally-Ann, one afternoon, pushes open the back door, hesitantly, shyly, and stands in the kitchen that is steamy from the boiling of broth and the ironing of sheets. Senga, slowly as if she is sleep-walking, reaches to pull out the plug of the iron and comes out from behind the table.

'Mum,' says Sally-Ann.

Senga feels an odd rush of anger, as if she would like to slap her daughter; at the same time she wants to rush at her and hold her tightly. What she does do is to walk up to her and hold her by the shoulders and shake her gently; it is Sally-Ann who tries to turn it into a hug, though only a brief one.

'I'll put the kettle on,' says Senga, pulling herself away. 'And don't you ever, *ever* do a thing like that again.'

Sally-Ann – no longer Zita – is looking round the kitchen as if to check that everything is the same as it was, which of course it is. She props her rucksack against the cupboard and sits down on a chair, and lets out a long breath as if she is exhausted.

'Tired?' says Senga.

'Not really. Just a bit. I've walked up from the station.'

'Come by train, did you?'

'No, I hitched. Just got dropped at the station and it wasn't worth trying for another lift.'

Senga pours water into the teapot. 'Do you need something to eat?'

Her daughter looks up at the clock on the shelf. 'I'll wait while teatime. A cup of tea will be lovely though. I haven't had a proper cup of tea in months.'

'What have you been drinking then? What do they drink over there?'

'Coffee. Wine too.'

'Wine,' says Senga. 'I hope you've no been drinking wine. Spending all your money.'

'It's really cheap. But no, I didn't drink much wine, don't worry.'

'I suppose your money ran out then?'

'I've got some left. I'll put it back in the bank.'

Why are we talking like this, wonders Senga, as if she never went away, as if she's done nothing wrong, and nothing has happened, and nobody's been crying themselves to sleep. She sets the cup of tea in front of Sally-Ann and opens the cupboard for a packet of Garibaldi biscuits.

'You look thin,' she says.

'Do I?'

'And brown,' says Senga. 'I've never seen you so brown.' Sally-Ann, with her Scottish skin, has never before managed a tan in her life.

'I'm not very brown,' she says. 'Not next to some of the others.'

'You went with a group of people then? You were no on your own?'

'Oh no,' says Sally-Ann, but does not expand on her answer.

'I suppose you've got some washing to do?' Senga directs a nod towards the rucksack.'

'Some. I'll put it in the basket when I've had my tea.' She sips her tea even though it is too hot to drink. 'Is it all right if I have a bath?'

'I'll put the immersion on for you.' And Senga goes upstairs. Why aren't I shouting at her, she thinks. Here's me, wanting to give her a good telling-off, and there's her sitting like she's done nothing at all, and what Willie will be saying to her I can't imagine, when he gets home. She goes back into the kitchen where Sally-Ann is still sipping her tea. She looks different – as well as being thinner and slightly sun-tanned, she has tied back her hair and it gives her a look that Senga feels might be elegant and slightly foreign, in spite of the shabby clothes she is wearing. 'Give it half an hour to get hot,' she says. 'Do you want more tea?'

'Yes, please,' says Sally-Ann, and smiles for the first time. 'There's nothing like a nice cup of tea. At least, take it from me, in France there's nothing like a nice cup of tea.'

Senga smiles too, appreciating the effort. 'Your bed's made,' she says. 'You can go for a wee lie-down if you feel like it.'

'I'll have a bath,' she says. 'Then I'll wait for Daddy to come home, but I'll probably have an early night. I started at seven o'clock this morning. I've come all the way from Dover, all in one day. I thought I'd only get about halfway home, but I were really lucky with lifts. I usually am lucky. People always said it were good, hitching with me because I get good lifts.'

'How would you do that then?'

'I don't know. There isn't a reason. I'm just lucky that way.'

'You had a good time then?'

'Didn't you get my postcards?'

'Sure we did. But you didn't tell us much, did you? Same every time – "Don't worry about me, the weather is nice." What good is that to anyone?'

'I'll go and run the bath,' she says.

When she comes down from the bath her hair is loose and damp and she is wearing slippers and pyjamas and a thick sweater. She sits back down in her chair, the one she has always sat in to eat with her parents, the one that faces the back door, the one she sat in as a small child, waiting for her father – or for Douglas – to come in through the door, home from work or school.

'It's toad-in-the-hole tonight,' says Senga.

'If there's not enough, don't worry,' she says. 'I can have a sandwich, I don't need a proper meal.'

'As if there wouldn't be enough,' says Senga – who has in fact nipped down to the shop to buy a couple of extra sausages while Sally-Ann was in the bath. 'I bet you haven't had a square meal in months.'

'French food is nice,' says Sally-Ann mildly.

'Do they no use oil for everything? And garlic, I've heard.'

'It isn't the same as your home cooking, Mum. And I haven't had toad-in-the-hole, not once, while I've been away.'

'You'll be looking forward to it, then?'

Willie gets home at his usual time. They hear the latch of the gate and the click of the pedals as he wheels his bike into the back yard. Senga turns to the cooker to stir the gravy rather than see his face change at the sight of Sally-Ann, who remains still and expectant – steeled.

Willie sees her the very second he pushes open the back door. His face transforms into a rare and wide smile. His eyes shine and he holds out his arms. 'Come here, lass,' he says, and she stands up and walks round the table towards him and he hugs her tight and pushes her away so that he can see her, and then hugs her again. Senga looks on in some surprise; this is not the behaviour she would have expected from him.

'Sit down there,' he says to Sally-Ann, 'and don't move while I go and wash myself. Stay there now, till I get back, don't go running off again.'

Senga and her daughter exchange looks. 'Jings,' says Senga. 'That's no what I was waiting for.'

Zita – she can be Zita again in the privacy of her bedroom – sleeps well for the first part of the night and wakes early, while it is still dark. It is a strange feeling, waking and knowing exactly where she is, in her own bed, in her own room, different from waking up on a beach, or a bench, or in a dormitory, or even in the room above the café in Arles. It's her own room, where everything is known, in her own house where she has lived all her life, and in the next room her own parents, so familiar and at the same time so changed – her mother so stiff and suspicious, her father so volatile, his laughter and jokes so forced, his silences so unsettling. She does not know if they were always like this. Has her going away changed them, or has it just changed what she sees in them?

She lies in the dark and thinks about Terry, and about France, and sunshine, blue front doors, baguettes for breakfast, dinner and tea, schoolchildren shaking hands with each other when they meet on their way to school, people drinking wine in squares with the sun shining down in patches through the leaves of the trees. She thinks about getting a blister on her heel when they had to walk miles because there was no traffic on the road, about having to sleep in doorways when there was no hostel to go to, or they arrived to find it shut, or full. She makes herself remember Terry's unchanging commitment to Rosalind, how he talked about her every day, how he kissed her photo at night before he went to sleep, whether Zita was watching or not. Shameless devotion, she thinks. She remembers the bad lifts – sliding about in the back of vans, ending up, when there was some misunderstanding, in the wrong town, or the wrong side of the right town and having to find their way through unwelcoming streets where men stood under streetlights and called out to her. She thinks of the laughs she and Terry had, laughing about nothing, mostly: just laughing because things had gone right for a change, or had gone more wrong than usual. They had not quarrelled once – not what you'd call proper quarrelling anyway, just bickering over which way to go, or what to buy to eat; nothing that made her regret being with him.

She turns over in the bed and closes her eyes and tries to go back to sleep. But she has a list of tasks to do, starting in the morning. Unpacking, obviously, and sorting out her belongings. Getting a new, proper, ten year passport to last her through all the travelling she dreams of doing. Finding a job to see her through till Christmas, because the last thing she wants to do is to hang around the house getting in her mother's way and feeling guilty for everything she does or doesn't do. Telling Marion about everything. Getting in touch with Ros and finding out from her where to send a letter to Terry. Going to see Terry's mother to reassure her that he is fine and happy.

Finding Douglas. That, it becomes apparent to her now, is the reason she has come home.

'If it were me,' Terry said – on the promenade in Nice – 'if I had a brother that I didn't see, I'd go and search him out. There's got to be ways.'

'He might not want to see me.'

'You don't know, do you, till you try?'

'I don't know where to start.'

He looked at her so sharply that she looked away. 'You know more than you let on,' he said. 'You know his friends, who he was at school with. Never mind what your mum and dad will say – don't tell 'em. Just do it.'

'All right,' she said. She would always, whatever the evidence, then and later, believe that Terry knew best.

She has to go and see Rosalind. She does and doesn't want to do it, is both drawn and repelled, but can't put it out of her mind. She decides to wait until Sunday, fidgeting and fretting about it, wondering if Ros will want to be friends with her and if so, how she will manage. She imagines cosy evenings talking about him; she invents scenarios where she and Ros are waiting together at Dover for Terry to step off the boat – maybe Ros would fall in the water and drown and Terry, after a suitable period of a week or so would know that it had really, all along, been Zita that he loved. She considers not going to see Ros at all, but she promised. She has her excuse – she wants to know where Terry will be next so that she can write to him. As he has asked her to.

She takes her thoughts away from Ros, to some degree by doing other errands. She calls into the local library to see Beryl and apologise for leaving without letting her know.

'It's all right,' says Beryl, without smiling. 'At least it is now we've got someone else.'

'I'm not asking for my job back,' says Sally. 'I'll be here for a few weeks and then I'm going back to France. I've been offered a job there.'

'Your mum will miss you,' says Beryl.

'I have to leave home sometime,' says Sally. 'She must know that.'

'She was very upset you know. It was naughty, what you did.'

'It's all OK now,' she says. 'I've told her I'm going back; she's got to get used to it. In the meantime – I know I can't have my job back, but I do need to get a job for a month or two.'

'Try the shops,' says Beryl. 'They might be taking on staff for Christmas.'

'OK. Thank you,' says Sally; she understands that she will not be working in the library ever again. She looks around at the tall bookshelves, the parquet floor, the high counter and has the vague feeling that she will never even come in there again.

'And while you're down town,' says Beryl, 'you might call in and make your apologies to Miss Bunting. She took it very badly you know, very worried about you she was. She deserves an apology.' She sees the face Sally is making and adds, even more briskly, 'I know you don't want to, but you've a duty.'

Sally shrugs, tries to smile.

'It's not funny,' says Beryl. 'She's not young, Olive Bunting, she shouldn't have to be worried about her subordinates. I know she's a funny old thing to you young people but she means well.'

'All right,' says Sally. Her visit to Beryl has proved less comfortable than she expected; Beryl disapproves of her; there will be no interesting conversations about where she has been or what she has done.

'You see, Sally–' says Beryl, and Sally, for the first time ever, interrupts her quite rudely.

'Actually,' she says, 'they don't call me Sally any more. My name is Zita.'

Beryl gives her a look that she has never seen before, a look that says she is childish, or affected, or showing off. Sally – Zita that is – is certain now that she will never be coming into this library again.

It is surprisingly easy to get a job. Just by going into Walshes and asking to speak to the manager, and offering to do anything in any department gets her a job in the tea room. She will be clearing tables and washing up and doing whatever anyone tells her to do. It will not be as professional-seeming as working in the library, not as skilled ,some would say, but she is quite happy to do it for a few weeks.

She calls in, that same afternoon, to the reference library, but does not stay long. The other assistant there smirks behind Miss Bunting's back and Miss Bunting herself is flushed and flustered and has clearly not forgiven her. Five minutes is enough to assure her that she is an unwelcome visitor.

'It's a shame,' says her mother. 'You should never have thrown up that good job. You won't get anything like that wage at Walshes. It's not a career, is it, wiping down tables? You'll be sorry.'

'I'll never be sorry,' says Sally. 'I could have ended up like Miss Bunting. I could have worked there for forty years and never seen anything but them dusty old books.'

'You've let yourself down,' says Senga. 'It's no even a waitressing job is it? It's menial, that's what it is.'

'I don't care,' said Sally. 'You know I'm going back to France after Christmas anyway.'

'So you say,' says her mother. 'You'll be sorry, if you ask me. On your own, in the winter. It won't be fun then, I'm sure.'

Senga is confused. My own daughter, she thinks, and I don't get it. Why did she go? Why did she come back? Sometimes she's the same, sometimes she's like a person I've never met before. It's not like when Douglas came out of the army and he was so pleased to be back and everything was fine, until it wasn't. Or is it just I'm waiting for something to go wrong, like it did with him? She's always been a good girl but now I can't tell whether she's good or no. She's behaving herself right enough, our Sally-Ann, but hasn't she always behaved. Always been the good girl. But she's no the same, and I can't get a grasp on what's different.

Willie is not a help. She's home, he says, that's all that matters. He doesn't seem to believe what she says about going away again. He seems to believe the clock and the calendar have been turned back and the household is back to normal. She's got it out of her system, he says, she'll be fine now. But Senga has sneaked a look at Sally-Ann's little notebook that went with her all round France; she has seen the names and addresses of people she's never heard of, some of them foreign names, with addresses in other countries, as far away as Australia. And also two addresses in Sheffield: Ros is one, and the other is Mr and Mrs Brown and an address on Arbourthorne.

Chapter Ten

It isn't hard to find Ros; she lives in a shared rented house down off the Ecclesall Road. Rosalind herself opens the back door when Zita knocks on it, and seems to know straightaway who she is. 'Terry said you'd call,' she says.

'Last time I saw him,' explains Zita, 'he didn't know where he was going next, so he said by the time I got home you would know, cos he keeps you up to date doesn't he, and you could tell me. He wants me to write to him, see, he loves getting letters.'

'I write to him,' says Rosalind, a bit coldly.

'I know. He is so happy when he gets them. Honestly, you should see him.'

'He doesn't let other people read them, I hope.'

'Course he doesn't.'

'So is that all you came for?' says Rosalind. She clearly has no intention of saying, Come in, have a cup of tea, tell me all about your travels. 'He said, next letter, send Poste Restante, Naples.'

'I'll write to him tonight,' says Zita.

'You don't have to,' says Rosalind. 'I'll be writing in a day or two.'

'OK,' says Zita, though without changing her intention, and walks away wondering if Terry really knows what a cold welcome Rosalind is capable of. She considers briefly that she might be jealous but dismisses it. No one who knows Terry could doubt how much he is in love with Rosalind and she knows that no one who sees Rosalind next to her, Zita, could doubt which one of them is the most attractive.

The tearoom is fine. It is not as much fun as working alongside Terry; it is not as challenging as trying to understand the language of French customers; it does not, as her mother says, pay as much as the library but it is fine. When the Christmas rush gets going she is often sent to help out in departments that are short-staffed, moving from toys to kitchenware, from men's socks to Christmas decorations. She enjoys, in spite of the aching feet at the end of the day, the feeling of being a part of a big establishment and the knowledge that she is good at being helpful. She couldn't, she thinks, have been so competent and confident a few months ago. Her pre-France life seems to belong to someone else, someone much younger and less impressive.

She writes letters to Terry and receives one back, from Naples. He is with a small group of Canadian travellers. Naples was dirty, he says, and not welcoming; they are going to go North again, maybe into Switzerland. Has she seen Ros? Did they have a good talk? He likes to think of them being friends. And she mustn't forget to go and see his parents and his brothers; they are waiting to see her, he has told them so much about her.

She visits his parents one Sunday. Sleet is slanting into her face as she waits for the door to open. It is one of the brothers who opens it, and the sight of him brings back so completely Terry, his grin and his eyes, that she almost gasps, but instead says, 'Are you Lol?'

'Lol's out,' he says. 'Football. I'm Barry.'

'Is your mum in?' And then she emerges from the kitchen, drying her hands on a tea-towel the way Zita's mother would do, and saying, 'Is it Zita? It must be. Come in, come in, don't stand out there in the rain.'

And then it is just as Terry told her it would be – cups of tea and jam tarts and telling stories of their travels, and Mr and Mrs Brown – Peggy and Lawrence they insist – telling her about their boys, and especially about Terry, especially about how he always wanted to go places, so much about Terry that Barry, who is thirteen, becomes either bored or jealous and kicks out at his little brother and spoils his carefully choreographed array of toy soldiers. He looks guiltily round at his parents – they are both looking sternly at him and his father says quietly, 'That'll do.'

Zita is looking round at the room, noticing the ways in which it does, and doesn't, look like her parents' house. Just as clean, a bit less tidy – well, naturally with three boys and their belongings and their toys. A family of boys would also explain the worn look of the carpet and the sofa cushions. Coal fire, just like home, though with the addition of a fireguard in front; same brush and shovel and coal bucket, same smell. Above the fire there are family photos on the mantelpiece – a wedding photo, school photos of the boys, so many that they are jostling for position, and in the corner, on the sideboard, more photos:

grandparents, it looks like, in deckchairs on the beach, holding a baby in a garden, crossing arms at some sort of party, singing Auld Lang Syne most likely. Is it, wonders Zita, the presence of all these images – or is it just the presence of three boys – that makes the room feel more homely, more welcoming than her parents' home? What is it that makes the fire seem to burn brighter, and the room feel warmer? Do they use a different sort of coal over this side of the city?

Peggy offers more tea and another jam tart and asks why Zita has come home and she explains that she thought she had better see how her parents were getting along, since they hadn't agreed to her going in the first place.

'So you went without telling them?' says Lawrence. 'My wife would have died if our Terry had done that.'

'They would have stopped me,' says Zita. 'I sent them postcards.'

'Every week? Terry writes to us every week.'

'Yes,' she says, though she knows it isn't true. At the beginning she intended to send one every week, even congratulated herself for being so punctilious but now she can tell that intention was half-hearted. Not good enough. And she didn't even keep to her intention for long.

'And I bet they were pleased to see you,' says Peggy.

Zita smiles a little. 'Relieved, I think. Next time they won't mind so much.'

'Next time? Are you off again? Going to catch up with our Terry in Italy?'

Why not, she thinks to herself and it hurts her somewhere inside, but she smiles and says, 'I'm going to work in a hotel over the winter. Where people go skiing, in the French Alps.'

And she tells them about the lucky lift and the business card that he left her with and how she had to go to the Post Office to make an international call, and how her French went all wrong –'Now, I don't believe that,' says Peggy. 'Our Terry always says how much French you knew. Mind, he's in Italy now so French wouldn't be much good to him.'

Lol comes home then, all covered in mud, and Zita gets up to go.

'Come and see us again,' says Lawrence. 'Come at Christmas, bring your mum and dad. We always have a do on Boxing Day, why don't you come?'

'I don't know,' she says. 'Are you sure?'

'He's sure–,' says Peggy. '–Lol, get upstairs and in the bath – We'd love you to come and tell Terry's aunties and cousins what he's been doing.'

'I don't think my parents –'

'Then just come on your own. I mean it.' And she smiles her big smile and pats her on the shoulder in a friendly and motherly way.

Is it love? wonders Zita, that makes the difference between her home and Terry's, but she knows her parents love her, even though it is never said. She knows that her mother goes without in order to buy treats for her daughter; she knows her father cares about her even while he is criticising. Happiness, she thinks, is what makes the difference. There is more happiness in Terry's home, that's what it is.

'Have you tracked your brother down yet?' writes Terry from somewhere near Milan. He was no longer with the Canadians – they had turned left into France. He and an English couple – a crazy pair, he called them – were heading for Germany; she could write to him Poste Restante Munich. His letter is at home waiting for her when she returns from a busy Saturday in the tearoom, and also waiting for her, sitting at the kitchen table, is Marion, back in Sheffield now for the winter, filling the space as always, flashing her engagement ring and bewildering Senga with a full account of her wedding plans.

'So what's all this then?' she says. She has Terry's letter in her hand and is waving it as if it is Exhibit One. 'He's got to like you Sal, to be writing actual letters. Brian wouldn't write to me if I was stuck at the South Pole.'

It would not be beyond Marion to actually open the letter and read it aloud; Sally quickly takes it from her teasing hand and tucks it into her own coat pocket.

'Where's Brian?'

'Gone to his mum's. Come to the pub with us tonight?'

'OK.'

'And I'm going to do something with your hair. You've let yourself go, Sal, since I saw you last.'

'I've been working all day. We've been run off our feet.'

'Come over when you're ready. I'll do your make-up for you.'

'OK,' she says again. 'I'll have a bath and then I'll come over.'

'Your tea's ready,' says Senga.

'Mine will be too,' says Marion and gets up to go. She suddenly opens her arms and pulls Sally to her; Sally finds there are tears in her own eyes. 'I've missed you,' she says.

'I've missed you too,' says Marion. 'We'll have a good catch-up, all right?'

There is so much to tell, on both sides. Great Yarmouth and France, Terry and Brian, the wedding preparations, Sally's plans, and a million small details, the people they've met, the differences they've been exposed to, the enlargement of their worlds. The people they are now. Sally sits on Marion's bed, looking at her extensive collection of every Avon product her mother can provide for her – but arranged in tidy rows, by size and purpose, lids all in place, not like her own untidy jumble. Even at school Marion was always neat and tidy with her books and her pencil case.

'So,' says Marion, 'you even slept in the same room and he never tried anything. Is there something wrong with him?'

'He's faithful to Ros,' says Sally. 'He loves her very much.' She meant it to sound sweet but it came out rather on the bitter side.

'But you fancy him.'

'Well –'

'Give over. Give over being, Oh we're just friends. I can see right through you Sally-Ann Grey. You'd take your knickers off for him, I know.' Sally can see Marion's reflection in the mirror; can see her smirking knowingly.

'Actually,' says Sally, 'I should tell you – I go by a different name now. They call me Zita now.'

'Your mum doesn't.'

'She doesn't know. But everyone that I've met since – they all think I'm Zita.'

'Zita,' says Marion. 'Unusual. Whose idea was that?'

'Mine.'

'Does Terry call you Zita?'

'Or Zee. Mostly Zee.'

'What did his letter say?'

'Oh, just about these people we know, and Italy, and where he's going next. And reminding me about something.'

'What?'

Zita hesitates. Her parents have always told her that she is not to discuss family business – by which they mean Douglas – with other people. Particularly, they would say, with the neighbours. Marion turns away from the mirror and spits into her mascara.

'What? Come on Sal, no secrets.'

'I suppose – it's not a secret to you, is it. You know all about Douglas.'

'What about him?'

'Terry says I should try to find him. He's got brothers you see, he thinks it's awful, having a brother that I can't see. He thinks it's unnatural.'

'So are you going to?'

'What?'

'Find him. Do you want to?' She turns back to her reflection and works on her eyelashes.

'I do *want* to. I can't believe that he could do something so bad that we can't even mention him at home.'

'Who says?'

'Says what?'

'That you can't mention him. It's your dad isn't it. I bet your mum would mention him if you asked her. I bet she even knows where he is. Have you ever asked her?'

'I used to ask her. But she would never tell me anything. I started to think he must have gone to prison for something really terrible. But I can't believe that.'

'That's ridiculous,' says Marion. 'My mum says he was a very quiet boy. Wouldn't say boo to a goose, she says.'

'Does she know where he is? Does she know what happened? Have you ever asked her?'

'I've asked her, when I was younger. She wouldn't say much because she said I was a loudmouth and I'd tell you and get you into trouble. It was something to do with a girlfriend.'

'He had a girlfriend?'

'That's all I know – something to do with a girlfriend. Maybe he got her pregnant. Maybe your parents had something against her. Maybe it's like West Side Story.'

'I wonder if he's still in Sheffield.'

'Look in the phone book.'

'I looked. When I worked in the library. But he wasn't there. But *we* haven't got a phone, a lot of people haven't got one.'

'Ask your mum. In fact, tell you what, *I'll* ask her for you.'

'No don't. It's my job. He's my brother.'

Marion gets up, her make-up complete. 'Come and sit here, I'll do your hair for you.' She brushes it out. 'I'm going to call you Zee. Is that all right?'

Sally-Zita smiles gratefully.

'Your split ends are in a state. You've not been looking after it have you.'

'Too busy,' says Zita. 'And travelling – well, there's not the facilities in hostels. You're lucky if you can dry it.'

'You've been out in the sun.'

'Course I have.'

'Do you know what,' says Marion. 'I could cut it for you – not now cos we're going out, but I could cut it tomorrow. You'd look good with short hair – a sort of Mary Quant look. Twiggy, Cilla Black, you know, neat and short. It would suit you.'

Zita considers. Her hair has always been a problem. It's both thin and coarse, it never does what she wants it to. In France she wore it in a pony tail for convenience and the rubber bands have damaged it. There has never been anyone, not even her mother, who has complimented her on her hair so what has she got to lose? 'All right,' she says.

Senga is finding these few weeks a trial. Right enough, Sally-Ann is home. She is safe and well, and not pregnant. She is calm and reasonable, she is kind. But distant. Not herself. Her mother has seen the letters that arrive every couple of weeks; she has seen that they are addressed to Miss Z Grey. She has said nothing and she has not drawn Willie's attention to them. Sally-Ann has also said nothing. Secretive? wonders Senga. No, not really, she will answer questions, she will tell stories, but you have to ask. And then she will tell you wee funny stories and make you forget what it was you were asking her. Willie sees none of this. His little girl is home and he brushes away her open intention to go away again. He does not seem to care to listen to her travellers tales; he asks her about her day at work and encourages her to work hard, make herself noticed, be indispensable, get a job in the office, better herself. She does not argue with him, just sometimes reminds him gently that she will be going away again after Christmas. Senga would like to slap both of them.

'Mum,' she says, 'are you going to the market this week?'

'Aye,' says Senga. 'I'll be starting to put by for Christmas. Wednesday probably.'

'Can I meet you there in my dinner hour? We can have something to eat in the café.'

'Why would you be doing that? You get your dinner for nothing don't you.'

'I thought it would be nice.'

'Well, all right, I suppose so.'

So they are sitting at a Formica-topped table in a noisy café, a cup of tea and a sandwich in front of each of them, Sally-Ann checking her watch because she must not be late back.

'Mum, I want to ask you something.'

Here it comes, says Senga to herself. She knew there was something funny about this. She's not pregnant, I know that, so what is it?

'I want to ask you about Douglas.'

Senga stares at her, hearing what she just said but allowing herself to be distracted by the new short hairdo. Her lovely long hair and she let Marion cut it all off.

'Mum: Douglas.'

Senga looks about her, as if Willie might be there, listening. 'What about him?'

'I want to know where he is. Is he in Sheffield? Do you know where he is? What happened?'

'Oh jings,' she says. 'I canna tell you.'

'Mum. Just tell me something. Why did he leave home?'

Senga says nothing. She does not dare to start speaking.

'Marion says it was to do with a girlfriend.'

'What does Marion know about it?'

'That's all she knows. She thinks Dougie fell out with you and Daddy because of a girlfriend. Is that right?'

'Oh, I can't say,' says Senga. She takes a large bite of her ham sandwich and chews as if it will save her.

'Do you know where he lives?'

Senga shakes her head, unable to speak through bread and ham and pickle.

'Not even roughly where he lives? Not his address, but which part of town?'

Senga takes a large gulp of tea to wash the bread down, and grimaces because she has forgotten to put the sugar in.

'Mum, he's my brother. I would like to know him. What's wrong with him that I have to be kept away from him? It's not fair on me.'

Senga spoons sugar into her tea and stirs it for longer than necessary. 'It's just how it is,' she says.

'It's not the way it should be,' says Sally-Ann. 'When I tell people I don't know my own brother they all think there's something wrong with our family.'

'Which people? What have they to do with it?'

'Anybody. Terry –'

'Oh Terry. What does he know? How is it any of his business?'

'It's not his business, that's not what I mean. Just tell me, where does he live? Our Douglas. Or have I got to go to the police station and ask them. Have I got to put an ad in the paper for him? Have I got to go round all the boys he was at school with?'

'You don't know them.'

'I bet I do. I could find out.'

Senga puts her sandwich down on her plate. She grips the handle of her teacup as if it will support her. 'Your father,' she says, 'would not hear of it. I'm not saying, mind, that I agree with him, not on everything, but he's the man of the house. He's told your brother to go away and stay away, and your brother has done that. It's not for me to change the way things are. What can't be cured —'

'Don't say that stupid stuff,' says Sally. 'Just tell me what you know.'

But Senga has had enough. She pushes back her chair and picks up her bags, and Sally — Zita — looks sadly at her retreating back in its old brown coat.

In truth, Senga does not know where Douglas is living; neither does Willie. He was given a choice by his father and he made his choice. He went up to his room and filled a carrier bag or two with his few possessions — the few civvy clothes he had that still fitted him, a small record collection, his Box Brownie camera. He left behind his school books and his story books and his Dinky cars and his Airfix models. The business took no more than ten minutes and then they heard him come down the stairs — they were sitting, tense and silent, in the front room — and they heard the back door close. And later, when Sally-Ann asked where he was Senga lied and said he's had to go back to the army for a wee while, and Willie shouted at her, and told Sally-Ann that Douglas was gone for good, and good riddance because he was not welcome here.

Senga did not exactly share Willie's view but she understood it. Live and let live, she might have said, but she wouldn't have liked it. She and Willie had never seen a coloured person before they came to Sheffield. They didn't have them in Scotland. They didn't have them in Sheffield until the war brought them. Maybe in London, who knew, but not around here. After the war Willie worked in the forge with some men from Yemen — 'Good workers,' he said. 'Hard workers. Wouldn't keep 'em on otherwise.' But West Indians — he couldn't take to them. He used all sorts of names for them – spades and jungle bunnies was the nice end of what he would say. Senga put it down to being in the army during the war; everything that was wrong with Willie was because of the war. And they had never met this young woman, didn't even know her name, but Willie had seen his son with her, outside the swimming baths, holding hands, laughing, and that had been enough.

Where Douglas had gone when he walked out – they didn't know that either. He could have married her. They could have children by now, little brown children – would Willie call them nasty names? They could be living in the flats, they could have gone to another town. They could be in Jamaica, or Australia, or anywhere. Senga had given up looking out for Douglas. It took a lot of energy, walking round streets on a Saturday, peering in the faces of young men, wondering what she would do if she did meet him. Would she even recognise him after nearly eight years? Would he even speak to her? And if he did what could she say? – Your father's sorry? Because he wasn't, he wasn't sorry at all. He had ripped up all the photos of Douglas as a little boy – though Senga had had the presence of mind to take the negatives and hide them in her underwear drawer where he would never look.

Sometimes it has occurred to Senga, in a vague sort of way, that Willie never really took to Douglas. He had hardly had time to get used to being a father when he was called away to Catterick for training. Other men working in the steelworks were considered to be necessary to the war effort and told to stay at home and carry on making the wherewithal for planes and ships and tanks, but Willie, somehow, got called up. Maybe it was his own decision; maybe with the baby on its way he thought the army would be a better bet. Senga never asked him, and it was surely too late now. But it did mean that he saw his little son seldom, and briefly, and it was never satisfactory, and when he finally came home to stay, Douglas was well past his sixth birthday, and, said Willie, disgusted, a proper mammy's boy who would prefer playing quietly in the house to running in the street with the other kids.

When Sally-Ann was born though, it was a different matter. Willie would even push the pram if they went out on a Sunday. He would sit her on his knee and sing to her. 'Clap hands Daddy comes, with his pocket full of plums.' He spoiled her, he favoured her over Dougie, she could do no wrong and it was a wonder that she grew up as pleasant as she did, thought Senga, having been the centre of her father's world for the whole of her life. Count your blessings, Senga often told herself. She wanted Willie to leave her when she realised that Douglas would never be coming back while he was there, but of course he wouldn't hear of it. Why should he? If it was her that wanted to separate – and it was – then it was up to her to find herself somewhere else to live. But how could she, she thought, because then Dougie wouldn't ever find her. And what about Sally-Ann? Willie certainly would do his best to keep her. 'My best girl,' he called her, though she was into her teens now and he'd have been better being firmer with her. There she was with Marion Ward, putting on make-up and writing the names of boys on their school books, and hanging round after the youth club, hanging round on street corners instead of coming straight home as they'd been told to do. If Dougie had been late home when he was that age he would have got a good hiding, but Sally-Ann would get away with a stern look and a threat that would never be carried out. And look where that ended up, says Senga out loud.

Chapter Eleven

On Christmas Eve, at the end of a long busy day, Zita collects her wages and her insurance cards from the office. One of the assistant managers is there, cashing up and generally seeing to the end of Christmas, as far as the shop is concerned. He recognises her as the girl he has redeployed over the previous two months to fill in the gaps in his staffing.

'Sorry to lose you,' he says. 'If you want a job here – permanent – you can have one. And if you ever need a reference just let me know. Good worker,' he says. 'Never missed, picked up quickly, got on with everyone. I'll make a note of it now – don't forget, just call in and ask if you need a recommendation.'

'Thank you,' says Zita. 'I'm going to work in France for the winter, in a ski hotel.'

'All the best then,' he says, and shakes her hand.

She will always remember – Zita – the sadness of that Christmas. The awkwardness, as if her parents were strangers to her, and she to them. All through Christmas Day her mother kept looking at her warily, as if she was going to say something about Dougie in front of her father; questions filled the air between them like static. Her father pretended not to notice and kept up some sort of seasonal cheer, laughing too hard at the television and drinking more than he was used to. And Sally fidgeted and chafed, and went to her room to write a letter to Terry, and found nothing to say to him, although in her head she talked to him much of the time, rehearsing her letters, saving up the small everyday things that he said he wanted to know about. She hadn't heard from him and it was another thing that made her anxious.

On Boxing Day afternoon, after the subdued and awkward festivity of Christmas Day at home, Sally-Ann becomes Zita once more and goes again to the Browns' house and tells the stories once more to a wider audience of friends and relatives and neighbours, all crammed into the little house, eating from the buffet in the kitchen and talking loudly over the noise of the record-player in the front room. Terry's Nannan is there, sitting by the fire with her Advocaat snowball and Zita is taken to her and introduced.

'You're not Rosalind,' says the old lady.

'No,' agrees Zita.

'He brought that Rosalind to see me,' she says. 'Never said a word, not a word, to me. Stuck up, I call her.'

Zita knows she shouldn't let a satisfied smile show, but she is unable to stop it.

'From down south,' says Nannan. 'Nothing good ever came from down south if you ask me. I suppose he's with her now. Down south.'

'He's not,' says Zita. 'He's in Germany.'

'What does he want to be there for? They're a nasty lot, them Germans. They bombed us, tha knows.'

'He's only just passing through,' says Zita, soothingly, and is rescued by a passing aunt, and taken to the kitchen to be given her first ever gin and tonic, until she finds herself dancing to the Rolling Stones with a cousin and shouting above the noise that yes, she is the girl who went travelling with Terry and no, she doesn't know where he will be going next. She drinks her second and third gin and tonic and sits on the stairs with a very pregnant young woman, the neighbour from next door, who keeps taking little sips from Zita's glass, apparently believing that someone else's drink doesn't count.

'My sister got drunk every weekend when she were expecting,' she says. 'Baby were fine. But this doctor I've got says I've got to keep off it. Only a week to go, though, now.'

It is well after midnight when the party begins to break up. Zita becomes a little tearful as she wonders how she is going to get to the other side of the city. But Peggy has thought of that and shouting over the sound of the Beatles singing Hello, Goodbye, tells her that one of the uncles has been given the job of driving her home, in defiance of the possibility of being caught with one of those new breathalyser things.

The next day she packs her rucksack again, openly this time, and says a civilised goodbye to her parents, who do not seem to be too upset – her mother seems almost relieved – and goes to catch a train to London, reasoning that hitching so soon after Christmas could be difficult and would certainly be cold – and sets off for the Alps.

'Well, she's gone again, then,' says Senga.

'And she'll be back again,' says Willie serenely. 'Just wait and see. She won't last the fortnight over there in the cold, waiting on folks and making beds. She'll come crawling back. Have I to put the kettle on or are you going to do it?'

And that journey is one full of mishap. Hostels closed for Christmas, lifts where she misunderstands the driver and ends up miles from where she wants to be, days when she fails to buy food while the shops are open and has to be hungry all night. And having Douglas on her mind. She had made no progress whatever in finding him and can see no way forward. She worries about telling Terry, and what he will think of her; she daydreams about meeting her brother at the hotel she is working at – she would see his name on the register, he would not recognise her, she would have to tell him who she was, he would be with his wife, and maybe a child, they would welcome her into their lives. It distracts her and stops her concentrating. She finds herself unable to remember how to speak in French; she is not a good hitchhiker, not grateful enough, not talkative enough.

But she arrives there in the end. M. Felix has gone back to the south, his son tells her, and she does not know whether to be glad or sorry. She sleeps in a cupboard-sized room up in the attics, with a tiny window that does not quite face the mountains, shared with a girl from New Zealand. Two other girls – Italian – share the room across the landing. And soon after her arrival there is a letter for her from Terry, forwarded by her mother. Zita can imagine her taking it into the post office, that worried look on her face, to ask how she could send it on, would she have to pay extra? Telling them things they didn't need to know.

Terry's news is that he is leaving Munich and Germany. He and the crazy couple have been approached by some men who need someone to drive a car through Eastern Europe, through Turkey and into Iran. There they would hand over the car to a person who would give them money. 'So,' he wrote, 'next letter Poste Restante Istanbul. Wish you were here, it's going to be a laugh.'

She feels desolate at the idea that he is moving further and further away from her, although slightly comforted by the idea that he is even further away from Rosalind.

The Italian girls are cousins, Vittoria and Sofia; they are there for the work, not for the experience of being abroad. They speak a little French but hardly any English and apart from work-related exchanges about clean sheets or the whereabouts of a mop and bucket, they do not speak to Zita. The New Zealand girl is called Cecily. She has been in Europe for a year, she says, travelling a little, working a little, moving on. At first Zita feels rather as she felt when faced with Dora, all those months ago; she feels inadequate and ill-informed, but Cecily is not so brisk as Dora, not so opinionated, not so bossy. Her French is rudimentary, less useful than Zita's, and it becomes routine for them, at the end of the day, after the dinner and the clearing up of it, for the two of them to sit on Zita's bed – or on Cecily's – and eat chocolate if they have any, and speak in English.

'Have you been to Turkey?' Zita wants to know.

'Only to Istanbul. It's really good. I want to go back there, there's lots more to see.'

'Ruins?'

'I guess so. It's old. There are things in Istanbul that have been there for centuries. But the writing on the buildings – the old ones – it's in Arabic or something, so you can't tell when they were built. But you should go there.'

'My friend,' says Zita, 'the one I was travelling with, he's gone to Istanbul, and then he's going to Iran.'

'Then to India I suppose.'

'Is that what people do?'

'It's what the hippies do.'

'He's not a hippie. At least he wasn't.'

'He will be, I bet, by the time you see him again.'

'Oh.'

'Why do you say it like that? It's the hippies that go East.'

'He's not like that.'

'Not like what?'

'Well,' says Zita, faced with the task of describing Terry to a stranger. 'Well, he's very clean for a start. He doesn't have long hair. And he doesn't smoke that pot. He doesn't even smoke cigarettes. He told me his girlfriend used to smoke when he first knew her but he made her throw them away.'

'As if it was any of his business,' says Cecily.

Zita, later, recalls some of the things Terry said to her, his prohibitions about women in shorts, his dislike of women who dyed their hair or laughed too loudly. His pronouncement that he could not marry a girl who had been with even only one other man. His certainty that Ros would be content with having four babies, his strictures on smoking and other ways of being unfeminine. Maybe he was rather old-fashioned. Maybe that was why Zita always felt safe with him. Some of the other men she had met on her travels had looked her up and down to see whether they fancied her; most had clearly decided no they didn't, others could have considered perhaps she might do, at a pinch, and she would have been somewhat nervous if Terry hadn't been there. Like a brother, she thinks, more like a brother than a boyfriend.

India. Her ideas about India are limited. Famines, she thinks, poor people. Goodness knows why anyone would want to go there. Too hot, and isn't that where they have monsoons. What will Terry be like when he gets back from there? In a sense, Europe never touched him. He liked it, he liked being away from home, on a sort of adventure, but the thing that excited him was moving. Moving on, another town, another sight, another country. In Arles he had chafed at the waiting, wanting to get on, on, somewhere else, impatient, restless, unsatisfied. He was bored by it after a couple of days. Would India offer him more? If it did, would he ever come back? Or would Ros have to go there to marry him?

Cecily is a small girl, with brown curly hair and curiously yellowish eyes. She has a pointy little face and a habit of compressing her lips so that she looks as if she disapproves of whatever is going on, although in fact she is cheerfully tolerant most of the time. She says she is an orphan, which Zita feels she has to doubt, since she has never met a real live orphan before.

'You must have somebody,' she says.

'No, I don't,' says Cecily. Her accent sounds like someone talking with their jaw clenched. 'Somewhere in Ireland there may be some third cousin or something, but I wouldn't know about that.'

'What happened to your parents?'

'My mum left – oh, years ago, when I was young, and my dad married again and then he got killed in a car wreck and my stepmother, well, let's say we didn't get on that well anyway.'

'Have you got brothers and sisters?' She always wants to know this about people.

'I have a step-brother,' says Cecily.

'How old?'

'He's sixteen – no, seventeen now. I've known him since he was a baby, they lived in the same street even before my mum left. In fact, that's *why* she left, I believe. He might even be my half-brother, that affair was going on a long time.'

'Do you get on with him?'

'I'm kind of fond of him,' she says. 'He's a pain in the backside, of course, but I guess I like him really. Or I did. I probably won't ever see him again.'

'Like me,' says Zita, half sad and half delighted. 'My brother had a row with my dad and he left home.'

It is a bond between them and occasionally they revisit the subject of brothers, bringing up memories and descriptions. Cecily's brother was a lovable rogue, it seemed, known for wagging school to go fishing, and hanging round with older boys who gave him ideas that never worked out except to get him into trouble. Dougie, as far as Zita could remember, was a quiet boy, sensitive (their mother used to say) and easily upset. Mostly, he and his sister had very little to do with each other, but on Sunday afternoons when they were not allowed to play out, he would sit on the front room floor with her and play snakes and ladders or ludo, quietly, while their parents had what they called 'a wee five minutes' in their respective armchairs. Then, when their mother woke up, she would cut slices of cake and her children would compete to see who could make theirs last the longest.

'It's strange,' says Zita, 'how things come back to you. I'd not given a thought to all that for ages. It kind of brings him back to life.'

'At least I know where mine is,' says Cecily. 'I could go back and walk in though the door and there he'd be, eating at the table most likely. He eats all the time and he never puts on an ounce.'

'Terry says I should try and find my brother,' says Zita. 'I did ask my mum but I didn't get anywhere. She just closed up on me. I don't know if she even knows herself where he might be. Terry keeps asking, in his letters.'

'It's not his business, is it?' says Cecily. 'He should keep his nose out of it.'

'He's only taking an interest.'

'He's poking his beak in where it's not wanted,' says Cecily. 'If you ask me.'

By the time the skiing season ends Cecily and Zita are sufficiently used to each other to contemplate going somewhere else together.

'A little holiday,' says Cecily.

Zita feels like she has not had a holiday since before Douglas went into the army. She somehow doesn't think of bumming round France as a holiday; holidays are beaches and ice cream, bingo and chips. The last time she went to the seaside for more than a day trip was when she was about eleven – yes, eleven because she had her birthday there and the boarding house lady made her a cake and Dougie wangled a day's leave and came by train from Catterick to share it. It was Filey, on the Yorkshire coast; there was sea and sand and a cold breeze and nothing to do except sit on the beach or walk along the promenade. One day it rained and they went to the pictures in the afternoon. All in all, it was not a big success and discouraged her parents from ever trying it again. Once or twice since then Marion's mother had invited Zita – Sally-Ann – to go on holiday with them but no one ever expected that her parents would allow it, they were not going to be forced into being grateful to anyone, or being in a position where they might be thought to owe a favour.

'A holiday,' says Zita, now, to Cecily. 'At the seaside?'

'Greece,' says Cecily. 'Nice weather, and you can sleep on the beach.'

Zita thinks with a pang that she will not meet up with Terry in Greece. His last letter, much delayed, said that they had delivered the car to Tehran, and been swindled out of the money they'd been promised. The crazy English couple were going back west, back to Europe and proper medical treatment –'only a little bit of dysentery' said Terry – but he had decided to go further and joined a group of Australians in a bus that was being driven to India. 'Might be going all the way to Australia,' he added. 'Will keep you posted.'

Zita thinks of him as she and Cecily wake up on their own tiny beach in Corfu and look at the unfeasibly turquoise water moving with a gentle restlessness as far as they can see. Behind them is a small rocky area thick with flowers, real flowers, like spring and summer all at once – what sort they are Zita does not know, except that some are just like tulips, though smaller. A few hundred yards away there is a village – or a hamlet, a settlement – where they can buy bread and eggs and the locals call them hippies and shrug their shoulders at them.

Here there are no guests to be cleaned up after, no manager to come checking how hard they are working, no Italian girls skimping on their work and blaming it on Zita. No kitchen staff shouting that the tables needed setting, or clearing, or moving for a larger party than usual. No guests who cannot go skiing – because of the weather, or because of being injured – just sitting around in the lounge and asking them very reasonably if they could just maybe go to the bar and order them a coffee, or a hot chocolate, or a glass of wine. Here there are no demands on them; they are on holiday.

It is quite boring. They can swim, they can walk among the flowers, they can lie on the sand and talk, or be silent. They can wonder how long it would be before they could reasonably eat more bread.

They walk up the hill behind the village. Overhead there are three large birds – eagles? vultures? – and almost at their feet a green snake stirs and slides behind a rock. As they reach the top of the hill – almost a mountain – they meet an old woman coming the other way carrying a great tin of oil by holding it on to her head with one hand. She greets them without a smile and strides on.

'Could you stay here for ever?' says Cecily.

'Only if I had a proper toilet,' says Zita. 'And some books. Actually, no, I couldn't, not even then. It's too quiet.'

'I think I wouldn't mind if I was old,' says Cecily. 'I'd have one of those little houses and keep chooks and have a donkey to take me around.'

They continue walking until they reach another village, bigger and more developed than the one by the beach. There *is* an old lady astride a donkey, who glares at them for walking in what she considers her space. There is a café with men sitting outside wreathed in smoke and loud talk. When they go in to buy lemonade the owner asks if they want to rent a room. He shows them the room – spartan and bare with what looks like two army surplus bunks, the window looking out on to the side of the next house, close enough to touch. But next to the room there is a toilet and a washbasin and a rudimentary shower. They drink their lemonade, discussing their position. He has written down a price – it seems very little; they could get better food in this village; it would be a long way to the beach but they are tired of the beach, and of trying to cook eggs on a driftwood fire, and of peeing in the sea and going behind a rock to do a number two, and they have each been wondering how they would cope when their period came. One week? they ask each other, and decide yes for one week they would live here and walk over the mountain and look at the eagles and learn to say some things in Greek, and think about where to go next.

Chapter Twelve

Senga picks up the postcard from the mat. So we're back on postcards again, are we? She has had a number of brief letters from Sally-Ann in France, mentioning the weather – sunny – and the number of guests and how she is learning more French. Nothing revealing, not even anything affectionate, but to Senga they have been an improvement on the postcards, more serious, more daughterly. The last one included: 'So now the snow is melting Cecily and me are going to Italy, and maybe further. Don't worry, I have enough money.' As if money was the only thing to worry about.

This new postcard has two pictures, one of a huge fountain, the other of a grandiose church at the top of some grandiose steps. It says on the front, Saluti di Roma, which Senga takes to mean it comes from Rome. But on the back it says, Dear Mum and Daddy, we are on a Greek island. The weather is quite hot, I hope you are both well. Love, Sally.

'So,' says Willie when he comes home. 'She couldnae be bothered to post it while she was in Italy. She's forgot all about us, hasn't she and then she's looked in her bag and found it and just stuck some rubbish on it and put it in the post. I'm inclined,' he says, 'not to bother with her. You wait, she'll be writing one of these days asking for money and I'll tell her no, and serve her right.'

'You wouldn't Willie,' says Senga. 'You wouldn't go so far.' But he might, she thinks. He's sent Douglas away, why shouldn't he do the same to Sally-Ann.

She does not put the postcard on the mantelpiece, but straightaway in the box in Sally-Ann's bedroom, with the others. On the dressing table are two blue airmail letters – to Miss Z Grey. She knows, from the name on the back, who sent them, though why he thinks her name starts with a Z is a mystery. And in her apron pocket is another letter, addressed to herself this time; one that she does not want to read again although she knows that she must. Her sister Maggie has written, as she occasionally does, but this time it is not a bland summary of how they are getting on – their father's retirement, Kirsty's mumps and Donal's exams and the awful snow they had last winter. This time it is to tell Senga that their mother is in hospital. Maggie doesn't say precisely what is wrong but she is in hospital in Glasgow which must surely make it more serious. 'They are going to try to operate,' writes Maggie, and at the end, an afterthought, a P.S. – 'I think she might be happy to see you.'

*

By Easter, when the air is full of the smell of roasting lamb, Cecily and Zita have become members of the village. Cecily, a country girl, feeds the poultry that scratch around behind the taverna; Zita sits in the square and tries to master the Greek alphabet, and people come up to her and ask her to teach them English words. Children come in small groups to look at her, an English person; they tell her how to say things in Greek: house and car, bread and lemon and potato, tree and flower and bird, hello and goodbye. 'Yassas,' she says to them and they laugh and run away and she doesn't know why. Everything is slow, everything is sunny; it is as if she has never had another life, until she wakes up one morning and feels the need to go home.

'Why,' says Cecily. 'It's great here. Don't you think?'

'I know,' says Zita, 'but I just feel I should go home. You could come too.' The idea of turning up at home with Cecily and expecting her parents to find her a bed – Dougie's room obviously – makes her pause, but then again, why not. Other people take friends home, why shouldn't she.

'I think I'll just stay here,' says Cecily. She has been getting quite friendly with Spyridon, who drives the only taxi in the village, and has big plans to open a restaurant down by the beach. So friendly that Zita is often left on her own, wandering through olive groves – though she doesn't know that's what they are – or along the road to the next beach in the next village.

'Is he your boyfriend,' she asks.

'Well, kind of,' says Cecily. 'Only we're not going to let on to his mother just yet. She might not take kindly to it, he says.'

'But do you love him? Are you in love?'

Cecily laughs at her. 'You've been reading too many soppy magazines. I like Spyro, I fancy him too. We get on.'

'Maybe,' says Zita, 'he thinks you would be able to get him to New Zealand. I've heard of things like that.'

'You think I haven't? Don't worry about me, Zee. I can look after myself.'

But as the days go by Cecily looks after herself more and more by being with Spyro, sitting in the front seat when he takes passengers to the next village, or to Corfu Town, waiting outside the church for him to emerge on Sunday and wandering off together, coming home late at night, after Zita has gone to bed, waking her up to apologise, and to tell her more about Spyro's attractions.

'Anyway,' she says, 'you're all right on your own aren't you. You don't seem to need anyone else.'

'Of course I'm fine,' says Zita.

So she sets off again by herself, ferry to Italy, hitching into France. France feels a bit like home, travelling up again from south to north; it makes her think of Terry with renewed longing. She hasn't written to him, or heard from him since she left the hotel weeks ago. She even wonders if when she gets home she might find him there, in Sheffield, telling all his adventures to his admiring family. She can see him, sitting there with his parents in their little front room, his brothers sitting on the floor – and Ros sitting by his side. His arm around her. The vision pops like a bubble, as if it's a dream in a cartoon.

She is dropped off by a lorry on the outskirts of Calais; she buys her ticket for the ferry. She is tired, grubby, she feels the cold after the spring warmth of Greece. She reaches Dover, she reaches the centre of London and suddenly she has had enough. She changes her money into pounds shillings and pence and takes the Underground to Kings Cross. She will go home on the train; there is nothing that says she shouldn't.

It's Sunday, though she hadn't really noticed that fact; and the train is quite full. She walks through the carriage, looking for a seat with room for her and her rucksack – she doesn't fancy trying to get it up on the rack. Something makes her stop, and step back, and look again at a group of young people she has just passed. Yes, it is, she's almost sure it is – Ros, sitting with another girl and two young men, sitting next to one of the boys, as if they are a couple. Zita decides she can after all put her rucksack up on the rack and sit behind Ros. Why not?

What she hopes for she couldn't really say – some evidence that Ros is being unfaithful? But that would hurt Terry badly. Some evidence that Ros thinks about him night and day, so that she could write to Terry and tell him? She wouldn't do it; she wanted Terry to be happy but she wasn't prepared to make herself quite so *un*happy in the process. As it happens, she listens to their conversation all the way from St Pancras to Sheffield Midland and Terry's name does not cross her lips. The talk is of assignments, practicals, essays, final exams; it is of other students and their oddities and their prospects; it is of landlords and flatmates, keys and deposits and cooking and cleaning, or lack of it. The boy next to Ros gets up and wanders off and Ros is not heard to speak while he's gone. He comes back with chocolate bars and Zita hears Ros laughing at something, and then they talk about their families and the unreasonableness of their allowances. They are going back to Sheffield for their final term; they talk about the jobs they are applying for.

'London,' says Ros. 'I'm not staying in Sheffield. I want a job in London.'

'Me too,' says the boy next to her.

London, thinks Zita. That's certainly not Terry's plan. Interesting.

She follows them off the train and up to the bus stop where they wait. Ros and the boy are not holding hands, as she hoped they might have been, but they could be said to be standing closer together than absolutely necessary. Zita stands and watches them until their bus comes, then she turns in the opposite direction. And once again she arrives at home, through the back door, just as her mother is finishing the dishes and is about to put the kettle on. Her mother cries when she sees her.

Terry's letters tell of motoring mishaps, of the mountains of Nepal, of the kindness of strangers, of crowded trains and buses, of the heat, of seeing a dead person. He asks her if she has heard from Ros, Ros hasn't been writing lately, have her letters not reached him, have his not reached her? 'Find out for me, Zee. She'd love to see you I know.' You know nothing, says Zita, out loud, sitting on her bed with his letters in her lap. She wishes she had managed to look and see if Ros was wearing the unofficial engagement ring, the ring that Terry talked about so much.

There is a tap at her door; it is her mother, clutching her own letter from Maggie.

'So would you come with me?' she ends up by saying. 'Come and see your Granny before she dies. Your Aunties and your cousins.'

It is not a very enticing prospect, but what can she do but go. She's been through France and back, twice, she's been through Italy and stayed on a Greek island; it should not be difficult to go to Glasgow with her mother.

The preparations are intense. All the bedding in the house is washed and ironed and put away, labelled with instructions for Willie on how and when to use it. His shirts and underwear likewise. Senga leaves lists of what he has to buy for his sandwiches. She goes into town and orders a fridge to be delivered; it has to live at the foot of the stairs because there is no room for it in the kitchen. She sets about baking and preparing meals to leave for Willie to heat up.

'Couldn't he buy something?' says Sally. 'There's a chip shop down the road.'

'A man needs meat,' says Senga. She writes instructions on how to heat them up and sellotapes them to the fridge. And instructions on when the binmen come, and when the milkman has to be paid, and a pile of shillings for the gas meter as if he didn't have his own shillings in his pocket.

'Can't he look after himself?' says Sally. 'He's a grown up you know.'

'You wait till you're married, you'll find out.'

'I will never marry,' says Sally.

She says the same to Marion, in a letter; Marion being back in Great Yarmouth for another season, with Brian, both of them saving hard for furnishing the house they hope to have when they are married. 'Only going out one night a week,' she wrote back. 'It was more fun when we weren't engaged.'

Marion and Brian have been together since school, since she was in the third year and he was in the fourth and just about to leave and start his apprenticeship. He caught up with Marion and her best friend on the way home from school.

'Hey, Long and Shorty,' he shouted, and they turned round and waited for him to catch up.

'I don't need you, Beanpole,' he said, and Marion gave her a nudge and said, 'Wait for me at my house.'

And Sally-Ann waited on the corner of their road, out of sight of her mother, until Marion arrived, more pink in the face than usual, and said that she was going to the pictures with Brian Miller on Friday evening. She did not invite her best friend to come with them, and Sally-Ann did not expect her to. Since then, since that afternoon seven years ago, Marion has had to share herself between Sally and Brian, and has done it fairly and kindly, and gradually giving more time to the boyfriend, and then a little less, when they got engaged and he started to work overtime so as to save money for the wedding.

And now the wedding, so long promised, is imminent, and they have enough in the bank to put down on their first house. Marion wanted a June wedding but they will be working until October, so it's been booked instead for the week before Christmas, honeymoon put off till they can afford it.

Chapter Thirteen

Senga and her daughter travel to Scotland by coach. It makes Senga anxious, just being away from home; she fidgets and worries about whether they are going the right way, will they get to Glasgow in time? Will visiting time at the hospital be over? Will they be allowed in? She has made sandwiches for them both but she is too nervous to eat; Sally, however, feels that this is quite luxurious, having no need to wonder where she will end up, or what she will be eating during the rest of the day.

They arrive, they make their way to the hospital; it is evening visiting but, sorry, the sister says, Mrs McHarg had her operation today; she's not come round properly from the anaesthetic just yet and there's already a visitor by her bed, two more wouldnae be allowed.

'Will you tell her please,' says Sally, 'tell the visitor I mean – that we are here. We've come a long way,' she adds, and her English accent goes some way to prove it.

So they are sitting on two hard chairs outside the ward, when Senga jumps up and cries out, 'Betty!'

'Senga?' says the woman.

'Betty,' she says again.

'I'm no Betty,' she says. 'I'm Jeannie.'

'Whit is it?' says Senga. She has hardly been in Scotland five minutes but her accent has returned; her daughter looks at her almost in alarm.

Jeannie is ten years younger than Senga and doesn't even look her age. She is trim, prosperous, nicely dressed; her hair is softly permed, her handbag matches her shoes.

'You don't know?' she says. She opens her eyes wide and points to her breast, the left one, and mouths, without sound, the word, Cancer.

Senga's hand goes to her own breast and she looks at her daughter as if to protect her from the word.

'Go in and see her,' says Jeannie. 'She's sleeping, she won't know you're there, but you'll have seen her. You too,' she says to Sally. 'You need to see your Granny, even if it's the only time you do.'

The hospital smell is more intense inside the ward. Senga goes to the side of the bed and sits on the chair; Sally stays by the end of the bed, unsure. How should she behave, what expression should she have on her face? But there is nothing to be learned from looking at the woman in the bed – she is still, she is pale, her eyes are closed, she has a tube in her right arm. Senga touches her left hand, which is lying on the cover as if someone has put it there for the visitors.

'Mammy,' she says.

As they walk out of the ward Sally notices, but does not let on that she's seen, that her mother is brushing tears away from her eyes, surreptitiously, as if she is ashamed of them. Jeannie is waiting for them.

'Come on home then,' she says. 'Did you tell Maggie you were coming?'

Even when she is old, Zita will remember how bewildering were the two days she spent with her mother's family, a country as foreign as any other she'd been to in her life. She will never go back there, to Glasgow or Dumbarton, but not because she's never asked by her aunts and cousins, not because they don't keep in touch – Christmas cards and the occasional letter will be sent through the years, and her cousins never forget her birthday – but going back there – no, she will never do it, never.

She will recall that they went first to her grandfather, retired from work now, fidgeting in his chair as if he is unaccustomed to sitting still, wanting news of his wife.

'So, she'll be home when?' he said, and Jeannie patted his hand and told him it's early days, she'll have to stay in the hospital until she's well enough to come home.

'But look,' she said. 'Here's your Senga, come all the way from Sheffield to see you.'

'Hello Da,' said Senga shyly. 'How are you?'

'And this is Sally-Ann,' said Jeannie, pushing her forward a little.

'Hello,' said Sally-Ann softly. The old man had such intimidating eyebrows and so few teeth that she felt quite afraid of him. He might easily, it seemed, jump up and shout at her, and her mother to get out of his sight, waving the stick which she could see he kept by his chair.

But he seemed to accept the sudden presence of his runaway daughter with no surprise, and took no notice at all of his granddaughter, although Jeannie made more efforts to push Sally-Ann into his line of sight.

'Put the kettle on, hen,' he said, and Jeannie went into the kitchen. Sally-Ann remained standing, by the open door, almost in the tiny hall, but Senga approached his chair and knelt down beside it.

'I seen Ma,' she said. 'She was sleeping, but I've come all this way and I'm glad I've seen her. Tomorrow I'll go and see her again, when she's come round.'

'Come round?' he said.

'Aye, Da. The anaesthetic you know. It has to wear off and then she'll be awake.'

'Where's Jeannie with that tea?' he said. 'A man could die of thirst waiting for someone to come and put the kettle on.'

'You're not an invalid, Father,' said Jeannie, coming back from the kitchen. 'You could do it yourself if you'd a mind to.'

He reached for his cup. 'No cake?' he said, just the same as, thought Sally-Ann – though he didn't know it – her own father would have done.

'We've all been too busy,' said Jeannie briskly. 'You'll have to have a biscuit.'

'Well, if I must, I must,' he said.

'Your dinner's in the oven,' said Jeannie. 'You'll be all right till tomorrow. I need to take Senga to Maggie's now. Betty'll be in tomorrow to see you.'

'I'll no be coming with you,' said the grandfather. 'Switch the telly on for us, Jean, I'll just stay here on my own.'

'Well, you've seen him,' said Jeannie to Senga when they were back in the car. 'It's no wonder our mother's poorly, running after him the whole time. Put the kettle on, bring in some coal for the fire, go up to his bedroom and bring down that wee pullover, for he feels the cold, just one thing after another.'

Maggie's house was old-fashioned in a different way, different from the grandparents' house and different from her own home in Sheffield; the furniture seemed larger than necessary, a long dining table with – she counted – eight chairs with carved backs and red plush seats. In the sitting room the chairs were huge, brown leather, and there was a smell of pipe smoke; the television was the biggest she had ever seen.

She had to sort out which aunt was which. Jeannie was the modern one, the youngest, who drove her own car and had a full time job at a lawyer's office. She was bossy, Jeannie, but usually right; her sisters let her make decisions because she wanted to, and because she was good at it. Maggie was the conscience of the family. She was the one who kept up with everyone, writing to Senga in Sheffield, to aged aunts in Fort William and Perth, to her daughter in Liverpool and her son in Edinburgh. She visited her father more than the others did, though it was Betty who lived nearer to him; she was a churchgoer and her husband, a dry stick of a man, was an elder of the church. Betty was the scatty one. She forgot what day she was supposed to do things; her knitting always came out wrong and Maggie had to undo it for her and show her again how to decrease. Her housekeeping was uneven; she would spend a morning worrying at the grouting round the bath and neglect the soup boiling on the stove downstairs. No one burnt as many pans as Betty did.

Then there were the cousins. Betty's daughters were close in age to Sally, as was Maggie's son, the one who was in Edinburgh, studying to be a doctor. Others were mentioned as if Sally knew them and would understand references to 'all the trouble there was last year' or 'that big disappointment.'

'She's very careful of Kirsty, of course,' said Betty about Jeannie's fussing, but Sally was only bewildered as to what to say; Senga had never told her any of this.

And they wanted to know about Douglas. Sally could hear Jeannie leading the questioning.

'So how is Douglas then?'

'He's fine,' said Senga.

'He's how old now?' said Maggie, and knew the answer. 'Thirty next birthday, that's right isn't it. And is he married? You'd have told us if he was.'

'No,' said Senga. 'Not married.'

'Steady girlfriend then?'

'Oh yes.'

'Nice girl is she?'

'Oh yes.'

'And tell me again – what does he do. Douglas?'

'He works – he manages – a shoe shop.'

Sally could not believe what she had heard her mother say. Was she making it up? Or could it even be true?

A car stopped on the road outside and a couple of teenagers arrived; one was Betty's younger daughter, the other a cousin from her father's side. The room suddenly felt too full, too hot. Sally felt faint, what with the early start, the long journey, the sick grandmother, and now the press of people, the questions, the lies her mother was telling. She feared that she might be sick and hurried out of the room, found herself in the kitchen. It had fluorescent lights that made her feel sicker than ever, fluorescent light bouncing off shiny surfaces – white fridge and washing machine, dazzling kettle and an array of copper saucepans all catching the light. Maggie had followed her.

'Sit down, hen,' she said. 'Are you hungry? I should have thought, you'll have had a long day of it.'

'I'm all right,' said Sally. 'Just need a bit of fresh air.'

Her Aunt Maggie opened the back door – a neat green lawn and a narrow border of bedding plants, red, white and blue – and Sally breathed, and felt better.

'So – Douglas,' said Maggie. 'I'm thinking there's something your mother's not telling us, am I right so?'

Sally was too tired to think up a lie; and anyway, she said to herself, What would Zita do? 'I don't know,' she said. 'We haven't seen Douglas for a long time. I don't know anything about where he is or what he does.'

'That's what I surmised,' said Maggie. 'And can I get you something to eat?'

'Could I just –' said Sally '– would you mind if I just went to bed?'

Maggie kindly escorted her to her cousin's vacant bedroom, showed her where the bathroom was, checked again that she wasn't hungry, equipped her with a glass of water and left her to sleep, which she did, immediately and thankfully. Which was why she missed being present later when the phone call came from the hospital to tell them that her grandmother – their mother – had not come round from the anaesthetic and had in fact died.

When she got up the next morning much had already been done. Betty had gone to tell their father the night before. Preparations for the funeral were getting under way – the church was already booked, on account of Uncle Fraser being an elder. Betty and Maggie were in the middle of a telephone marathon, taking turns to call up yet more aunts and uncles and cousins, friends and ex-friends, neighbours and ex-neighbours. Sally could hear them as she came down the stairs, almost apologetic as they passed on the news. 'Och yes, I know,' they said. 'I know.' Jeannie was using her own phone at her home in Kilwinning, getting through her share of the list.

Senga had been left in charge of the kitchen; already she seemed to know where everything was. She made a pot of tea, she showed Sally-

Ann where to find cereal and milk – 'Or I could make you porridge.'

'You know I hate porridge, Mum.' She spooned a thick covering of sugar over her cornflakes.

'You've heard?' said Senga.

'What?'

'Your Granny died in the night.' Senga wiped her eyes on a tea towel and then pretended she hadn't.

'Oh.'

'They're arranging it all the noo,' said Senga, flapping the tea towel in the direction of the big sitting room. 'There's a wheen o' folk to let know.'

'Why are you talking like that?' said Sally, but she muttered it quietly so her mother wouldn't hear.

'I've to tell you,' said Senga. 'Alison – that's Betty's daughter – she'll be coming by to see you. She'll be taking you to see the sights o' the toon.'

'Like what?'

'There's the castle. And the rock.'

'Mum, I want to go home. I've got things I need to do.'

'You'll no get home today,' said Senga, 'being Sunday. And are ye no staying for your Granny's funeral?'

'When is it.'

'Friday next.'

No, she was not staying for her Granny's funeral.

After the confusion of aunts and uncles the day before, there was now a blur of cousins. Cousins and their girlfriends, fiancés, best friends and casual boyfriends, turning up through the day to take a look at Senga, their missing auntie, and at Sally-Ann, their English cousin. And – what they hadn't expected – to hear that their grandmother was no more, the story told over and over as each new set of people arrived. Sally-Ann was impressed by the way they all seemed to know the right thing to say and do. Some cried a little, but not enough to be embarrassing; they all said something appropriate to their aunts; they kept their faces solemn and respectful. They were, in short, well-brought-up, she thought.

'We'll see you at the funeral,' each one said to her as they went away. And to each one she said politely, 'I'm afraid I have to go home tomorrow.'

'Are you not staying for the funeral?'

No, she was not staying.

Chapter Fourteen

She arrives back in Sheffield on Monday evening, walks up from the bus station to home, feeling secure that her father will welcome her as he has done before when she returned home.

And is disappointed.

'Been managing just fine,' he says, offended when she offers to cook, or wash dishes.

'Anyone would think you'd been gone for half a year,' he says when she says she's glad to be home.

He cuts her off when she tries to tell him about the aunts and the cousins. 'I've got brothers and sisters of my own,' he says. 'It's not just your mother who's got a family.'

She has never heard him mention his brothers and sisters before, and she isn't going to hear any more now; he turns the TV on and lights a cigarette and opens the newspaper. Only then, she sees on the mantelpiece, a letter, a blue airmail letter, face down.

'Is that for me?' she says.

He looks up from the Daily Mirror. 'It's not,' he says. 'Unless some fool has put the wrong name on it.'

She turns it over. Miss Z Grey, it says, but it has been scribbled out and written over – Not known at this address. She says nothing but takes it and leaves the room.

In her bedroom she finds that she is trembling, sitting on the bed and looking at the letter quivering between her fingers. He could have thrown it away, she thinks, he could have put it into the post again – 'Not known at this address' – she could never have received it, ever.

What is the matter with him? Is he missing her mother so much? Does he think she's never coming back? Does he want to be left on his own entirely? Does he want to get rid of his daughter like he got rid of his son? What is it?

Early though it is – not even dark yet – she puts on her pyjamas and gets into bed. She sits and opens Terry's letter. He's in Nepal, he writes, it's amazing, incredible, she should be there to see it, there are mountains, he can't even describe what he is seeing, it's unreal. And what about this, she'll never believe it, does she remember from Nice, a big lairy Aussie called Ray? 'I had to have a fight with him,' writes Terry, 'and you won't believe it but it was over you. He was saying vile things about you, I won't tell you what he said, but it was bad enough for me to hit him. I won of course, but my nose got a bit mashed.'

She smiles, then she is stunned. Fancy Terry sticking up for her when she wasn't even there to hear herself being insulted. She imagines being there and putting Ray in his place without needing Terry to take over, but still she is gratified. No one has ever before had an actual fight on her account. Then she thinks, If he'd do that for me, he'd probably commit murder for Rosalind.

When she gets up the next morning her father has already left for work. She notices that he has not had his usual fried breakfast, just a cup of tea and a slice of toast. She looks into the new fridge; it seems as if he hasn't touched any of the provisions that her mother left for him. He's been sulking, she realises, all weekend, living on nothing but tea and cigarettes and working up his feeling of being badly done to. He's gone to work hungry – no sign of a sandwich being prepared for his pack-up – and will come home hungry. She will not be there to see him.

She has some tea and toast herself, runs a bath, packs her rucksack once more and leaves him a note. 'I have gone to see Marion. P.S. it would be a good idea if you could get a phone in the house. Zita.' There, she has done it and it is quite possible that he will never let her in the house again.

She makes her way, as she did before, to the Parkway, and by one lift, and then another and another, makes her way to Great Yarmouth, there to surprise Marion and get herself taken on as a cleaner of chalets and maker of beds.

'My jobs get worse every time,' she says to Marion. 'Library used to feel like almost a professional sort of job – since then I've been a kitchen hand, a kitchen hand again, then a chambermaid, and now I'm a cleaner.'

'You're looking all right on it,' says Marion. 'I'll cut your hair again and we'll get you fixed up with a boyfriend.'

Zita – what a relief to be Zita again – sends a card to her Aunt Maggie thanking her and apologising yet again for not attending the funeral, and then, briefly becoming Sally again, she phones Maggie's house to speak to her mother.

'I just wanted to tell you Mum, I'm with Marion and I'm working here for the summer. And I wanted to tell you Daddy's in a foul mood.'

'What's all this,' says Senga, interrupting, 'what's all this about you being called Zita? That's what Alison's told me.'

'That's right,' says Zita. 'I've changed my name.'

'You've no right to do that,' says Senga.'

'I've done it,' she says. 'So you can like it or lump it. And I wanted to tell you, can you forward any letters on to me – don't let Daddy get hold of them. And I've told him to get a phone installed; if you were on the phone I could let you know where I am.'

'Oh,' says Senga. 'Oh. All right then.'

*

Ten days after leaving Willie to fend for himself, Senga is back home; her accent has returned to its usual hybrid. Within hours Willie is back to his normal self, more or less. He is not good, she realises, at being left on his own. She cleans and tidies and re-organises. She throws away the food he hasn't eaten; she empties the fish and chip wrappers out of the pedal bin; she pulls out the twintub and turns the temperature up as far as it will go, all the while replaying in her head conversations with her sisters, her last sight of her mother, her visits to her father, her walks round the town she grew up in, how it had changed, how it was just the same.

Willie is not very interested in her account of what happened up there in Scotland, though he says the right things about the sadness of losing her mother. They have talked about Sally-Ann and her future, and how she seems to have itchy feet and where will she go next. And Willie has agreed readily, to Senga's surprise, to having a phone installed and she is waiting, this very day, for the man from the GPO to come. So she is not surprised to hear a knock on the front door, even though she had asked them to come to the back. She is not surprised to see a young man standing on the step, smiling, although she had thought he would have been in some sort of uniform. She is surprised, though, to hear him ask if Zita is at home.

'If you mean Sally-Ann –' she says. 'Sorry,' he says. 'I thought you'd know her as Zita by now.'

And to tell the truth, Senga and Willie have disentangled the issue of what their daughter has been doing with her name – swapping a perfectly reasonable, pretty, normal name for an outlandish and frankly ostentatious one. They are not happy about it, but she is old enough to do what she wants, they say, gloomily, and they know they will become used to her postcards from now on being signed from Zita.

'She's at work,' says Senga.

The young man looks disappointed. He's a thin thing, Senga notices, and his hair is too long, well over his collar at the back and falling over his eyes at the front. He wears khaki shorts and a tee-shirt that has seen better days; he's very tanned and his right foot seems to be heavily bandaged.

'What time does she get home?' he says.

'I couldn't tell you. She's not staying in Sheffield just now.'

Looking past him Senga sees that there is another person standing in the road; she's almost certain it's the girl who knocked at her front door back there before Christmas, the first time Sally-Ann went away. It is all falling into place.

'Are you Terry?'

'That's right.' He grins, charmingly. 'She must have told you about me.'

Senga indicates the young woman standing out there as if she's on sentry duty, or as if she doesn't want to be seen with him.

'Come here Ros,' he calls, and says to Senga, 'This is my fiancée. This is Ros.'

Ros takes a couple of steps closer and stops; this is obviously as far as she's going to come.

Senga decides it will not hurt to tell him. 'In fact she's in Great Yarmouth – she works there now, at Pontin's. With Marion.'

'Back at the weekend?'

'Weekend's her busiest time. Changeover day.' It is Doris Ward who has told Senga this.

'I guess then,' he says, turning to include Ros, 'we'll have to go there and see her.'

'It's a long way,' says Senga. 'But you can get there by train. Or by coach.'

'Or in my girlfriend's car,' he says. 'She got it for her twenty-first.'

More money than sense, some parents, says Senga to herself.

'And anyway,' he says. 'I've been halfway round the world and back. I should be able to manage a trip to the seaside.'

He stands there as if he would say more, as if he'd like to be friendly but by now Senga is in the act of closing the door.

*

It is Ros that she recognises first.

Sunday evening. Zita and Marion have finished working for the day and are sitting in the bit of the cafeteria where staff are allowed to sit, finishing off a pasty and chips each. From the sound system – installed by Brian – comes someone singing that this guy's in love.

'Well,' says Marion, 'there's another couple of pounds on me hips. That dressmaker, she's going to have to let out the seams on that wedding dress.' She never says "the dress," or "the guests," – always puts the word "wedding" in her sentences as many times as she can.

'Are we going to the show tonight?'

'Might as well.' Marion sighs. One of her complaints is that Brian, being employed as an electrician –'and dogsbody' she says – has to work every evening dealing with the lights and so forth for the nightly entertainment.

Zita puts her knife and fork together and picks up her mug of tea. She looks idly towards the door and does not believe that it is Ros she is seeing. Why should it be?

'See that girl by the door,' she says. 'That's what Terry's girlfriend looks like.'

Ros is wearing a straight up-and-down dress of printed cotton, very short; a floppy white hat dangles from her fingers.

Marion looks with interest. 'Oh yes.'

It's only then that Zita notices, behind Ros, holding open a door for a family who are on their way out, someone who looks a bit like Terry. Even now, she can't put the situation together. Terry's last letter was from Bombay; he was planning to move on to Australia to find work for a few months. Equally, Terry is not recognising her; he has never seen her with her hair cut short. But Zita keeps looking, because if it's not Ros then it's not Terry, but it looks like Ros, and the more she looks, the more it looks like Terry, thinner and browner and with longer hair, but the eyes, the smile, they are Terry's, and if it's Terry it must be Ros. She stands, she waves. Marion looks on, slowly catching up. Ros does not smile, or move, but Terry – all of a sudden – is hugging Zita, laughing; she is laughing and crying too. Marion is looking gratified, Ros is keeping her face impassive, but Zita and Terry are not watching them, they are exclaiming and explaining, both together, all at once, and hugging again.

'You know Ros,' says Terry, taking her by the arm and pulling her into the circle.

'This is my friend, Marion,' says Zita.

'I've heard a lot about you,' says Terry. 'I'm pleased to meet you. This is my fiancée, Rosalind.'

Later, they are all four sitting in the bar, having two separate conversations.

'Terry wanted to go somewhere, just the two of us, and get married,' says Ros. 'But my parents would be so upset if I did that. And me and my sister promised each other when we were little that she could be my bridesmaid and I would be her Matron of Honour.'

'I want Zita to be my bridesmaid,' says Marion. 'She thinks I'm joking when I say it. She says I've got enough with my cousin's little girls but I think I should have a chief bridesmaid too, don't you?'

'Definitely,' says Ros.

'You're not having Zita too are you? As well as your sister?'

Ros looks shocked; Marion understands her point.

'But I thought you were going to Australia,' says Zita.

He lifts up his foot to show her the bandage. 'Poison foot,' he says. 'That's why I came back. Went to a hospital in India – well, you wouldn't want to stay there for long. Come out worse than you went in.'

'Did it hurt?'

'I should say so. Agony. I thought, if this goes right up my leg, it'll be the end of me.'

'So how did you get back? When?'

'It's all down to Ros,' says Terry. 'She wired me the money for a plane ticket. Of all the journeys, that was the worst. I was in a bad way.'

'You look fine now,' says Zita.

'Antibiotics,' he says. 'That's all it took. I tell you, Ros didn't recognise me when she saw me.'

'She will have been so happy to see you,' says Zita, wincing at her own insincerity.

'She wanted me to come back.'

'She didn't want you to go in the first place, but you did.'

'It was getting so I thought she might not wait for me,' says Terry, and Zita thinks, Dead right, she wouldn't have.

'Satin,' Marion is saying. 'Lace sleeves.'

'Terry's not really happy about the church.'

'Red velvet with white fur trim,' says Marion.

'What was Greece like?' says Terry.

'We were in Corfu. Beautiful. Spring flowers everywhere. People were so friendly, so nice.'

'And that Cecily, where's she now?'

'The hall isn't booked yet,' says Ros. 'My mother is seeing to all that.'

'When will it be? The wedding?'

'February. That was the earliest date I could get at the church, three o'clock was what I wanted but they were all booked up. Everyone wants three o'clock, don't ask me why. So they couldn't fit us in before Christmas, and I didn't fancy getting married in January.'

'What about that fight?' says Zita.

'What fight?'

'You wrote to me about it. With Ray. What was it about?'

'Nothing,' he says, 'nothing at all.' And she understands that he will not talk about it when Ros might hear.

'On the pill,' Marion is saying.

'Me too.'

'But the weight I've put on! I can't believe it. I'm never going to get into my wedding dress.'

'Oh dear,' says Ros. 'What a shame.'

'So what will you do now?' says Zita. 'I'm here till the end of the season, then I'll find something else.'

'You could do better than this,' he says. 'Tell you what, Zee, I like your new hairdo. Suits you.'

'I don't want to do better,' she says. 'I just want to save enough to go abroad again. I want to go further, like you did. I wish –'

'You wish you came with me,' says Terry. 'Is that what you were going to say?'

'Sort of,' she says.

'My travelling days are over,' he says. 'I'll soon have a wife and family to support. I owe my dad money, I owe Ros for the air fare.'

'Family?' she says.

'Not yet,' he grins. 'I've not been back long enough for that. But after the wedding – maybe aim for Christmas after this next one –'

'Aim for?'

'Our first baby.'

Zita looks over at Ros, so neat and pretty, so still and detached. It is not easy to imagine her pregnant, with swollen ankles, hiding her bump under ugly smocks. She looks at Marion – she can see Marion being a mother, loving but brisk, practical but jolly – and then again at Ros. Selfish, she thinks, and looks at Terry. He is looking at Ros, and Zita is shocked by the love and joy on his face.

Chapter Fifteen

'Telegram for you,' says the office manager, opening the door of the chalet and interrupting Zita in her cleaning of the bath. She holds out the yellow envelope.

Zita has never had a telegram before. They are famous as bringers of bad news and she knows straight away that her mother is dead. Or her father. Their house has burnt down. She opens it.

'News' it says. 'Ring evening. Terry.' And a telephone number, which she recognises as his parents' home.

What the news can be occupies her for the day. He and Ros have split up. He is going abroad again. He wants her to go with him. His foot has been amputated. Ros has failed her exams. Ros is pregnant.

Maybe, she thinks, dropping her four pennies into the slot, maybe five-thirty is too early to be called evening but she really will go mad if she has to wait any longer.

She dials. His mother answers. 'He's not home yet,' she says. 'I'm expecting him any time now.'

'Is he all right?'

'Oh yes,' she says.

'Only he sent me a telegram.'

'I told him. I told him it would only get you worried, but he wouldn't listen. They never listen, boys.'

'So it's all right? I mean, everything?'

'I tell you what – I'll give you a clue, and then you can talk to him later and he'll give you the whole story. It's about your brother.'

'What about him?' Douglas is the last person she would have thought of.

'Our Terry thinks he's found him.'

'He's met him? I mean, he's talked to him?'

'Not as I know, not yet. Look, give me the number of that phone box and you just stand there and wait. He'll be in any time now. I'll get him to ring you there before he has his tea. All right? I won't give him his sausage and mash until he's put you in the picture. All right love? I've got to go or the spuds will be boiling dry.'

Zita leans against the wall of the phone box, trying to make sense of it. It seems a thing both too big and too small to be happening, and too ridiculous that she should be waiting for a call that might never come, if Terry doesn't get home till much later, if someone else wants to use the phone, if ... luckily the holiday camp guests are mostly in the dining room eating their teas, or else cooking their own in their chalets.

'What you waiting there for?' Marion is passing by. Zita explains.

'A telegram? He's off his head, that Terry. What was he thinking? What's so urgent he can't write a letter?'

And then the phone rings.

'Slow down.' Those were his first words. 'Let me tell you a bit at a time.' He has had a night and a day to get his story polished for her. 'Right, so you know I've got this bad foot?'

'Yes I know. Is it all right?'

'Never better. Well, could be better I suppose, but coming along nicely. Let me speak, will you. I had to go to the doctor's to get the dressing changed, right? So I've made an appointment and I've gone in to see this nurse, right. And I'm sitting there and she's taking the old bandage off and prodding me foot, like, to see if it looks all right, and I'm just looking at her and she's got this little badge on, with her name, right, and her name is Angel Grey, and I think that pretty funny, being as she's as black as they come, but just to make conversation I say I know someone called Grey and does she know Zita Grey, and she says no, and then I remember and I say, Oh no, I mean Sally-Ann Grey, that's her proper name, and she says how do I know her, this Sally-Ann, and she's proper calm you know, casual, not excitable at all, so I say, Oh she's just a good friend of mine, and she says, Oh, where does she live and I tell her – not the whole address, just like roughly where your mum and dad live, and she says, Oh, and she carries on mopping this stuff on my foot – stings a bit – and she puts a new bandage on and tells me to come back in three days for another look at it, and then she says – and I'm not expecting this at all – she says, My husband might know Sally-Ann, I'll ask him. And she gives me this big smile as I go out and I know – I just know, Zee, she's married to your Douglas.'

'Angel?' says Marion later when Zita has told her all about it. 'What sort of a name is Angel?'

'I don't know.'

'Maybe she's Angela and the 'A' fell off her badge,' says Marion. It's all a bit of a joke to her. 'Do you really think your Dougie went and married a coloured girl?'

'Why shouldn't he?'

'No wonder your dad went off like that. My dad would have if it was me.'

'She's a *nurse*, Maz. She's got a better job than you or me. More educated.'

'Yeah but still.'

'You're prejudiced.'

'What if I am. There's no law against it is there.'

They are in the canteen, eating pie and chips. Zita does not know what she is feeling; Marion is ready to stop thinking about it and to start talking about wedding catering.

'Well, it's just –' Zita doesn't know what it is. Dora comes into her head, the girl who would run over a black person and drive away without stopping; Cecily, who seemed as if she might marry a Greek; Terry and his tales of India, the welcomes and the selfless hospitality; and at the same time, John who was in their class at school, hers and Marion's class, and his thick lips and his squashed-looking nose, and how none of the girls would ever have fancied him.

'Remember John?' says Marion, as if she's read Zita's mind. 'Wonder what he's doing now.'

'What do coloured boys do?' says Zita. 'I mean what jobs? I mean, he's never going to be a champion boxer is he? And I don't think he could sing.'

'He wasn't good at anything,' says Marion. 'Couldn't even fight. What do you think about mince pies? As it will be Christmas – instead of canapés?'

'My mum does lovely mince pies,' says Zita. 'She'd do them for you, she'd like to.'

'Actually,' says Marion, 'I was going to tell you – I don't think I can ask your parents to the wedding. Brian says we've got to stick to a limit in the hall. I'm sorry –'

'She wouldn't come anyway,' says Zita. 'They never go anywhere. She'll probably stand outside the church though, just to see you go in and come out.'

'And see you in your bridesmaid dress.'

'I'm not doing it Maz, I'm really not. There'd be you and Brian, and there'd be me, about a foot taller –'

'You're not a foot taller.'

'I'm a lot taller than you. Taller than Brian. I'd *feel* a foot taller. I'd feel like a freak, all dressed up. I can't do it, not even for you.'

'I bet you'd do it for Terry.'

'I would *not*. Seriously, do you even think I *want* to go to their wedding. Even if they invite me, which I bet *she* won't.'

'Stuck up cow, isn't she,' says Marion, and Zita smiles at her, gratefully.

She goes to sleep in a hopeful glow – finding her brother, reconciling him with their parents, getting to know his wife, having a sister, maybe being an aunt – and wakes early in the morning, worrying.

Her father will be furious; there will be no forgiving from him. What if they make her choose – Douglas or parents? What if Dougie doesn't want to know her? What if his wife doesn't want to know her? And suppose she's not a nice person after all, then what?

She gets up and puts on her green overall; goes to the canteen for tea and toast; absentmindedly sits letting her tea get cold. How is this going to work anyway? Has she to follow the woman home? – wait outside the surgery until she comes out and trail after her, hiding behind bushes if she seems about to turn round? And anyway, she won't be back in Sheffield until after October – suppose by then Angel Grey is no longer working at that surgery? What if she's never there again, only been filling in for some absence? What if she tells Dougie that someone was asking about him and they up and leave the city?

It's lucky her work routine demands very little concentration; she's cleaning and tidying automatically, straightening bedclothes, rinsing out sinks, putting away pots and cutlery. She sweeps the floors and empties the bins, touching the family's belongings only so far as necessary; some are worse than others for leaving damp swimming costumes on the floor, damp towels on the beds, magazines and colouring books on the surfaces she is supposed to wipe down, glasses that should have been returned to the bar on the draining board. It strikes her, unexpectedly, that there are never any black families at the holiday camp, never any mixed families. Why is that? she wonders. Where do Dougie and his wife go on holiday? Or don't they go? Is it too difficult to find somewhere that will accept them? Have they been turned away from places? Will she be even able to ask them something like that, when and if she meets them?

And back again to the problem of just *how* she will be able to get in touch with them.

*

Senga is pleased that they now have a phone in the house. Now that Sally-Ann no longer sends postcards there is no need to prop them up on the mantel piece, to remind Willie that she has gone away again. Instead she phones once a week, on a Sunday. There is never much to say, only a few words about the weather. Senga never has any news; her weeks follow one after the other, every one the same, unless there is some domestic misfortune, like breaking a bad egg into a cake mixture, or needing to buy a new broom head. She would ask after Marion and Sally-Ann would tell her that she was fine and about that week's wedding dilemma. Then Sally-Ann would say, Should she have a word with Daddy? And Senga would make some excuse – he is asleep, or watching something on TV – because he would have already said that he isn't going to speak to his daughter until she is back under his roof.

Most weeks now Senga has a conversation with Doris Ward. They can compare what their respective daughters have told them about the weather in Great Yarmouth; Senga can ask about the wedding preparations; Doris can ask about Sally's plans for the winter.

'She has not told me a thing,' says Senga. 'I don't know if she'll ever settle down.'

'She's just waiting for the right man to come along,' says Doris. 'You'll see.'

It is pleasant, reflects Senga, after all these years of being neighbours, and their daughters being friends, to become more friendly themselves. A friendship that will not, of course include their husbands. Willie would certainly have nothing to do with it, and Senga would not dream of having a conversation with Mr Ward; what, after all, could she talk about?

She wonders why it has taken so long for herself and Doris. The Wards were already living there across the street when the Greys moved in. Willie was home from the war; Douglas was six, Senga was pregnant with Sally-Ann, Doris was further on in her pregnancy. Senga saw her from her front room window, bending down to pick the milk off the step, straightening up with that hand to her lower back. When she told Willie, he showed no interest, except to say that he doubted that they'd have much to do with their neighbours. About that, he was right; but even so, as soon as they could walk and talk there was friendship between Sally-Ann and Marion. They watched for each other from the front windows, and each demanded and clamoured to be allowed out to play if the other one so much as showed their face. It was a quiet little street, Boyce Street, with no through traffic and the infants' school at the far end. Douglas was allowed to play out; there were other wee boys around, to chase and play at marbles, or kick a tennis ball back and forth. He could easily keep an eye on the little girls as well, and stop them from wandering off.

The two girls started school together, and stayed together, constantly in and out of each other's houses, shut up secretively in their bedrooms, or making a mess with glue and paper in the front rooms on rainy days. The eleven-plus worried them, for the risk was that one might pass and the other not, but as it turned out neither of them did and they continued together all through secondary school, a comical pair, Marion like a little blond barrel, Sally-Ann so tall and spidery that her nickname was Longo, derived from Long Tall Sally. Still, not more than half a dozen words per year would pass between their respective mothers. And yet she's a nice woman, says Senga now to herself. They've a bit more money than we have, but it doesnae worry her, and it shouldnae worry me. You've got to be pleasant with your neighbours, for who knows when you'll be needing them. Or when they'll be needing you. And Willie needn't be told anything.

Now it's autumn and the holiday camp is closed till the spring. Senga bakes a fruit cake and a batch of drop scones. Sally-Ann has told her she will be home by the middle of the afternoon, but four o'clock comes and goes, and five o'clock, and Senga guesses that she must have missed her train. She looks across to the Wards' house, but it is not clear whether Marion has arrived or not. She remembers now, Sally-Ann said that Marion was coming in the car with Brian, but there was no room for Sally-Ann because of all the things Marion had been buying for their new home.

It's almost six before she arrives, with Dougie's old rucksack on her back, looking excited, but weary, with no explanation for why she is so late.

'And your Daddy will be home any minute now,' says Senga. She is disappointed that she hasn't been able to have some time alone with her daughter. And sure enough, they hear him wheeling his bike down the passage, and he's in the kitchen taking up space, almost before Senga has finished explaining that the cake has been ready for two hours at least, and the kettle's been boiled umpteen times.

'Never mind,' says Sally-Ann.

She eats with them – it's a steak and kidney pie, home-made of course – and says nice things about being home, but she seems distracted, quiet, absent. Not unhappy. Could it be, wonders Senga, that there is a boyfriend at last. Is there some young man on her mind?

Afterwards, she helps by drying the dishes.

'Mum,' she says. 'I've got something to tell you.'

This is it, thinks Senga. There's a boyfriend.

'But you mustn't tell Daddy. You have to promise.'

'I don't know.'

'If you don't promise I can't tell you. He doesn't want Daddy to know.'

'Who doesn't?'

'You have to promise first. I mean it Mum. I'm not playing a game.'

'But who are we talking about? Who says –?' Then she knows. 'Is it Douglas?'

Chapter Sixteen

The wedding of Marion Ward and Brian Miller takes place just before Christmas. It's a bright day but icy cold, and Marion looks to have made a good decision with her velvet cloak to wear over her lace sleeves, while Brian is shivering in his suit.

'Something to be said,' he whispers to Zita later, 'something to be said for woollen undercrackers. Should have borrowed me grandad's.'

Zita's Asti Spumante goes down the wrong way and she has to be patted on the back.

'You next then?' says Marion's mother. 'Any plans – you and that Terry?'

'He's got a fiancée,' says Zita. 'Marion must have told you.'

'Sounds to me like he can't make up his mind between the two of you,' says Doris. 'Just don't play hard to get. Do you hear me?'

'So you didn't want to be bridesmaid to our Marion?' says her father. He has a large stomach and a red face and holds a full glass in one hand and a half full bottle in the other.

'It wasn't...' says Zita. She does not know how to finish the sentence.

'It wasn't to be,' he says, nodding. 'Saved me the expense of another dress, that's how I look at it. And you're a bit of a beanpole aren't you, really. Might have looked a bit comical –'

'That's what I thought –'

'What with our Marion being such a bonny girl.'

'Yes, she is –'

'But short,' he says, as if confiding a secret. 'Look a bit stumpy next to you. Takes after me you know.'

More people come in the evening, after the meal, people Zita knows from school, the more distant relatives of the Wards, young women from the hair salons where Marion has worked, one or two neighbours. Marion in the end had sent an evening invitation to Zita's parents, but Senga replied that they were unable to come, thank you, and sent a salt and pepper set from Walshes as a present.

There is a proper DJ and after Marion and Brian have started the dancing there is general taking to the floor, encouraged by the sight of Mr Ward, still holding his bottle, doing the twist, or something fairly like it, to whatever tune is playing.

'He better not give himself a heart attack,' says someone standing near Zita. 'There's nowt puts a damper on a do worse than a heart attack.'

But he survives, although one of the little bridesmaids is sick on the floor and the caretaker of the hall is sent for, to come with his bucket of sand and his mop and clear it up.

'Excitement,' judges someone – a different someone.

'Or chicken pox,' says another someone. 'It's been going through the school like a dose of salts.'

'Want to dance?' says a young man to Zita – someone she was at school with who has never spoken to her in his life before.

'Norman?' she says, as they move on to the floor.

'You're Sally aren't you?' He's a tall young man, with glasses and acne scars, in a shiny suit and a nylon shirt that is sticking to him already. 'They used to call you Longo.'

'I've changed my name,' she shouts into his ear. 'They call me Zita now.'

'Why's that then?' he shouts back. 'Going on the stage are you?'

She laughs.

'Or a model,' he says. 'I mean, they have to be tall don't they.'

'But being tall isn't – I mean, on it's own being tall isn't enough, is it?'

Now he laughs. 'If it was, I could be a model. You've got to be a girl.'

Maybe, she thinks, he's just very short-sighted; maybe he doesn't know that she is – well, the kindest word is 'plain.'

He escorts her off the floor with a hand under her elbow, as if she is delicate, and tells her to sit down while he fetches her a drink. She watches him waiting at the bar, she weighs his tallness against his spectacles. He stands very straight, shoulders back – and she realises that she herself always tries to appear shorter than she is; she always rounds her shoulders and pokes her head forward, especially when she is around boys and men. It doesn't do to look down on them, or even to be tall enough to look them straight in the eye. She is the same height as Terry – she knows that if she were to stand up straight and look him squarely in the face, even if Ros fell under a bus tomorrow, she would never have a chance of being his girlfriend. He wouldn't like it. It wouldn't do.

Norman is on his best behaviour. He brings her a port and lemon – 'I didn't know what you wanted' – and tells her that he works in the Yorkshire Bank on South Road. He tells her that he was not at the actual wedding that afternoon; he was at the football instead, but he restrains himself from giving her an account of the match. They talk a little about people they knew at school; they remind themselves of significant teachers and hilarious incidents; they have to shout above the noise of the music.

Suddenly the floor clears. Engelbert Humperdink is singing The Last Waltz; Marion and Brian are taking to the floor, a little uncertainly after all the alcohol they've had, having their last dance before leaving for their wedding night in a hotel. The guests look on, some of them applaud; then there are kisses and calls of Good luck, Lots of Love, and they stumble out to the waiting car (Brian's cousin's) and are gone. The hall is booked until eleven thirty, the disco starts up again, but the older people are leaving, as are the ones with children ready to be put to bed. Soon only Mr and Mrs Ward remain of the older folk; the music, on Doris' instructions, is turned down in volume and slowed down in tempo. Girls are hanging on their partners now, resting their heads on shoulders, some have taken off their shoes and are ruining a pair of tights.

'Do you want to–?' says Norman but she can tell he's not too sure about it himself and she shakes her head.

'I probably should be going home,' she says.

'Shall I walk you?'

'If you like.'

'Where do you live?'

She tells him. 'Same as Marion. I've known her since we were babies.'

Doris gives her a kiss, and a piece of wedding cake wrapped in a paper serviette to take home for her parents. 'You look nice tonight,' she says. 'Is he taking you home?'

'It's on my way,' says Norman. 'I'll see her safely to her door.'

When they reach her house she can see him looking for the number so that he will remember. The house is dark: only the light has been left on at the bottom of the stairs. She is not sure how to say goodbye; if he was Terry she might hug him briefly and chastely, but he's not. She looks at her shoes and he ducks his head under hers and gives her a kiss, wet but brief. It might have been aimed for her mouth but only touches her cheek. 'See you soon,' he says.

'Thank you,' she says.

106

'What for?'

'Oh, you know, everything.'

She turns down the passage before he has gone more than a couple of steps, and before she has even let herself in through the back door the whole day has disappeared from her thoughts and she is thinking again about Christmas, and Douglas, and his children; and making plans.

Senga puts the lid back on the cake tin, after she has dribbled the Christmas cake with its twice weekly ration of brandy – its last measure before the marzipan, the icing, the silver balls and the frill – and puts the tin back on the top shelf, where Willie will not go looking for it. He is a devil for cake, is Willie. She tucks the brandy bottle away at the back of another cupboard, hidden behind a bag of flour. More and more things now have to be kept from Willie – real solid things, the presents for the grandchildren she has not yet met, and real but more ethereal knowledge. Wishes, thoughts, plans, hopes. Memories. Blame.

Sally-Ann had been very careful about how much she told her. 'I promised our Dougie,' she said.

'He doesn't trust me, then,' said Senga sadly.

'He doesn't want Daddy finding out. I mustn't tell you where they live, or where they work.'

'I wouldn't tell him.'

'He might find out. They don't live near here anyway, I can tell you that.'

'You've been to their house then?'

'I've been to the end of their street, that's all. We met in a park.'

'Which one?' said Senga but Sally-Ann shook her head.

'So what's she like?'

Sally-Ann stopped to think. 'She's nice,' she said. 'She was a bit – quiet. Careful I suppose. I mean – what did Daddy *do*? It must have been bad. She is really scared of him. I think Dougie is too.'

'Your Daddy wouldn't hurt him.'

'I think it was things he said. The language he used.'

'What did he say? Because I don't remember, myself.'

'Yes you do,' said Sally-Ann. 'You wouldn't forget that. *I* don't know though. And, if I did know, I wouldn't repeat it. I could be wrong that they're scared of him. More likely they're just angry.'

'So,' said Senga, 'did he have anything to say about me?'

'He asked me how you were. I said you were the same as always. I told him about your mother dying and he said to tell you he was sorry.

He said – he said he was sorry the children couldn't know you –'

'Children,' said Senga.

'There's a boy and a girl. I said I wouldn't tell you their names.'

'How old?'

'He's just little. About two. She's just started school in September so I suppose she's five.'

'If I could only see them.'

Sally-Ann – Zita – had not had any intention of doing what she did next; it must have been pity for her mother and, maybe, just a little bit of one-upmanship too.

'I can show you a photo.'

It was an odd-shaped photo taken with one of those new cameras that developed almost instantly. It was a rather blurred image – the little boy must have moved – of the two children on a park seesaw, one behind the other. The colour was dull, as if it was taken in the dusk of the evening and both children wore hats and gloves. Senga looked at it for a long time and then Sally-Ann moved to put it back in her bag.

'Can I keep it,' said Senga. 'You can get another one next time you see them.'

'I don't know.'

'You will be seeing them again?'

'Yes. But I don't want Daddy finding it.'

Senga takes the photo from her daughter's hand. 'Don't worry about that. There's plenty in this house your Daddy doesn't know about.'

Chapter Seventeen

On Christmas Eve, after her work at Walshes finishes, Zita goes to Terry's parents, taking gifts – sweets for the boys, cigars for Lawrence, a poinsettia for Peggy. Terry, she knows, will not be there. He has a new job, one which has surprised everyone – he is working at a school, not an ordinary one but a Special School, for children with what they call difficulties. He drives the minibus, and helps in the classrooms and, apparently loves the job so much that he is planning to go to college and be trained to do it properly, as a career, for ever. But term is over and he is down in Guildford. He will spend Christmas with *her* family, but be back in Sheffield for the Boxing Day party.

'He'll not miss that at least,' says Peggy. 'But you'd think they could be here for Christmas Day. Our Darren's been crying already, thinking his big brother won't be here. It were bad enough last year, but at least then he weren't *able* to get home. And it'll be his last Christmas before he's married too.'

'Maybe he'll bring her here next year for Christmas,' Zita says to Peggy. They are in the kitchen, where Peggy is making the stuffing ready for the next day, chopping onions and celery and putting stale bread through a Spong mincer.

'I'm not counting on it,' she says. 'I don't think we're posh enough for Madam.'

'But by next Christmas,' says Zita, 'she'll be part of the family, won't she? I mean, they're in Sheffield, you'll be seeing a lot of her.'

Because Ros's plans to work and live in London have come to nothing and the job she has started on is at the big Northern General Hospital. She is still living in a student rented house, along with, most of the time, Terry. Her parents are not supposed to know. 'We'll see,' says Peggy. 'I don't mind telling you, I'd rather he was getting married to someone from round here. Someone of our sort, you know, that we could get on with.'

There is a silence while Zita wonders what she should say. The poinsettia stands on the kitchen table between her and Peggy and suddenly she sees that there is another one in the room, already, on the windowsill.

'Stay for tea,' says Peggy. 'Lawrence will like to see you.'

'I can't stop,' says Zita. 'I'm going to see my brother. I've got presents for the children, and presents from my mum as well. I'm not allowed to tell her where they live.'

'Terry told me all about it,' says Peggy. 'It's a shame your dad was so against it.' She stops and thinks. 'I mean, I'm not all that keen on our Terry's choice, but she'll always be welcome here. We might have to work on it, Lawrence and me, but she'll be family, whether or not.'

'Of course she will,' says Zita. It comes out rather sadly.

'So how do you get on with her?' says Peggy. 'Your new sister-in-law? Must be a funny do, finding out about her after all this time.'

'Well,' says Zita, 'I've not really seen her much. She's nice. I mean, I like her. She doesn't fuss about things you know. She's nice with the kids I think, you know, doesn't spoil them or shout at them —'

'Is that what you think parents do?' Peggy is laughing at her.

'My dad can be a bit of a shouter,' says Zita. 'He's not very patient. And he goes into a sulk. And then my mum is scared of him, so she doesn't say anything, but she'll always buy me sweets or something when he's not there, to make up for him.'

'It's not right,' says Peggy. 'Respect is one thing but it works both ways. Nobody should be scared of the person they live with. Just you remember that.'

'She says it's him that earns the money —'

'So it is. And it's her what does the cleaning and the shopping and the cooking and the washing and the ironing and the mending, and brings up the children. I've told our Terry —'

'Terry wouldn't be nasty. Ever. He's too nice to throw his weight about.'

'He may be nice,' says his mother. 'I hope he's nice. But he's not a pushover, and that one, she'll want to rule the roost, *I* know. When all the lovey-dovey stuff wears off there'll be ructions, I'm telling you.' She tips a saucer of dried herbs into her stuffing mix and stirs vigorously. 'You'll be coming on Boxing Day? To the party?'

'Yes, please,' says Zita. 'Is it all right if I bring a friend? Norman?'

'Boyfriend is it?'

'Just a friend really. Someone I was at school with.'

'Not serious then?'

'Not serious,' says Zita firmly.

'Bring Norman,' says Peggy. 'The more the merrier. Will you be bringing him to the wedding too?'

Zita pauses, takes a deep breath. 'I'm not coming to the wedding.'

Peggy says nothing for several long seconds, then: 'Why not?'

Zita mumbles, 'I don't know.'

'But you've had an invitation?'

'Oh yes.' It came earlier that week, and she recognised Terry's cramped, sloping handwriting on the envelope. Inside it was a stiff white affair embossed with silver, Ros' parents requesting the pleasure of her company. She had to take it to her room and sit looking at it for some time while the decision not to go formed in her head and became inevitable. Then she sent her reply.

She takes a deep breath. 'I can't do it Peggy. I'm sorry.'

'He wants you there though. He told me. I was going to ask if you wanted to come down with us, all the Sheffield folk together. He really means it when he says he wants you there.'

'I can't,' she says again. 'And besides, I'm going back to France straight after New Year. Back to the hotel for the skiing season.'

Peggy looks at her until she has to look away. 'We'll miss you,' she says.

'I'm sorry,' says Zita.

'It's not too late to change your mind.'

'I'm sorry,' she says again. 'I'll be thinking of you.'

'Of course you will,' says Peggy. 'And don't forget – Boxing Day, party – you'll be here for that, you and Norman.'

'Yes,' says Zita. She adds, just as the idea comes into her head, 'Most likely, I'll be going on to Spain in the spring.'

For the Boxing Day party, Zita wears the red dress she wore for Marion's wedding. She has not, having had second thoughts, troubled Norman with an invitation. They have been to the pictures together, twice, and the second time he held her hand in the dark, and kissed her on the mouth on her doorstep when he took her home. But it was no good, she knew it was no good. He wasn't Terry, and they had nothing to say to each other. She was glad that she would not have to see him in the same room as Terry, looking even more inferior.

It is Ros who opens the front door to her. She is wearing trousers, very tight round her bum, very flared at her ankles, and hasn't taken off her coat yet. She does not smile, or greet Zita in any way, just holds the door back to let her in. Mardy, thinks Zita.

She finds Terry talking to his mum in the kitchen; something's wrong, she can see at once.

'It's me Nannan,' he says, turning to her. 'She's been taken to hospital. Fell down steps as she were coming through front door. Me dad's gone with her in the ambulance.'

'Oh dear,' says Zita. Nothing more seems to be appropriate, but she asks anyway. 'Is there anything I can do?'

Peggy is pulling a tray of sausage rolls out of the oven. 'I wish I knew,' she said. 'It seems right heartless having a party when the poor old lady's been carried off to casualty. But what can we do? Folks have come all the way from Barnsley —' She slides the sausage rolls on to a plate and stands looking at them.

'I've unplugged the record player,' says Terry. 'It don't feel right either way does it.'

'Shall I take some of this food through,' says Zita. 'Maybe when they've had something to eat they'll think about going home. Under the circumstances.'

Peggy seems to notice her for the first time. 'We can't chuck em out,' she says. 'They'll want to know how she's going on. But you've done right, our Terry, shutting the music off.'

Zita ferries a number of plates of food from the kitchen into the front room, and then stops by Ros, still stationed by the front door.

'All right?'

'I suppose so,' says Ros.

'I think I'll go home,' says Zita. 'It doesn't seem right, hanging around. It's different for you, you're family.'

Ros makes a face which seems to indicate that being family is not a lot of fun. The phone, on a small table at the bottom of the stairs, begins to ring.

'I have to answer it,' says Ros. 'Will you go and tell Terry's Mum. Yes,' she says into the phone. 'Someone's just gone to get her.'

'Phone,' says Zita, and Peggy puts down the plate of cakes, slowly, as if it matters, and goes into the hall.

Terry says, 'Is it bad?' but Zita doesn't know. Shyly, but unable to stop herself, she puts an arm round his shoulders, only to comfort him, and it's him who turns it into half a hug.

'Why won't you come to our wedding?' he says.

'I can't,' she says.

Then he kisses her on each cheek, like the French do, just as Ros comes through the kitchen door, followed by Peggy.

'I'm sorry,' says Zita, though no one is listening. She edges out of the way, leaves the kitchen without being noticed, takes her coat off the banister, and steps out into the night.

She has not reached the end of the road before a car pulls up beside her.

'What do you think you're doing?' It's Terry, winding down the window of his dad's big old Hillman.

'I thought I'd better get out of your way. I'm sorry about your Nannan.'

'She'll be fine,' he says. 'Shock, they're saying, and bruising. They're keeping her in overnight. I've to go and fetch me dad though. Get in.'

She gets in. 'I'll be going home anyway,' she says. 'I thought – well, I had an impression – that Ros –'

He laughs. 'Oh Ros is insanely jealous of you. Didn't you know? She always thinks there's something going on between us. We've had words, more than once. But then there's always making up, isn't there?'

'I wouldn't know,' says Zita, a bit stiffly, feeling foolish.

'What I tell her is – you're my best mate – apart from our Lol – but she's the love of my life. Then she has a little cry if she's feeling that way out and then we kiss and make up.'

'You can drop me off here,' says Zita.

'Come to the hospital with me. Come back to the party with me. Party hasn't started yet. You can't go home now.'

'Let me out,' she says. She will not look at him and she cannot recognise her own voice. He has no time to persuade her; they have arrived and his father is waiting in the hospital doorway. Zita gets out and holds the door open for Lawrence. Terry has turned his face away from her; she wishes he would ask her again to come back to the party but no, he's not going to ask again, not even going to wait long enough for her to speak to his father. She hears the engine change its sound and steps out of the way as he performs a lurching three point turn. She watches his tail lights wink round the corner, and as she turns towards home the thought comes to her head that she will never see him again.

'I've been thinking,' says Willie. 'What we're going to do, we're going to buy this house. There's a scheme now, you know – landlord has to sell it to us if we ask to buy it.'

'Surely there's not the money for that,' says Senga. 'I've heard about it, there was a notice about it in the post office, I saw it. But I never thought –'

'It's time we did,' he says. 'We've paid enough in rent to buy it by now, more than once over.'

'Well, I know that,' she says (because isn't it her after all who has to open the door to the rent man twice a month and hand over the money Willie works so hard for.) 'But is there enough money?'

'I think there is,' says Willie. 'I've looked into it. We might have to borrow a bit.'

'Borrow?' says Senga. 'We surely don't want to borrow. And who from?'

'From the bank, woman,' says Willie scornfully. 'Where did you think? And think, lass, once it's ours we can do it however we like.'

'What do you mean?'

'Change things. Paint the front door. Have it however we want.'

'Like what though?'

He pauses to think. 'Like – what about this – a new bathroom?'

Senga shakes her head. 'Now that,' she says, 'I know we cannot afford.'

'We'll save up,' he says. 'After all, we'll not be paying rent out every week, will we? You'd like that wouldn't you – a nice new plastic bath that you don't have to scrub clean.'

'Oh, I would,' she says. 'Could we have a pink one? And everything to match?'

'Well,' he says. 'I wasn't thinking pink myself, but we'll see. And another thing, when we're gone our, Sally-Ann will have a house to inherit. We'll tell her, we'll say, this house will be yours my girl, as long as you do the right thing by us. Do the right thing and you'll have a house all of your own and it will never cost you a penny.'

'Do you think–?' says Senga, but Willie has turned his attention to his dinner.

'That's it,' he says, through a mouthful of liver and bacon. 'Leave it to me now, I'm not discussing it any more. I'll deal with it.'

They eat in silence for a while, then Senga says, 'She says she's thinking about going to Spain after she finishes at the hotel.'

He tips his plate forwards and uses the spoon – that should be kept for his rice pudding – to scoop up the gravy.

'She's told you that?'

'She mentioned it. In passing, just.'

'It's time she was getting married, not mucking about in foreign countries. It's time she was giving us some grandchildren.'

Senga feels a familiar stab somewhere below her heart, above her stomach. 'Marion's expecting already,' she says. Is that to change the subject, or to affirm the truth of what he has just said?

'There you go, then,' he says. 'It's about time. She's what: twenty-two? You and me had got a child of three by the time we were twenty-two.'

Willie has spent most of his life in a state of puzzled anger, as probably his father did before him. His brothers and sisters, all younger than him, all scrabbling for whatever was going – food, space, attention; his mother anxious, poorly, pregnant, exhausted; his father, worn out with working and worrying. And himself a teenager, before the word was invented, working of course, pretending to be a man, longing for a bit of softness in his life, and a bit of fun. When Senga smiled at him on the promenade at Girvan was it any wonder that he smiled back? Was it any wonder that when he found her on his doorstep in Motherwell one Monday evening that it seemed a clear and natural thing to walk out of his home and go with her?

And after that, it seemed as if life picked him up and whirled him round, and when his feet touched the ground again he, somehow, without having wished it, had been married, fathered a son, been through a world war, come out of it with a hatred of cold food, and ankles that would be still stiff and painful thirty years on, and then, still a young man, with a son who seemed to be nothing to do with him, another child on the way, a wife he hardly recognised, now all he had to do – *all* – was to get a job and get on with the rest of his life as if nothing had happened.

How can he talk like this, she thinks, as if he's never thrown Dougie out of the house, as if Dougie isn't still someone they know, isn't still their son? If he wants grandchildren he's got them, if he only knew it, if he wasn't such a pig, if he hadn't put himself, and her, out of reach of them. So what if they're black, or brown, or sky-blue-pink? Little harmless weans is what they are and all she wants to do is to give them a wee cuddle, sit them on her knee, hold their hands across a road, tuck them into bed, sing them a wee song. She wonders again – she wonders this every waking hour – if she should not maybe, this time, leave Willie and go to live on her own, somewhere he couldn't find her, and in time Dougie would come round to the idea of her again; he would know it was never her that made him leave. But where could she go, and how could she manage? Where could she even begin? You did it once, she says to herself. You left Dumbarton without a worry, you found your way to Motherwell, where you'd never been before, you found his house by asking people in the street, you knocked on the door without any fear that he'd send you away. You were a bold lass then.

*

The Italian cousins are back again at the Hotel Mimose; the fourth chambermaid is a tiny French girl, who lives locally and goes home every evening, allowing Zita to have a bedroom to herself.

'The door,' advises Vittoria, miming the bolt. 'Shut it. The old man–' She waves her arms to indicate that the old man can be anywhere, even up here under the roof.

Zita has not forgotten his hand on her knee, but it was nothing, she knows it was nothing. He remembers her, which she finds flattering, and kisses her on both cheeks, the way he greets his daughter-in-law, and calls her *'ma petite 'itch–'iker'* which makes her feel especially welcome. Vittoria, she knows, does not understand that she, Zita, is special.

Saturday sparkling sunny day in the French Alps. Zita is busy getting rooms ready for new guests, sometimes taking off her overall and doing a stint on reception, if staff are being called elsewhere to deal with items unexpectedly missing from places where they should have been, or newly arrived guests who have lost their way to their rooms. It will be a long day and she will be tired at the end of it, and she is glad to be keeping busy, although she has to admit to herself that pictures come into her head. Ros having her hair done, getting dressed in the famous silk dress, Terry waiting at the altar, going through the service, his responses loud and confident, kissing the bride, signing the register. The group on the steps of the church, arranged for the photographs. Happy.

From her bedroom in the attic area of the Hotel Mimose, looking out of the small window to see the mountains dissolving into the dark, Zita writes her letters on Sundays. She writes to Marion – weather, anecdotes, awkward guests, lovely news about the baby, hopes that Marion's washing machine will be delivered soon, *regards to Brian, and your mother. Love from Zita.*

She writes once or twice to Norman and the third time she tells him that she has decided not to come back to England after her job finishes – *I want to see Spain, and no, I can't give you a forwarding address, I don't know where I will be. With best wishes for the future, from Zita.*

She writes to Douglas, to Mr and Mrs D. Grey, enclosing some postcards for the children. She hopes they are all well and she is looking forward to seeing them when she comes home, probably in the summer. *Love from your sister.*

She writes to her parents. *Dear Mum and Daddy, I will be leaving the hotel after the end of next week and I am heading off to Spain. I will keep in touch.* She does not put a name at the end; it is easier not to.

She writes to Terry – to *Dear Terry and Ros*. She hopes the wedding went off all right and that they enjoyed their honeymoon. She is looking forward to seeing them both when she gets home.

She reads what she has written and scores it out, roughly, tearing the paper. She starts again:

She thinks about him all the time, she only wants the best for him and she knows that Ros is not what he believes she is. She, Zita, has seen her on a train from London with a young man – they'd been together in London for the weekend, they were kissing on the train. *Did Ros ever tell you about that?* She's only married him for the wedding – all she wanted was the wedding and all the attention. She doesn't deserve him. No one, and especially not someone as shallow and stuck-up as Ros, could ever love him like Zita does. *I will never love anyone else. You are the only one I will ever love.* And folds the paper without reading it over and slides it into the envelope, writes the address, licks and sticks her last stamp and puts it, with her other letters, in the tray on Reception from where it will be sent.

Chapter Eighteen

'So,' says Douglas, 'you didn't stay in Spain for long. Something wrong with it, was there?'

'Not really,' says Zita. It is a cold Sunday in December. They are sitting on a park bench while Angel pushes Dexter on a swing. 'But I didn't feel very comfortable there, on my own. They're not used to girls hitchhiking you know. And I couldn't find places to stay overnight. There may have been hostels, other people have told me there are, but I just didn't find them, so I got as far as Barcelona and I saw the sea there and I thought, I'll get on that ferry and see where it takes me.'

'Someone I know went to this place called Lloret del Mar,' says Douglas. 'Had a great time, he said, really cheap drinks, hotel pool, you know. Angel were thinking we might be able to go there with the kids one day. Not much more expensive than, say, Filey, and you can trust the weather will be good. What do you think? One of those package holidays?'

'Oh yes, do it,' says Zita. 'It's only that I was on my own. But go, the kids would love it.'

'So, where did the ferry take you?'

'Majorca. But then I got another one and another one. I went right across the Med on little ferries, till I got to Corfu again, and I went to see Cecily – she's the girl I went there with last year and she's still there, so I stayed with her for a bit and then I went down to Crete – that's another Greek Island – and I stayed there. I think I could live there for the rest of my life.'

'So, what have you come back for?'

She feels a little hurt; it sounds as if he doesn't want her to come back. 'I just felt like seeing everyone here –'

'Marion I suppose.'

'Yes, Marion. And the baby. Faye, she's called. You should see Maz being a mum, you wouldn't believe it. And she's right excited about her new house, showed me everything, how it all works, you know, Brian's done it all up, central heating and everything. And there's Mum, I always feel like I have to come back and see Mum once a year at least.'

'She's all right?'

'Seems fine. She asked after you of course. She'd like to see you.' Zita is a little shy of saying this.

Douglas shrugs, dismissing the idea. 'While she's with our father I'll never see her. He'll never come near me or my wife or my children and that's the end of it.'

'But Mum –'

'I know, she's told you to ask me. I know you'll be telling me it's not her fault but I don't trust her. She'll never keep her mouth shut.'

Zita nods; there is no arguing with his position. They sit in silence. It's never easy, being with her brother. He says he likes to see her but it's hard to keep up a conversation. Angel makes it her practice to let them have time together, when in fact a meeting would go more smoothly if she were part of it.

'So,' he says, changing the subject. 'Seen anyone else?'

'Not really. I've been working.'

'Back at Walshes are you?'

'For the time being. I'm staying till the January sales are over, then I'll be going away again. Probably.'

'That's how you want to live is it? Back to the Alps again?'

'No, not this time. I'm not going back there.'

'Don't they want you?'

'It's not that.'

He doesn't ask any more. He doesn't really want to know, she thinks. He's just struggling to make conversation; I don't have to tell him anything. I don't have to tell anyone, no one has any right to know.

'You'll have seen that Terry?' he says.

'Not yet,' she says.

'Thought you would have.'

She shrugs. 'Been at work.'

He shrugs too. She can see him casting around his mind for something else to say. 'Terry's married now,' she says. 'And with work and everything.'

'Right,' says Dougie.

Angel has extracted Dexter from the swing and comes across with him. 'We have to go now,' she says. 'I have to fetch Nic from her friend's and get them home for their tea. Will we be seeing you at Christmas?'

'I've got a few things for the children,' says Zita. 'Is it all right if I pop round Christmas Eve?'

'Don't tell *them* where you're going,' says Dougie.

'I know,' she says. 'You don't have to keep telling me. I'll tell them I'm going to Marion's. They don't question me so much these days.'

'I don't know why you can even stay in their house,' he says, scowling.

'Where else would I go?'

He shrugs. How, she wonders, does Angel put up with such a moody man. 'He's our dad after all,' she says. 'He's not so bad.'

'You don't know him, then,' says Douglas. 'Not like I know him.'

'You could go and see mum though. Some time when he's not there.'

'I do have work to go to,' he says. 'Anyway, why would I want to see her? She was on his side.'

Whose side am I on, wonders Zita.

She hugs Dexter – who squirms away from her – and says goodbye. She walks across town, not wanting to arrive back home but having nowhere else to go. Marion is busy with her baby and her Christmas preparations, and anyway she would ask about Terry, has Zita seen him, is that Rosalind pregnant yet? And Zita would wish she could tell her friend about the awful letter she sent, but she would be too ashamed; she could tell no one, not even Marion.

(And the other thing she hasn't told anyone – hiding the knowledge even from herself – is that M. Felix, the old gentleman, did in fact try her door, her unbolted door – late one night, did come in and sit on her bed, talking all the while about poetry, did lift her nightie and stroke her gently, while she tried to push the material back over her legs. That he did take off his own trousers and his underpants – they were made of silk, she thought and wondered why she was noticing such a thing at such a time – and slid into the bed beside her.

She sat up straight in the bed then. '*Non*,' she said, but not too loudly because she was already embarrassed enough; she didn't want Vittoria to hear.

'*Si*,' he said softly. '*Tu ne veut pas perdre ta place, non? Ne crie pas.*'

So, she did not cry out. She said, in a whisper, '*Je ne veut pas –*' and he answered as if she were a child refusing its breakfast, '*Soit mignonne. Ca va bien, n'est-ce pas?*

And so she lay as still as she could while he did what he did and after he had gone she got out of bed and quietly moved the bolt into its housing – the very movement made her blush and shiver – and got back into bed and lay there trying to pretend that nothing had happened.

What would happen next, she asked herself. She imagined scenes in front of his son, the manager, she imagined being denounced in front of the guests, of being told to pack her bags. She imagined Vittoria shouting at her – Why didn't you listen to me? Why did you think you were something special? How could you let that happen? You slag. You slut. All in Italian so she wouldn't understand the words, but she would know very well what was being said.

And what could she have said? I didn't know. I didn't mean it.

She got out of bed in the morning and put on her overall and went to the linen cupboard to collect fresh laundry for other people's bedrooms, and her cloths and dusters, and a bag for removing the rubbish. She worked her way along the corridor while the guests were at breakfast. One more week, she said to herself, then I go to Spain.)

So she has told no one about what happened to her in the Alps. She cannot tell her mother, or Marion, she does not have the words. Interfered with. Taken advantage of. These could mean anything. She can imagine Marion saying, 'But *what*, exactly?' and she would not be able to say. The word 'rape' occurs to her only to be pushed away – besides, rape is what happens to drunken girls in alleyways, it's followed by murder and a body dumped in a ditch for a sniffing dog to find. Whereas with her, nothing happened. Well, something happened but she was not hurt. Not hurt at all – he had been, in fact, very gentle.

It was her own fault. She should have bolted her door; she should have told him no. She should have pushed him out of her room – he was only a small man – and gone to Vittoria. She did not do any of the things that she should have done and it was her own fault. And what was more – this thought came to her as she set off westwards towards Spain – it was a punishment for something she had done wrong, and she knows what that is. It is the letter she sent to Terry. It was wrong. She said things about Ros that might have been true, but were embellishments. She had not seen her kiss the boy on the train; she suspected but she had seen nothing. And it was malicious. She wanted to spoil their marriage and their happiness. She had done this to someone she called her friend and something bad had to happen to hers in return.

Spain had not relieved her of what had happened. Getting into cars with lone men became something to avoid. She stood at the kerbside, she put out her thumb, a car stopped, she leaned in through the window and then the smallest thing would put her off – a man with clean fingernails, a man old enough to be her father, a polite man, a smiling man – she would make them understand – sorry, thank you but she was going somewhere else. She waited for a car with a woman in it, or a lorry driven by a young man, and if they did not appear she walked long distances. She slept in doorways, she looked dishevelled and disreputable; she refused all offers of assistance; she believed that she deserved to die; she believed that she wanted to die.

She woke up early one morning on a bench by the sea in Barcelona and watched as the sun rose out of the sea. East, she thought. She and Cicely, a year ago – was it only a year? – had stood on the deck of a little steamer ferry and watched the island of Corfu rise out of the sea. Here was a port, here were boats, that could take her east. She would go east.

Chapter Nineteen

'Didn't you get the invite?' says Cicely. 'I sent it to England but I put Please Forward on it.'

'Sorry,' says Zita. That's two weddings she's missed.

'See, here,' says Cicely, 'it's very old-fashioned. No way can you sleep together if you haven't had a proper wedding. Even being engaged – you're still only allowed a peck on the cheek.'

They are sitting on the front doorstep of the very small house in which Cicely and Spyridon live. 'His parents wanted us to live with them,' she says, 'but I ask you, who wants to do that? It's bad enough being in the same street.'

'Handy for baby-sitting though,' says Zita.

'Don't start,' says Cicely. 'I've had enough of that already. I want to live a bit first. In fact – don't say anything to his mother will you – we're planning to go back home. You know –'

'Back to New Zealand? Does he want to?'

'Sure he does. What's for him here?'

There is no room for Zita in their tiny house so she is installed in the room she and Cecily stayed in the previous year. It feels like a very long time ago.

'Sorry,' says Cecily, 'I couldn't get it for more than a week – they're going to knock a wall down or something.'

'It's all right,' says Zita. 'I would be moving on anyway.' It hadn't been her plan but now it seemed to be what she had intended.

'Do you know what?' says Cecily. 'You've hardly said a sentence all week. You used to talk all the time about that Terry boy. Did he come back? Where is he now?'

'Married,' says Zita.

'Well, you knew that was going to happen.'

'I know.'

'So, what was the wedding like?'

'I don't know. I wasn't there.'

'Didn't you go? Why not?' And I can never see him again, thinks Zita. 'And you haven't said anything about the hotel –'

'What hotel?'

'Don't pull that – "What hotel?" Was Vittoria there this year? Was Madame in a vicious mood again? Did your old fella turn up?'

Zita hesitates. It would be the right opportunity to tell someone. She can hear Marion in her head saying, Go on. Get it off your chest. But no, it's not possible. She does not have the words.

By the time Spyridon has driven her in his taxi to Corfu Town and she has boarded the ferry she wishes she had managed to tell Cicely. She would have liked to be told what a sleazy man he was; that it wasn't her fault; that at least she wasn't pregnant. But suppose Cicely had thought as she herself did; suppose she had said, What did you do that for? Why didn't you keep the door locked? Why didn't you shout? Why didn't you kick him in the nuts? What would there have been for her to say? Anyway, she says to herself, she's still alive. No harm done. Best not to think about it.

After the first ferry, a night in a room. She lives mostly on bread although she has money. The days merge, the islands are seen in the distance, grow closer, resolve into a quayside, buildings, boats. She would get off – Could this be the place? She would stay a day, or two, or three, then embark on another ferry, further on, or – twice – even back to where she had already been.

People are kind to her, this tall, pale woman who seems to have no home, no family. At last, less pale now from exposure to the sun and wind in a dozen or more boats, little and big, she lands at Rethymnon. Apparently, this is Crete. Kriti. Maybe she has heard of it, maybe not, she really can't remember. She walks off the ferry, wanders through back streets, finds herself a room. Wonders where to go next.

*

It becomes a pattern that Willie and Senga know to expect. Their daughter will come home in the autumn, in time for a Christmas job at one of the big stores. She will spend Christmas Day with them, on her best behaviour – all of them on their best behaviour – she will help with the meal and with the dishes, and watch TV with them, politely, only glancing surreptitiously at the clock to see how much longer she will have to be there with them. She will avoid any arguments; she will not protest when they call her by her proper name; she will not set Willie straight when he makes remarks about hippies, or layabouts, or foreigners. She will admit to no opinions which might cause disharmony; she will tell them nothing that might cause them to worry, or protest, or even wonder.

Then, after the January sales, she will pack her rucksack – not Dougie's old one now but a newer, better one of her own – and set off back to Crete.

'See her, there,' says Willie 'She canna just wait to be off. You can see her counting the days.'

'At least she comes,' says Senga. Thinking, if Sally-Ann never came home at all, if she didn't go to see Dougie at all, then she, Senga, would never get news of them, never be able to buy the children presents, never be able to send a message. She would in fact, have to give up any hope at all of seeing them, and would Dougie, she wonders, even recognise her, given how big and fat she's grown. Even Sally-Ann was shocked, she could see it in her face.

'It's not good for you, Mum,' she said. 'You should go on a diet.'

'She eats no more than a sparrow,' said Willie, but Senga knows that she has never got used to cooking for only two. She still buys and cooks enough for a family of four, and if there are left-overs – which there are – they mustn't be wasted, they have to be eaten up. And if she bakes every week, which she does, as her mother always did, and her sisters probably still do, there is always cake, or scones, or biscuits, or all three, there to hand to help a cup of tea go down.

'You don't have to bake so much,' says Sally-Ann. 'One cake a week would be enough.'

But if the oven is on, Senga knows, it's a crime to waste the gas by not filling it.

'I'll ask Marion for you,' says Sally-Ann. 'She's always on a diet, she'll tell you what you should do.'

'I can ask her myself,' says Senga, with some dignity. 'I see Marion nearly every week, one way or another. I don't need you to go telling her my business.'

Marion lives close by, visits her own mother several times a week, always friendly, always ready to have a laugh; has two bonny weans, always clean and beautiful: grandchildren Doris is rightly proud of. Marion is a proper sort of daughter.

'If she's always on a diet,' Willie says, 'then it canna be working can it.'

Zita wonders why she keeps on doing this. Why come home (*home?*) for Christmas when there is no pleasure in it at all for her, and not much for her parents either. There is nothing for her here. She has not seen Terry since the night they all thought his Nannan had died; he has not, understandably she knows, tried to contact her. He will have told his parents about the letter so they are lost to her as well. Norman is married – he sent her an invitation to the wedding but she was abroad at the time; that's three weddings she's missed, or avoided; Marion's wedding remains the only one she has ever been to. But these days Marion is too busy to talk to her, too preoccupied with the children, with Brian, her house, with answering the phone to people calling about the re-wiring that Brian is to do for them. Zita can look forward to seeing Douglas and his family but it ends in disappointment; the children forget her year to year; she has nothing in common with any of them, Douglas least of all.

Her home is in Crete. She lives in Rethymnon, in what would be called a cottage in England; a tiny building rented from a family who have moved into a newly built house on the outskirts where they enjoy electricity and hot water. Zita is quite happy with candles and cold water. She works as a receptionist for the German dentist on the mornings he has patients, which is by no means every day. He has a sideline in guided walks and Zita often joins him and his party of holiday-makers in their rambles through the farms and the lower hills. She is learning about the history and the archaeology; she is becoming used to being the one at the back of the party, encouraging the slow walkers and the ones who have turned out wearing flip-flops; she practices her French with the French speakers and talks English to the English speakers while Uli manages the German and Italian ones. He is a moody character, Uli, up, down, cheery, morose; he came from Germany to see the place where his father died during the war, and never quite got round to going home again. 'My brain is German but my heart is Greek,' he said once to Zita. He seemed to think that explained everything.

And Zita often helps out at the hotel where Uli's Cretan wife is one of the managers. She can do a shift behind the bar, or help in the dining room or even the kitchen if they are short. She stands out as different – so much taller than the average local women, not remotely as chic as the French, more bohemian than the English and German; people are not quite sure what her status is, but she is pleasant, polite, self-contained. Who knows if she is happy.

This is the last time doing this Christmas thing, she promises herself, surveying her mother leaning back exhausted in her chair, out of breath after only getting up to close the curtains against the dark and rain of Boxing Day evening. Her father is looking through the Radio Times, hoping to find something to watch so he doesn't have to talk to his daughter. What's the point of coming here, she thinks. 'Of course I'll see you next Christmas,' Zita has promised, but now, bored and miserable in her parents' front room, she makes a vow – Christmas in Crete next year. And all the years after.

It is amazing how the years go by, here in Crete. Each spring, new hotels open; more visitors come. Shops open, cafes and restaurants; their owners build themselves new houses up in the hills. Sunbeds and umbrellas appear on the beach; boys and students find employment hiring them out, taking them down, locking them up for the night.

These new tourists have never been to Greece before; they are intimidated by the alphabet. 'It's not like Spain,' they tell Zita. 'They speak English there, and at least you can read their writing.' They are pleased to find Zita. She speaks English, she *is* English. She can tell them where the taxis are to be found; she can explain the items on a menu, she can reassure them about the non-existence of snakes and wolves when they go for a walk outside the town. She does not look like their tour rep – she does not have a uniform or painted nails or a clipboard – but she is a useful person to look out for. People come up to her in the street, once they've met her, to ask questions – the best café, the best leather shop, where is the best beach, how can they make a phone call?

Zita sometimes finds a newspaper in a guests' room, or left by the pool – one bought at an English airport and read on the plane. She takes it back to her house and skims through it, noticing dimly that stuff is going on in America with some president or other, that the Vietnam war appears to be over, or maybe not; that there seem to be soldiers in Ireland for some reason she cannot understand. She reads the front page, looks through at the photographs and puts the paper aside, feeling that England – Great Britain – is very dismal and very far away.

She is content. She owns little and she owes nothing. She speaks enough Greek to get by, and reads a little. She likes the climate; she gets on all right with Uli and Olga. She likes shutting herself into her tiny house – two rooms, one above the other. She likes watching the moon rise over the sea. She likes the hot and breathless days of summer when she is on her feet from early morning to late at night when the last hotel guests put out their lights. She likes the quiet of the winter when the tourists are gone; she writes occasional letters to her parents that tell them no more than they already know, and every autumn when the season ends she writes a letter to Marion in answer to the one Marion sent for her birthday back in August. She likes the spring best of all, when the streets are swept and the hotel cleaned and painted and aired and made ready for the next invasion of couples, families, retired folk – English, Italian, German. In spring flowers bloom beside roads and paths, the snow melts on the mountains and the rivers rush through the gorges. Zita works as hard as anyone; she has no complaints; this is her life.

At Christmas she receives a card from her parents, one from Douglas and Angel and one from Marion which includes a letter. Not so much a letter really, a note on the back of a shopping list. "Sorry about the paper," it says. "Total chaos here as you can imagine. But you remember that Ros woman – I met her. They got divorced – thought you might like to know? All the best for the New Year, Love Maz."

It really doesn't matter, thinks Zita. She still thinks fondly and sadly of Terry; but not very often. Mostly, she is content.

Chapter Twenty

Senga is worried. The miners are readying themselves to go on strike but it isn't that. There's an awful new disease called AIDs – who knew there could be new diseases? – and there are protesters on the news somewhere down south where the Americans have put some missiles or something, and the news is full of it. But it isn't that. She is finding it difficult to be content with her life. She worries about her health. Not that she is ill.

'Not ill,' she says to Betty on the phone. 'Just – not *well*. Do you not know what I mean? And there's not a thing to cheer you up, is there?'

'Aye, you're right enough there,' says Betty.

Willie watches the news. Every evening, every news programme, Panorama too, any programme that will show how bad the world is, how much worse it's getting, how little they are, these two people sitting in front of their TV watching hi-jackings and bombings, oil spillages and riots, guns and stones on the streets of Belfast, strikes and lockouts. Their TV is a colour one now, but that makes no difference to the news, only that you get a better idea of the blood.

'Is there no something nice to watch?' she says, but it seems that there isn't.

Sally-Ann – sometimes Senga even remembers that she is Zita now – is still away; hasn't been home for six years now. Senga has been counting. But she still sends a letter or a postcard occasionally– the weather, mostly, with maybe a mention of a walk in the hills, or some amusing incident. No mention of a friend, or a boyfriend; never a photograph of Sally-Ann herself, or even a view of where she is.

'You should go and see her,' says Doris Ward, on the occasions when they stop in the street to speak to one another. 'She could get you booked into that hotel she works at.'

'Oh, I couldn't,' says Senga. 'Willie would never go abroad again, he's said it many a time.'

'Go without him,' says Doris.

'Och,' says Senga, relapsing into Scottish, 'that I couldnae.'

Yes, she wants to see Sally-Ann, but she wants to see her *here*, at home, where she belongs. If she's not going to be a proper daughter and get married and have grandchildren for her, then the least she can do is be an unmarried daughter and come and live with her parents in their old age and when one of them dies, stay on and care for the other one.

That's what you have daughters for.

'Not that you ever stayed and looked out for your ma,' says Willie.

'I'd sisters though. She didnae need me.'

'We're not, right enough,' he says, 'a family that sticks together, are we now.'

Senga thinks he says it with some satisfaction in his voice; she would like to point out that it was not herself that drove Douglas away, and it was not herself that stopped speaking to Sally-Ann so that she must have felt unwanted and unloved. But she does not say these things, only heaves herself out of her chair and into the kitchen, holding on to door knobs and chair backs as she goes, in case she finds herself having – again – one of those dizzy turns.

She puts the kettle on to make a pot of tea – it is the middle of a Sunday afternoon – and sits on a kitchen chair while the water boils, chewing an indigestion tablet.

'No cake,' says Willie when she takes the tray through.

'I'm trying to cut down,' she says, lying back in her chair.

'I'll get it,' says Willie. This may be he first time he has ever offered to help. 'I'll bring you some, will I?'

'Och,' she says. 'Go on then.'

*

In Rethymnon it is a mild day in late October. The last of the hotel guests depart for the airport and Zita and Olga spend the morning going through the bed linen, checking for stains and tears and counting what they have and how much needs to be replaced. By early afternoon they feel like stopping, and do so.

'I go to see what Uli does,' says Olga.

'I'm going for a walk round the harbour,' says Zita.

The harbour is quiet. The bigger cafes are closing, stacking and tying up their chairs and tables, wrapping their lamps in sacking, and laying off their seasonal staff. The smaller cafes in the back streets will stay open for the benefit of local people who, after all, will still need a cup of coffee morning noon and night.

Zita walks round the harbour, not jostled by tourists, not accosted by people asking her urgent questions about buses and taxis, not disturbed by people's children complaining that they want to go to the beach, or they want a coca-cola, or their hair braided, or crying that they want to be picked up and carried, or put down. Today she is the only person walking along the harbour wall. Although there is someone else, not walking but sitting. As she gets closer she can see it is a young woman, sitting, drawing something, a piece of paper resting on a book on her knee. Not unusual – there are often people sketching here.

The young woman does not look up at Zita, but concentrates on the moored boats she is drawing. But Zita feels – somehow – that she is English, even that she might know her. She works out later that it is her niece Nicole that she is reminded of – same tea-brown skin and wavy black hair. So they do not speak, or even acknowledge each other until a few days later – three, to be exact – when Zita, on her way to the market, sees her in the street, walking towards her and wearing the very same Indian print skirt that Zita is wearing. This time they look at each other, smile, make some small gesture which they both know means that they acknowledge they are wearing matching clothes, and pass on in their opposite directions. And later, when they find themselves looking in the same shop window – a shop now closed, that when open sells knives to tourists – Zita speaks.

'Hello.'

'Hello,' she says. Sounds English, but then, anyone can say Hello.

'I saw you doing a picture. Down at the harbour.'

'Oh. Yes. I was.'

Definitely English.

'Been here long?' Knowing that she couldn't have been.

'About a week now. What about you?'

'I've been here years,' says Zita. 'I live here.'

'But you're English?'

'Oh yes.'

Then they make eye-contact, and smile, and turn away from the window with its display of vicious-looking weapons and walk in the same direction, together, each wondering what to say next.

'My name's Zita.'

'Heather.'

'Are you here on your own?'

'Yes.'

'On holiday?'

'Sort of. I was in Athens. I had a job looking after some children. But they've gone back to England and I thought I'd stay here and see a bit more of Greece.'

They have reached Zita's cottage.

'This is where I live.'

'It looks nice. I've got a room in the town.'

Zita knows she should invite her in, offer her tea. She opens her mouth to say the words but it doesn't happen; she remembers how untidy her downstairs room is, how she hasn't washed up a pot or plate for a day or two, how a pile of clothes for washing has been dumped on one of her two chairs. Even Uli and Olga have never been invited into her house. She is embarrassed.

'And that's where I work,' she waves a hand at the hotel whose balconies can be seen along the street.

'What do you do?'

'Anything,' she admits. 'Bit of cleaning, bit of reception, bit of bar work. Generally help out, you know.'

'I suppose they don't need any more staff?'

'No guests now. There's not much for any of us to do except get ready for next spring. So no jobs.'

'It's all right,' says Heather. 'I've got some savings. I might be able to sell a picture. Maybe.'

'Are you an artist?'

'It's what I do mostly. Then I'll take a job to keep me going if I run out of money. Actually my parents send me some too. I'm all right really.'

'I'll see you around,' says Zita.

'OK then,' she says and remains standing for some minutes after Zita has gone inside.

*

It is Doris Ward who, after weeks of discussion with Marion and wondering what is the right thing to do, finally puts in a long distance call to the hotel in Rethymnon. It is not easy, explaining to a Greek man – some sort of caretaker it seems – that she is calling from England, that she needs to speak to Zita, that it is important. Olga is brought to the phone and after some misunderstandings, promises to find Zita and ask her to call Doris back. Which she does.

'Where's the number?' says Zita, arriving at the desk. But Olga has assumed she would know it and has only written down the name. Even that is confusing – she's got 'Doris' all right but has written 'Wood', not 'Ward.'

Zita has to go back to her cottage for her own notebook and call Marion to find out Doris's number.

'Why don't I just call *my* mum?' she says.

'There's things you need to know,' says Marion. '*Your* mum will try to hide how bad it is.'

Doris, though, does not try to hide how bad it is.

'She sleeps all night in a chair,' she says, 'because she can't get up the stairs.'

'What about –?'

'Chamber pot,' says Doris. 'In this day and age. She won't have the doctor round. Even your dad has tried to get her to have the doctor and she says she wouldn't let him in if he came.'

'What's wrong with her?'

'How should I know?' says Doris. 'Am I a doctor?'

'Have you talked to her?' says Zita. She knows she should tell Doris not to worry, she will be on the next plane home; she will have to spend the rest of her life nursing her mother and keeping house for her father.

'She won't let anyone in,' says Doris. 'Back door's locked all the time.'

'What about my dad?'

'He's doing his best,' says Doris, 'which I thought I'd never say about him. But he's at work all day, and he doesn't know the first thing about cooking and cleaning. They're living on fish and chips – I see him come home from work and go straight down the chippie. That's no good for your mum, now is it?'

Zita sees an escape route. 'Do you think maybe Douglas –?'

'That's another thing. We thought of that, me and Marion.'

'His wife's a nurse,' says Zita as if the solution had been found. She felt herself smiling at the phone.

'Just wait while I tell you. Our Marion tried to phone Douglas the other day, when we were worried about your mum, and she spoke to his wife.'

'What did she say?'

'Here's the thing. I thought you might know already. Your Douglas and his wife have split up.'

'No,' says Zita. She says it softly but inside her head it is a wail of defeat.

'Yes. There's a lot of it around, Sal, you wouldn't believe it. I don't know what's got into folk. And she didn't say where your Douglas is – couldn't or wouldn't, I don't know which – though what help he would be in any case I don't know. But there you are, it's always the women who have to pick up the pieces.'

'Yes,' says Zita.

'So shall I pop across when I see your dad come home and let him know you'll be on your way home?'

Zita looks out of the glass doors at a slow winter drizzle. She is not needed here in Rethymnon; that is, there are jobs she would be doing but there are no guests to make them urgent. She will not be missed until the spring. Long before then, surely, she will have called the doctor to her mother, got her some medicine, tidied up the house, tracked down Dougie to keep an eye on things. She can be back here – home in Rethymnon – soon after Christmas if not before.

'All right,' she says to Doris. 'I'll have to find a flight. There's not many in the winter. But you can tell her I'm coming home.'

'I'll do that,' says Doris. 'I can knock on the front window and shout to her. She'll be thankful I know.'

'Yes,' says Zita, sadly. 'And thank you for all your trouble. Give my love to Marion.'

'You've never even seen her baby have you? And you haven't seen the other two since they were tiny. Just wait till you –'

'I have to go,' says Zita. 'I need to pack.' And she puts the phone down and stares with dull eyes at the quiet street outside, before going to Olga and telling her the news.

Chapter Twenty-one

Zita arrived home last night, phoned her parents from the airport to tell them to leave the back door unbolted, she would be arriving late, walked up from the bus station in a fine drizzle, much like the one she had left in Rethymnon, found the house silent, her father in bed already, as she expected.

There was a light on in the front room, a thin strip at the bottom of the door, and she pushed it open as quietly as she could. Her mother lay on the settee, under blankets. Briefly, Zita held on to the idea that she was dead – pushed the idea away – and was then disappointed to hear her breathing. The room smelled – a dirty body smell, and urine, and a mustiness which would surely distress her mother greatly if she had not become accustomed to it. Zita left the light on and pulled the door closed. She crept upstairs and lay on her bed – blankets, but no sheets. She felt she should go for a pee, and clean her teeth, but instead she fell asleep.

She helps her mother with the chamber pot and carries it upstairs to empty it afterwards. She has got her mother out of her clothes – smelly damp clothes – and washed her face and hands and under her arms where the rolls of fat wobble and hang, and found clean clothes and managed to get her into them. And then felt able to call the doctor who has visited and left a prescription as long as your arm, and instructions – no sugar, no biscuits – and has gone away with a promise to refer her to the hospital.

'How will we get there?' says Senga when he has gone. 'I canna be going on a bus.'

'They'll send an ambulance,' says Zita. 'Or if not, we'll get a taxi.'

Senga groans with distress. She has never paid for a taxi in her life.

'I'm going upstairs,' says Zita. 'I'm going to change the sheets and put the washing machine on.'

'It'll no get dry,' says Senga. 'Not with this rain.'

'It's not raining.'

'It is so.'

'Mum, it's a decent enough day for drying. If you'd have the curtains open you'd know.'

'Leave them shut,' says Senga. 'I don't want folks looking in at me.'

'Then I'll bring you a cup of tea. Then I'll go and get your medicine.'

She strips her father's bed – trying not to wonder how long these sheets have been on it – and opens the window to air the room. She loads the twin tub and then looks in the cupboards to make a shopping list. How long has this state of affairs been going on? For there is very little on the shelves, except ingredients like flour, gravy powder, suet; lard and margarine in the fridge but anything that does not need preparation – *cooking* – has been eaten already. Zita does not reckon herself to be much of a cook and her father will no doubt criticise her attempts but she knows it will be her job to do it.

She takes her mother a cup of tea and helps her to sit up and drink it. Is she really so ill – so *disabled* – that she can't get herself into a sitting position? Could this all be some desperate, elaborate scheme to improve her life, to get Willie to help more, to get Douglas to come back? To get her, Zita, to come home?

'Zita?'

She is on her way out of the chemist's with her mother's prescription, holding the door open for a woman coming in with a boy.

'Peggy,' she says, joyfully, and then remembers that she has something to be ashamed of and the joy goes out of her.

But Peggy seems to remain pleased to see her. 'You're back home. Since when? Terry never told us you were back. This is Adam, Terry's boy – got a bad cough, that's why he's not at school. That's why I've got him, Ros being at work.'

'It's nice to see you,' says Zita. 'I wish –'

'So do I love, so do I.'

Another customer needs to get out of the door; Peggy needs to take her place in the queue. 'Why don't we go to the café?' she says but Zita holds up her big paper bag of medications. 'It's my mum's medicine. I need to get back home with it.'

'I tell you what then.' Peggy is calling across the shop now. 'Come and see us on Sunday, just me and Lawrence. The boys have all gone. Come and have a cup of tea with us.'

'If I can get away I will.'

Four days, she thinks, walking back home through the wet streets, four days to wonder if she should go. Would Terry be there? She should have asked. But she'd said the words 'just me and Lawrence.' Terry would therefore not be there, but suppose – Peggy had been friendly enough – but suppose she knew about the letter. Even though it was years ago – nine to be exact – she might still be angry with her. But the idea of an afternoon with someone who could tell her about Terry keeps tugging at her. It would be a rest from her mum, huge and breathless on the settee, and the worry and the business of the house, and the nagging from her father when she failed to do things properly. The pleas from her mum to find Douglas and make him visit her before she died.

'You're not going to die Mum,' says Zita. 'Not with all this medicine.'

She closes the door to the front room firmly, so that – she hopes – her mother will not hear her on the phone. She dials the number which was once was Dougie's and is now only Angel's. A teenager answers and Zita has to do a swift calculation – yes, Nicole must be fifteen by now. 'Mum.' She hears her shout. 'It's for you.'

'Who is it?' comes from further away.

'Some woman.'

'I'm sorry to bother you,' says Zita. 'It's me, Dougie's sister. I need to get in touch with him.'

'What for?' Angel is not her normal polite self.

'It's my mother. Dougie's mother. She's ill. I thought he should be told.'

'He won't thank you for it,' says Angel.

'She might die,' says Zita, adding in her head, I wish she would, and then, quickly, No, no, I didn't mean it. 'I wouldn't want him not to know.''

'What's wrong with her?' Angel is, after all, a nurse.

'It's her heart, doctor says. She can hardly sit up. She's really poorly.'

'Is she in hospital?'

'She's got an appointment. An urgent appointment.' Zita is laying it on thick but Angel is not fooled. 'She can't be that bad if she's not in hospital. What medication is she on?'

'Um. Heart stuff. And she's on a diet.' Zita feels she might have lost this conversation. 'I just - I just would hate it if something happened and Dougie hadn't seen her before –'

'I'll let you have his phone number,' says Angel. 'That's all I know about where he is.'

The teenage voice – must have been listening to all this – says '*I* know where he lives.'

'Then keep it to yourself,' says her mother. But she tells Zita the number.

'What have you been doing all day?' says Willie, when his tea is not on the table at six o'clock, and she does not dare to stand up to him because it will agitate her mother – she will call out from the front room, 'Don't. Don't argue with him. Stop it.' And sink back into her cushions and close her eyes as if demonstrating how she will look when the two of them have succeeded in killing her.

Willie goes through and pats her on the shoulder. 'It's all right, lass. We'll be fine. She can bring it in here on a tray.'

And he will go and wash and change out of his work clothes and come back down and put the news on the TV, and complain loudly about the state of the country and predict the end of civilisation.

'That's enough,' says Zita. 'Look, you're upsetting her.'

'She'll be a lot more upset when she canna get a hospital bed. Just you wait my girl –' the way he says it sounds like 'growl' –'this is only the beginning. Look at Belfast – you've seen nothing yet.'

And Senga lies back exhausted by it all, and fails to eat most of her tea, which means she'll be hungry later and there'll be a need for cheese and biscuits, and maybe sweet cocoa to follow.

On Friday Willie gets off work a little earlier and is home soon after five.

'I'll do your tea,' says Zita, 'and I'll wash the pots – then I'm going out.'

'What about your mother?'

'What about her?' Pretending not to understand his meaning.

'And where are you off anyway?'

'I'm thirty-two years old,' says Zita. 'I don't have to tell you where I'm going.'

'Thirty-two,' he says. 'When are you going to start behaving thirty-two? When are you going to grow up?'

'Leave the back door unlocked for me,' she says.

'Oh aye. You want us burgled in our beds.' And he grumbles off upstairs to wash and change.

'I can't stand it,' says Zita to Marion later that evening. The children are in bed – Zita has been given a glimpse of them tucked in, the two boys asleep, Faye, nine years old now, sitting up in bed reading a book. Brian has agreed to go to the club for a drink. Marion and Zita sit opposite each other, the tea tray and the biscuit tin between them, and wonder where to start.

'How's your mum then?'

'I don't know,' says Zita. She feels like crying but it wouldn't do, Marion would only be embarrassed, and she would tell Doris, and they would think she wasn't up to the job. 'Honestly, sometimes I think she's just being lazy. Nothing hurts, she says, but the doctor says she has to go for tests. He listened to her heart for ages but he didn't say what he was listening for. She's got to have blood tests, and he said she needs to eat properly – vegetables. No fat, no sugar.' Marion must already know this of course, since Zita has met Doris in the street and Doris will have passed on the news.

'She'll be better with you looking after her,' says Marion. 'Men don't really know what to do. If I leave Brian with the kids, even for half an hour, I come back to chaos. Honestly – he tried to put Ryan into Mark's coat the other day, he gets their toys mixed up – there's ructions if he lets the baby touch Ryan's stuff, then there's a shouting match and he doesn't know what to do. The dishes are still in the sink, I say. What's he been doing? he says. How can he do anything with three kids underfoot?., I say: What does he think I do all day?'

'At least,' says Zita, 'my mother stays in one place. But she's forever calling out to me, bring her this, bring her that, turn the telly on, turn it off, she's thirsty, she needs a wee, she fancies a cup of tea, did I get any biscuits, do I know how to make a cake. I tell her she's not allowed and she looks like she's going to cry. And we have to have our tea in the front room with her, and she looks at Daddy's plate and she says, He's got more than me, and I tell her he's been at work all day heaving iron bars around and she's just been lying there, and then she cries and says nobody understands and he tells her to turn it off – the waterworks – and she mutters under her breath like a loony woman.'

'But she's your mum,' says Marion. 'You have to do it. Anyway, *I'm* glad you've come back. It's like old times. And now we've had our little moan, I'll tell you about that Ros.'

She met Ros, she says, 'at this Saturday morning thing that Ryan goes to. At the church hall – they just play games and run around shouting, you know what boys are like, but Ryan loves it. Anyway, I saw this woman and I thought, now where do I know you from? You know I only ever saw her the one time but I never forget a face and I'm thinking about the salon, you know, did I cut her hair, trying to see her, was it at Cutz? was it when I worked for Amanda? and I could only picture her in this big room, and I'm seeing a big white hat, and then it comes to me – Pontin's, she's that one that Terry went and married, when he'd have been better off with you. So I said to her, I just said, I haven't seen you here before, is that your little boy there, and she says yes, and I ask his name, you know how it is, and she says he's called Adam, and I say, Aren't you Ros, I met you once at Pontin's, and she says, What? and I say Pontin's holiday camp. At Great Yarmouth. We talked about our weddings, remember. You're married to Terry. And she says, not any more I'm not. And I say, Oh dear –'

'I met his mother the other day,' says Zita. 'She'd got the little boy with her. She's asked me round her house on Sunday, just for a cup of tea.'

'She never told you about him splitting up with her?'

'We didn't have time. I was going out the shop and she was going in. Anyway she wouldn't have said anything in front of the boy would she.'

'So will you go?'

'I'm thinking about it.'

'Don't think,' says Marion. 'Just go.'

'So do you still see her?'

'Ros? She lives near here, not sure exactly where. I see her sometimes, in a shop, say, but she looks straight through me and she hasn't been back to Saturday club.'

'So, did she tell you what happened? I mean what happened to split them up.'

'Well, no. I'd got baby Mark with me, didn't I – this is a year ago – I was feeding him all the time, you never saw such a baby for being hungry, and so we talked about babies, and that, and she told me she was training to be a yoga teacher, and I said I didn't know really what yoga is and she said it's good for getting your figure back after you've had a baby and I said I was a lost cause in that department, and I was just going to ask her where Terry is now when her boy got knocked over or something – they work themselves up these boys till they're wild. Anyway he was hurt and she went and picked him up and she never came back over my bit of the room, and as far as I know she's never been back, and as I say, I see her around but she never so much as nods in my direction. Proper stuck up, like I told you. Shall I make another pot of tea? And help yourself to biscuits, make yourself at home.'

Better than home, thinks Zita, gazing round the room – the clean white walls, the dark red curtains, the wedding photograph on the wall, photos of the children on the sideboard, their toys packed away into baskets half-hidden behind the chairs. She has no doubt that the rest of the house is equally organised – Marion was always methodical, she always liked her things to be tidy. She still cuts people's hair, in their homes, while Doris looks after the baby, and she still visits two sets of grandparents and takes their shopping to them, and makes time for Brian's mum. And she has learned to drive and often takes Brian to work and picks him up at the end of the day so that she can have the car and get done all that she needs to get done. And she listens to Faye's reading, and Ryan's, and cooks meals that they will consent to eat, and gets them to bed on time, and up in the morning on time, and I, thinks Zita, can't even manage one woman. I can't even *like* that one woman. She's dirty and she smells and from now on that's going to be my fault. And she won't get better and that's going to be my fault, and I will be here forever, waiting for her to die and, when she does, *that* will be my fault, and he – *he* – will want me to stay and look after him and I can't do it. I can't do it.

Marion returns with fresh tea. 'I should have asked you, would you rather have wine – I could nip down the offy.'

'No,' says Zita. 'I mean it, Maz, not at all. I'm not a big wine drinker and really, it's so nice to have a proper cup of tea. Over there, they just haven't got a clue. Their coffee is so strong it'll take the hair off your head and the tea is so weak you might as well drink hot water.'

'But you've stayed there all these years,' says Marion. 'There must be something good about it. Have you got a fella over there?'

'Nothing like that,' says Zita. For a microsecond she considers telling Marion about Monsieur Felix; then the impulse disappears. Too long ago.

There's a pause while they eat a biscuit apiece. 'I like your room,' says Zita. 'You've got your house very nice.'

'You should see it at the end of the day,' says Marion. 'It's not always like this, believe me.' She lets herself scan the room, pleased with it, and then comes back to Zita. 'Have you seen your Dougie yet? Or heard from him?'

'Not a word. I've tried phoning him but he's never there. That's what they say anyway.'

'What did she say – Angel – when you spoke to her?'

'Not much. She don't know me after all, does she, not very well. Just that he wasn't living there any more. I told her about Mum and she said she'd tell him when she saw him –'

'When she saw him, or if?'

'*When* – I think. He'll surely go and see his kids won't he? I don't know.'

It seems to her that she doesn't know her brother at all, nor what he would do under any circumstances. Terry now – that other separated father – she is quite sure that he will see his son on regular days. As long as *she* lets him of course. She knows now that she will, definitely, go to see Peggy on Sunday.

It is Lawrence who answers the door. 'She said you'd be coming,' he says. 'She's just in the kitchen clearing up. Come in out of the cold.'

He looks the same as he ever did, a little more jowly maybe, a little more bald; still smiling as he always did. Like Terry always did.

Peggy comes out, drying her hands. 'You've had your dinner?'

'I cooked it,' says Zita. 'First time ever I've done a roast dinner. Pork.'

'Oh,' says Lawrence, 'my favourite. Crackling – Peggy's crackling is the best in Yorkshire. And her Yorkshire puddings too.'

'I didn't do Yorkshire pudding,' admits Zita. 'Maybe next week.' Which, she realises as she says it, is a recognition that she will still be here next week, still cooking, still seeing the dissatisfaction – more from her mother than her father – at the quality of her efforts. By next week it will be December; her mother will be fretting about Christmas cake.

The front room has changed since she saw it the first time. Darren is not sitting on the floor lining his soldiers into their ranks ready for the battle; Barry is not sprawled on the settee reading the football reports in the Sunday paper. Young Lol will not be coming in caked with mud and being told to take his boots off on the doorstep. The mantelpiece and the windowsill are crowded now with photographs of the children of Lol and Terry, and one of Darren on holiday with a girlfriend, somewhere hot, with the sea in the background, and another one of the graduation of Barry.

Yes, they were all doing well. 'And you know what,' says Lawrence, 'I'm of the opinion – I really am and I've said it before haven't I, Peg – that if our Terry hadn't taken off for abroad he would never have come back and gone to college. And if he hadn't gone to college it wouldn't have opened their eyes – the other three I mean – and they wouldn't have done so well. They'd be in ordinary jobs, just marking time you know. But no – they're all going somewhere, even our Lol, he's proper qualified, he's a cabinet-maker, done all the exams –'

'These are his two,' says Peggy. Two small girls smile out from a silver frame. 'And this is Terry's boy, that you saw the other day.'

'Is his cough better?' says Zita politely.

'He'll be fine,' says Peggy. 'Ros is a bit over-protective of him really. He didn't need a day off school. But when you've only got the one – well, it's like all your eggs are in the one basket, if you see what I mean.'

'I suppose so,' says Zita. She cannot think of anything to say. Gone, she thinks. Lost. She lost Terry years ago; it was her own fault. His parents now, smiling at her kindly, she's lost them as well, there is no connection, no common ground, just politeness.

'Is Terry OK?' she says at last.

'He's doing really well.' Peggy sounds relieved – because Zita has asked, or because she really doesn't have to worry about Terry? 'He lives up your way now, near to Adam you see, so he can have him sleeping over.'

'He's had a girlfriend,' says Lawrence, 'but that seems to be over now. He never said much about her, did he Peg? His work, and Adam, that's all he has time for really.'

'What does he do? For a job I mean.'

'He's a teacher. We thought you knew that.'

'I don't know anything,' admits Zita, sadly.

'Who would ever think our Terry could be a teacher? Remedial they call it. Of course he knows all about being a rascal. He knows all their tricks, you can bet.'

'Does he like doing it?' says Zita.

'Loves it,' says Peggy. 'He's proper settled down now. There'll be no more globe-trotting from that one. Our Barry now: he's starting to get ideas about seeing the world. But we'll see. 'We thought,' says Lawrence, exchanging a glance with Peggy, 'that you might have seen him. I mean, he might have got in touch with you. Since you got back.'

Zita shakes her head. There is nothing she can say.

'We don't see much of him ourselves,' says Lawrence. 'Not enough anyway.'

Chapter Twenty-two

Walking back to her parents, making the walk last as long as she can through the December dusk, Zita finds the words – in touch, in touch – going round her head as her feet hit the ground. Left right, left right, in touch, in touch. She is not much of a one for touch, she knows that. She has shared a room with Terry, shared doorsteps and park benches with him on occasion; he has taken her hand to pull her into the back of a van, he has lifted her rucksack on to her shoulders and moved her hair, when it was long, out of the way of the straps. Sometimes, when they had to sleep in a doorway or a park, they would move closer together for warmth; she could have unpacked her winter coat from the bottom of her rucksack, but she never did. He has stood guard for her outside French toilets when there was no lock on the door. She has washed his socks and underpants in Youth Hostels; she has watched him sleeping, heard him sleeping, across from her in the room above the café. They were in touch then, even if there was no actual touching; they were close, laughing together, telling their stories, making plans. Mates.

And he hugged her. When he came back to England and turned up at Pontin's, in his mum's kitchen when he kissed her cheeks like the French do, and Ros came into the room. And before that, when he said goodbye to her on the road outside Nice and set off in the opposite direction. When, as she thinks of it now, he left her on her own to be picked up by the old monsieur, without which might she have been a different person during the last –how many? nine? – years. She imagines, briefly, a conversation with Terry where she would tell him everything; her old feelings for him, her regret about the letter, the business with Monsieur Felix. It was my own silly fault, she thinks of herself saying, I should have locked my door; I just thought that Vittoria was trying to scare me. What would Terry say? I can't believe you could be that stupid, that's what he would say. You asked for it. And, he would think to himself, You wanted it.

Her father, when Zita arrives home, is reading the News of the World; her mother is crying.

'What's the matter?'

Her father does not even look up, never mind answer.

'What's up Mum?'

'Nothing,' she says. She wipes the back of her hand across her nose, like a snotty child.

'Shall I make a pot of tea?' I'm like Marion, she thinks, placating a baby with a biscuit. 'There you go,' she says, pushing a chair up beside the settee. There's your tea beside you. You can reach it if you sit up a bit.'

She puts her father's cup on the mantelpiece, without speaking to him; he does not look at her, or speak, and she is on her way back to the kitchen when her mother calls after her.

'I don't smell do I? He says I smell. He says I stink.'

'You do,' he says. 'It's time you got yourself into the bath.' He calls out to Zita. 'Don't you go slinking off now. This is your job, keeping her clean. When are you going to get on with it, instead of going off visiting.'

Zita stands in the doorway, her back turned against both her parents. 'She can't get upstairs, can she.'

'See,' says Senga. 'I can't get upstairs can I?'

'With only a bit of help you could,' he says. 'A wee bit push from behind.'

'I'm going out,' says Zita.

'You only just came in,' he shouts at her back. 'This is your job –'

Zita stands in the shelter of the passage. After some minutes she goes out into the street. She walks to the end of the road. She turns and heads up the hill. It is properly dark now, rooms are lighted, light escaping through gaps in the curtains, the sounds of television laughter seeps through. The end of a weekend, people cooking tea, or making a sandwich from the end of a nice piece of beef; people watching a game show, or a variety show; children being asked if they've finished their homework, children pretending yes, it's all done; mothers ironing the school clothes for tomorrow; people already thinking of the next day's work: must set the alarm, get the lunch boxes ready, check the kids have got the right PE kit; doesn't the weekend just fly by. Other people.

Zita feels bereft. She longs to have a job to go to. Anything would do, anything except the job that *he* has just bestowed on her, that of unpaid carer, untrained, incompetent, unwilling, unsupported. *This is your job. She's your mother.*

At the top of the hill she stops, turns, looks across Sheffield. Makes a decision that is no decision at all. Turns for home.

They are in the same places, the same positions as when she left, but now he is excited, triumphant.

'All right now,' he calls as she comes in. 'I've worked it out. I know how we can do it. Sit down, lass, listen to this.'

This is his idea – Senga lies with her eyes shut, pretending not to hear – his plan is to move her upstairs, she'll be able to have a bath, there won't be all that malarkey with the chamber pot. Zita shrugs. It's not ideal; it will mean her running up and down stairs all day, but she can see that to be properly in her own bed might be preferable for her mother.

'But what about the telly?' she says. 'She'll need something to watch all day. All evening.'

'We'll get one o' they wee ones,' he says. 'It'll go on the dressing table.'

'Dressing table?' There is not, as she well knows, a dressing table in her parents' room.

'Not a problem,' he says. 'Stacks of room in there, once you've moved your clobber up to the attic.'

She takes a breath, ready to argue, ready to shout, ready to tell him what she thinks of his plan. She does not argue or shout, she folds her mouth tight, inwards; she goes out of the room. She goes upstairs.

Senga opens her eyes. 'Now see what you did,' she says, very quietly.

'I've done nothing. You wait and see, you'll feel better up there, with facilities. You'll be a new woman.'

'So then,' she says, still feeble, still soft. 'Why don't I go to my own bed, and you go up to the attic?'

He is shaking his head before she finishes the sentence. 'I'm a working man,' he says. 'It's only me around here that brings in any money. I need my sleep don't I. She'll be fine up there. It's not as if *she's* paying us anything for her board, now, is it. *She's* not earning owt.'

Zita, in her room that is no longer her room, sits on her bed. She picks up her pillow and lays it across her knees so that she can bash it with her fists. She would like to lose her temper. She would like to go downstairs and make a scene. She would like to walk out, with her rucksack, hitch a lift, get away. But there are obstacles. She has hardly any money; what she had was spent on her air fare home, and there is no hope of earning any when she has to be with her mother all day. Her mother has a hospital appointment on Tuesday – she has to go with her, because *he* won't. She briefly imagines her mother coming out of the hospital with a bottle of tablets that will cure her; she'll be back to her old self; she'll be able to manage on her own. The idea dissolves; Zita is not the sort of person to believe in a fairytale ending. She bashes the pillow a few more times, stands up, pulls open drawers, gathering the contents – underwear, knitwear, nightdresses – into her arms and makes her first journey up the attic stairs. Dumps everything on Dougie's old bed. There is no other furniture in his old attic bedroom, bare floorboards, a skylight with no curtain or blind to cover it. The wallpaper is what was there when Dougie was a small boy; by the bed it is scratched and peeling where a small boy has found something for his idle fingers to do.

She goes back to her bedroom for another load. Her books, her school memorabilia, her box of letters, the box of the postcards she sent to her parents. She pulls her dressing gown off its hook on the door, sweeps her few cosmetics into her handbag, pulls her rucksack from under the bed. The third time she comes out of her room, this time trailing her bedding, she sees her father at the bottom of the stairs, looking up at her.

'Will I help you?' he says. She does not answer. 'Suit yourself,' he says.

But he does not move Senga into Zita's room. The days go slowly by; Senga stays on the settee, Zita sleeps in Dougie's room, sulkily.

She walks to the shops. She stops outside the branch library, which is closed because the tanker drivers are on strike and there is no oil for the heating. It does not look like somewhere familiar – where she used to go and work every day. It does not look like somewhere she could go and work ever again. But that is what her life has for her to look forward to. Working somewhere nearby, where people will know who she is, where they will ask after her mother, who will be lying on that settee for ever. She, Zita, will be Sally-Ann again; she will have to nip home in her lunch hour to make sure her mother is all right; she will have to help her upstairs to the toilet, and back down again. Her suntan will fade, her serviceable Greek will atrophy, her smatterings of French and German will melt away. She is thirty two and until her mother is dead she will never go back to where she wants to be.

Douglas, she thinks. She has not told her mother what she has heard – that he has separated from Angel, nor that she has been told that he lives quite close by, in a room in someone else's house. There is no reason why, while their father is out at work, he should not visit her mother. His mother. His sick mother. Why did she not think about it before?

She has to telephone Angel again to find exactly where Dougie is living.

'Who?' says Angel.

'Dougie's sister.'

There is a chilly pause. 'What do you want now?'

'I'm sorry,' says Zita, thinking, Why am I sorry? I'm not sorry. About anything. 'I need to get in touch with Dougie. My mother's very ill. She's going into hospital tomorrow.'

'Oh,' says Angel.

'You gave me his phone number, but could you give me his address.'

Another pause and then, 'All right.'

'And if you see him, could you tell him. About our mother I mean.'

'That won't happen,' says Angel.

Though the tanker drivers are on strike, following the bin men, the trains are still running and Douglas is still at his station – The Midland Station, directing travellers to their platforms, moving trolleys of mail, waving the flag to tell the trains to begin their journeys and hoping one day to be an assistant station master.

She stands in the porch of his house and writes a note – *Our mother is not well. She has an appointment at the hospital. Maybe you could call round one day while Daddy is at work?* He does not answer and he does not call round.

On Tuesday an ambulance arrives. Two men, one jovial, one not, load Senga into the back, and Zita gets in and sits beside her. Across on the other side an elderly couple are sitting in anxious silence.

'All aboard,' says the jovial one.

'Oh. Oh,' says Senga.

'What's up Mum?'

'This sitting up,' she says, gasping. 'I feel like I'm falling off.'

'I'll hold on to you. You'll be right.'

She puts her arm through her mother's and with her other hand pats her wrist; it is the best she can do in the way of comfort and support. She has also done her imperfect best in the matter of washing her mother and dressing her in the most respectable garment that will still fit her.

It is not far to the hospital; in normal health Senga could have walked there. Now she is unloaded into a wheelchair and Zita walks alongside. Senga confirms her name and date of birth. They wait, in silence because it seems somehow rude to speak out loud.

At the end of the appointment Zita leaves on her own. Senga has been weighed and examined. She has had blood taken from her arm; her blood pressure has been measured on three occasions. She has been asked to stand, to sit, to blow into a tube for as long as she can. She has been asked questions. Zita has been relieved to find that her own opinions are not needed.

She stands again on the outside; it reminds her of coming out of a cinema into daylight, with that other world still in her head and the bright cold afternoon buzzing around her. Senga is not coming home. She is 'unstable.' Zita has to go home and bring back the things her mother will need.

'She'll be on the ward,' they said. 'Visiting between three and four, but if you can't manage that you can leave her belongings with Sister.'

As Zita turns into her road Doris Ward, who must have been watching out for her, emerges from her front door.

'I'm glad I caught you,' she says, a little out of breath. 'There's been people knocking at your door.'

'Who?'

'Two men, in a car, working clothes. Knocked on the door, went round the back. I went out and asked what did they want – they said – funny thing, this – they said they couldn't tell me, confidential, they said, but they'd come back later.'

'Oh,' says Zita.

'So how is she? How's your mother?'

'She's got to stay there for a day or two. She's got to have tests. I've got to get her some things together and go back.'

'Well,' says Doris, 'tell her I was asking after her. And if these fellas come back, what shall I tell them?'

'I don't know. Or – tell them my dad will be home about half past five. It'll be someone for him. It won't be anything to do with me.'

In the house she has a foreboding feeling. She tries to remember, has she ever – *ever* – been in the house without her mother being there, or at least no further away than the shops at the end of the road? It feels as if it's the first time in her life. Her smell is still there though, and Zita leaves the back door open wide, hoping that some of the smell will waft into the cold outside air and some of the cold outside air will fill the space.

She looks for a bag. Senga's handbag, almost never used, will be too small; her shopping bag, hanging on a hook inside the back door, is somehow too utilitarian for the occasion, besides being battered and scruffy. She goes up to the attic and searches among her own belongings and chooses – out of not many possibilities – one of those Greek fabric shoulder bags that every woman under twenty-five had at the back end of the sixties. She runs her fingers along the plaited handle and remembers that she bought it in Spain, in a market in Barcelona, bought it because it came from Greece. But never used it. She remembered showing it to Cecily who shrugged as if it was of no interest and said that they were cheaper in Corfu Town. It will do the job; it is the best she can do and it won't matter if it gets lost.

She assembles what she thinks is appropriate: nightdress, slippers, glasses. Toothbrush and denture fixative. Some magazines – probably been read already, but her mother won't mind that. Her purse, with some money in it – will she need money? Zita doesn't know. What else? She's run out of ideas. Should she go and ask Doris Ward? But decides not to, doesn't want Doris to know how incompetent she is. Marion would know – should she phone her? But no, Marion will be at the school gate waiting for Ryan.

Zita makes herself a cup of tea and eats a couple of biscuits and then – it is gone three o'clock – sets off back to the hospital in time to have twenty minutes by her mother's bedside.

'See I've been washed all over,' says Senga. 'Very nice they were about it too. I'll be seeing a consultant in the morning.'

'That's good,' says Zita. I suppose, she thinks.

'Now,' says the invalid, 'you'll be needing to get your father's tea ready. Tuesdays I usually make a meat pie. Just for once you could buy some of that ready-made pastry – you just roll it out. And he likes the gravy not too thick.'

Zita feels the weariness of defeat. 'Mum,' she says, 'if I do all of that we won't have time to come and visit you this evening. You know I can't cook as quick as you can. Fish and chips would be easier.'

'He's had nothing but since I've been taken bad,' says Senga.

'I cooked roast pork on Sunday,' says Zita. 'Did you forget? And all last week I cooked for you and him. Didn't I? Fish and chips won't hurt him.' She tries to smile but her face refuses to crease properly. 'I'll do a pie tomorrow, when I have more time.'

'Excuses,' says Senga. She seems to be tired now and lies back on her pillows. A bell rings to tell the visitors they have to leave. When Zita reaches home the men in the work clothes are waiting for her.

When they have gone – and it was not a long visit – Zita stands at the front room window watching them walk towards their car. What did they just say to her? What did it mean? Could she run after them and make them say it again, just so that she knows it's real? Or maybe: will it never be real?

There are things she should be doing, she knows there are, but what are they? Make a meat pie? No, not today, and never again. Tell someone? Her mother – but her mother is in the hospital – wait till she comes home? But shouldn't she be told? But what if it kills her? Tell Douglas – call Angel, ask her to tell him? But it feels wrong. Call Marion, yes, but what could she do? Would she know any better? Who is there who could direct her in what she has to do? Peggy? Doris Ward? But all the warnings she has ever been given by her parents – don't ask, don't presume, don't be in anyone's debt – all the instructions buzz through her brain like flies.

'Folks are good in their hearts, right enough,' Senga would say, 'but you don't want to be telling them your business.' But it doesn't feel to Zita like something that *is* her business. Why should I? she says out loud. Who else can do it, she answers herself.

She writes another note for Dougie. 'Mum will be home from the hospital soon, but I have to tell you that Daddy has died. So you can come round any time.' She hopes he will believe her.

This time Douglas turns up, knocking tentatively on the back door the next evening. He stands in the kitchen, dripping from the rain, refusing to sit down, as if she has laid a trap for him. Zita starts to tell him what happened.

'I know,' he says. 'I saw it in the paper.' He has it with him – the front page of the Sheffield Star telling of the fatal accident in the forge, the name of the person who died, the accounts of the other workmen, the statement from the management.

Zita makes a pot of tea; the two of them sit awkwardly opposite each other, either side of the fireplace, and the ghostly presence of both their parents stops any ideas that they might speak to each other. Zita pours the tea into the cups and passes one to her brother.

'Tell you what,' she says. 'Let's go and sit in the kitchen.' Thinking but not saying, It still smells a bit in here.

It's better in the kitchen. The table between them seems to give them something to hold on to.

'How's Mum?' he says.

'Pretty good. Looks a lot better. The medicine seems to really work.'

'I meant though – how did she take the news. About him.'

'Hard to know. I mean, she was shocked, like she couldn't believe it, but she didn't fall apart like you might think. Maybe it hasn't sunk in yet.'

'He's not such a loss,' says Dougie. 'He's a bad-tempered, selfish old bloke. She should have left him years ago.'

'Oh,' says Zita. 'So, is that why you've left Angel and the kids?'

'You wouldn't understand,' he says. 'You've never even had a boyfriend – or have you?'

'Not really,' she says. 'I'm sorry, Dougie. It's none of my business I know. I just wondered what went wrong.'

He lifts his cup to his lips, puts it down again, searches in his pocket for tobacco and paper and begins to roll a cigarette. 'You wouldn't understand,' he says again.

Zita sips her tea, wishing he would drink up and go away, knowing she has handled it all wrong.

'Women think they can change men,' he says. He searches for his lighter and takes a long drag at the thin cigarette. 'If I was all right to get married to – then you'd think I'd be all right to stay married to. But no, I don't talk to her enough, I don't take an interest in her work. I don't spend enough time with the kids – the kids are nearly grown up, they don't *want* my company. I don't do enough round the house – I work shifts for God's sake – doesn't she know what that does to your brain and your body?'

'So you had a row?'

'Many, many rows,' he says. He seems to sag lower on the kitchen chair. 'But I'm not going to stay where I'm not welcome. I've walked out of this family, haven't I, to be with her. I did it once, I can do it again.'

'So, that's it, is it? No going back?'

'She wouldn't have me back.'

'How do you know?'

'Trust me,' he says, 'I know. Once she makes her mind up to a thing, there's no going back.'

'But she didn't throw you out – *you* walked out.'

'And it was completely clear between us, If you go, she said, don't even let it cross your mind that you might come back. You go, you stay gone.'

'Oh,' says Zita.

Chapter Twenty-three

Senga is almost sorry to be going home. She could, she thinks, have happily stayed in the hospital for ever. People to talk to, other patients, orderlies bringing cups of tea and –rather skimpy – dinners; cleaners passing the time of day as they mop the floors, doctors taking an interest in how she was feeling, nurses checking her blood pressure and her heartbeats. True, there is no television and she hasn't been able to smoke her occasional cigarettes but they said she shouldn't be doing that anyway. People – other patients – complain that the time goes slowly, but for Senga, comparing it to being at home, the days have fairly flown by.

Of course it was a shock, when she heard what happened to Willie – when she saw Sally-Ann approaching the bed with the sister, and both of them with that look on their faces – well, she thought they were coming to tell her that she had no hope of ever getting any better. 'I'm sorry,' they would say, and she would know she was going to die. She was feeling better but she was going – soon, this week – to die, and all of a sudden she really didn't want to die, not yet, not without seeing her sisters again, not without seeing Dougie again.

And Sally-Ann took her hand – when did she ever do that? – and said those words. 'Mum,' she said. 'I'm sorry.' So she was sure, they were telling her there was no hope. And the sister joined in – you could tell she'd said these words before – 'I'm sorry Mrs Grey,' she said, and Senga could hardly take it in, what they were saying, – 'an accident.' 'Your husband' said the sister. 'Daddy,' said Sally-Ann. 'Died in the ambulance,' they said. 'So sorry,' said the sister. 'I'll just leave you with your daughter.' And she drew the curtains round the bed, very considerate, so that the other patients wouldn't be looking at them.

And after that she was a sort of celebrity on the ward, everyone being really nice to her, treating her especially gently, as if she was paying for her care, or as if she was the Queen or something. And Dougie came with Sally-Ann to visit and she did not recognise him, so tall and thin and bearded and *old*. He hardly knew how to talk to her, she had to do all the talking, told him about the other women in the ward, what they were in for, where in Sheffield they each lived. When she asked him about his children he just mumbled that they were fine as far as he knew – so Sally-Ann had been telling the truth when she said he and his wife had split up. Well, there was a lot of it about – Senga couldn't even deny that she had thought about it herself, thought about downing tools and walking out, as she'd done when she was a girl. As Dougie had done, and Sally-Ann, and Willie himself. She had never thought before – it was practically a family tradition.

And then they said – the doctors – that she could go home. She is home for Christmas, with her pills and her diet sheet, her ankles less swollen, her breathing easier, a card in her purse with the date for her out-patients appointment, home with Sally-Ann looking as if she was wishing she had died after all, and walking out of the room whenever Senga raised the subject of the funeral arrangements.

'You know it can't be this side of Christmas,' she says. 'You know they have to have an inquest.'

'Yes, yes,' says Senga. 'You told me. But we should still be making arrangements.' She is particularly bothered by thoughts of Willie's family – whether or not to let them know, and if so, then how. 'It was just a wee house,' she says. 'No front garden, straight off the street. A house, no a tenement. I canna just recall the name of the street.'

'Mum,' says Sally-Ann, 'It was probably pulled down years ago. There'll be flats there now.'

'They've a right to know, so they do.'

'His parents are probably dead by now.'

'He'd brothers and sisters too.'

'But what do they call them? You don't know do you.'

'George maybe? Or Joe? See, he never talked about them. It's over – that's what he used to say. It's over. Same as Douglas.'

Douglas has visited more than once but has proved to be worse than useless with the arrangements.

'Do what you like,' he says to his sister, and when she says 'OK then, just the one car to follow the hearse,' he says, 'Have it your way' as if he disagrees and hadn't just told her to make the decision. But he has sat with his mother, not talking very much, but not upsetting her either. They speak about the weather, and what is happening on the television. He says he will bring his children to see her, as soon as she is well enough, although they are teenagers now and he won't be able to force them to come.

'Would they be wanting to come to the service?' "Service" is the euphemism Senga uses for "funeral."'Their mother will never let them,' he says, and Sally-Ann, overhearing, says she does not blame her.

There is doubt all along, as well, about the state of the strikes – will the gravediggers have called off their strike, or will it have spread to Sheffield by then? They decide on a cremation, just in case. Will the crematorium – up there on City Road, near where Peggy and Lawrence live – even be heated if the oil tanker drivers were still on strike? Will the machinery be working? It is a precarious, fretful time all round.

Senga does not know what she feels. She talks to each of her sisters on the phone and each time she feels that she has been lacking in the right sort of feelings. Maggie would like her to mention God, and how Willie is now safe in Heaven; Betty would like her to cry when she has to say his name; Jeannie asks her questions about compensation and pensions and how she will manage without his wage. All three of them assure her they will be at the funeral, as long as she can arrange somewhere for them to stay overnight. Two nights. All three of them, too, as soon as they have done their duty by poor Willie, mention how difficult their father is getting, what with his bad temper, and his bad knees and his daily requests – orders – for messages (by which they mean shopping) to be brought, meals to be cooked and delivered, housework to be done. 'Of course,' says Maggie, 'we know Jeannie works full-time, but it would be a wee bit easier if there was another one of us to share the burden.'

'I would do more if I could,' says Betty, 'but there's just not the hours in the day, and do you know, the minute my back's turned Maggie goes and does something different and I never know am I coming or going.'

'I wish I could help,' says Senga, thinking, Haven't I just got shut of one difficult man, would I want to take on another one?

But in the end it happens, Willie Grey's funeral, on a freezing February day, Sheffield deep in snow so that the funeral car cannot get up the hill to their house and Senga's children have to practically carry her down the hill to where it has been waiting. Men from his work come in their best suits, but with their trousers tucked into big boots. They stand together, looking hopefully for there to be a bigger gathering of relatives and friends. But no, only Dougie and Zita, one each side of Senga, holding her up, and Doris Ward and her husband. Senga's sisters have not been able to make the journey, on account of the dreadful weather in the Borders. Peggy and Lawrence have sent a card with a kind message and a promise to attend but when the day comes there is a phone call to say Peggy has the flu and Lawrence has to stay and look after her. The men decline the invitation to come back to the house and set off to the pub, and the Wards claim that they have to go and babysit Marion's children. So it is just the three of them, Senga, Douglas and Zita, who sit down in the front room to a cup of tea and a plateful of slices of Christmas cake, which Senga has not been allowed to – and Willie has not been alive to – eat at Christmas.

Senga sits in a chair now – rather than lies on the settee – for much of the day. The telephone has been moved to within reach. Once a week she phones Dougie, though it's a slightly fraught business; he never answers the phone, which he shares with the other people in the house. It is often engaged, since five separate people live in the house. Someone else will answer it, call up the stairs and Dougie may or may not reply, because he may or may not be in his room, may or may not be in the mood to talk to his mother.

Other days she receives calls from one or other of her sisters; they have a strict rota: Mondays it's Maggie, who will tell her about the sermon in church on the previous day, and give details of her commitments for the coming week – Mothers' Union, church flowers, preparation for next week's Sunday School. Maggie's life revolves around the church, its cliques and its worries about the organ and the roof, its difficulties getting people to do the unpopular jobs, the strain it puts on Fraser, and so on. And on.

Wednesday evenings Jeannie rings, interrupting the TV – Senga has to struggle out of her chair to turn the sound down. Jeannie, though, is never on the phone for longer than a brisk ten minutes, mostly taken up with questioning Senga – how is she? has she been out for some fresh air? is she taking her medicine? is Sally-Ann settling down again? Senga appreciates the effort Jeannie puts in but is relieved when the ten minutes is up and she can go back to watching Coronation Street.

Friday afternoons are best, when Betty calls and they have a good hour – at least – of gossip and reminiscence, of enjoyable taking apart of their sisters – Jeannie so bossy, Maggie so holy – and of wondering whether Sally-Ann will ever settle down and get married.

'But she's thirty two,' says Senga every week.

'Aye right enough,' says Betty. 'Maybe an older chap then.'

When the phone rings next to her one Tuesday evening Senga wonders who it can be.

'Can I speak to Zita?' says the voice. It's a man's voice.

'I'll call her,' says Senga.

Zita responds to a shout of 'Sally-Ann'; she really can't be bothered any more, and comes into the room pulling off the rubber gloves with which she has been scouring the bathroom.

'Who is it?'

'A man,' says Senga.

'Zee?' says the man, and Zita says, 'Terry?'

'How's things?'

'OK, I suppose.' She is aware of her mother listening but the phone cannot be moved and neither can her mother.

'Well,' says Terry. 'How about meeting me in the pub? Can you manage that?'

'Who was that?' says Senga.

'Terry. No one you know. I'm going to meet him in the pub.'

'So I heard. Leaving me on my own.'

'You'll be fine, Mum. Or you can call Dougie and see if he'll come and keep you company. I'll be back before your bedtime.'

'I should hope so.' And when Zita has tidied herself and the door has closed behind her, Senga dials Betty's number to discuss what has happened.

Terry is there with a pint of beer in front of him. He stands up when he sees her come through the door but there is no hugging on this occasion. She remains standing for too long, wondering should she have bought a drink for herself on the way in, feeling out of practice, feeling as if she is in an unknown country where the customs have yet to be worked out. The music that comes from somewhere is unfamiliar – like nervous shouting, she thinks.

'Have a seat,' he says at last. 'What will you have?'

Again she doesn't know. Years gone by she and Marion would drink vodka and lime if someone else – usually Brian – was buying; in Crete she has drunk only wine, sometimes a little raki, which would often make her sneeze.

'Take your time,' he says, not kindly, she thinks.

'Same as you then,' she says. 'But only a half.'

He raises an eyebrow as if to doubt her but goes to the bar anyway and returns with her drink.

'Thank you,' she says and wonders what to say next. All the stored up stories and reminiscences and the things she wishes she could have told him have flown out of her head and she can do nothing except sip her drink and avoid looking at him.

'All right?' he says.

'Yes.'

He waits for her to say something else and then says, 'I was sorry to hear about your dad.'

She nods.

'My dad saw it in the paper. My mum said she would have shown up at the funeral but —'

'Yes I know.'

'Did it go off all right?'

'I suppose so.'

He seems to be thinking, then says, 'Your mum all right?'

'Much better, thank you. As long as she takes her pills. Still not going out, but she's better than she was.'

He frowns. 'I meant, is she managing her — you know — grief. Losing her husband like that.'

Zita wonders what to say. It seems to her that life without her father is an improvement. There is less tension, fewer arguments, not so many prohibitions and rules. Occasionally she and her mother even laugh together, and there is no one telling them they are misguided and foolish. 'She's OK,' she says.

'Because,' he says, 'if it was my mum she'd be — I don't know — destroyed, almost. We all would be.'

'You never met my dad,' says Zita.

'No,' he says. 'And — I forgot — you're the girl who left home without telling where you were going. And your brother walked out and left too didn't he. I don't call that a family.'

There have been times when Zita would have been ashamed and hurt, hearing that, and times when Terry's disapproval would have made her cry but now is not a time like that. 'We can't all be as lucky as you,' she says.

'Call me lucky?' he says. 'Yeah right, being married to Ros, call that lucky?'

'You've got a girlfriend haven't you? Your mum told me.'

'Did have. Had a few. Somehow they don't last very long.'

Zita is not surprised, given his present mood, but decides not to say so. She sips her drink and looks at him properly for the first time that evening. It seems to her that there is less of him than there used to be, although he has surely put on some weight; and his voice and his laugh are somehow softer, even while the things he says seem harsher. But of course, she thinks.

'I'm sorry,' she says.

'What for?'

'The letter,' she says.

'You've never written me a letter since I was in India,' he says.

'I remember that one. But I mean after that. After you got married.'

'I've still got them,' he says. 'All of them, they're at my Mum's house, along with all my travelling stuff. Ros never wanted all that in the house. It was like she thought I'd go off again. But nothing after we got married. So what letter are you on about?'

'From France. That winter.'

'I don't remember it.'

'You would,' she says, 'if you got it.'

'Where did you send it to?'

'Your house of course.'

'My mum's house? Or mine and Ros's.'

'Your house of course. Freedom Road wasn't it?'

'Freedom Road,' he says. 'Ros is still there. Freedom Road now, you might say, for both of us. So what did it say, this letter?'

'I can't tell you.'

'Can't or won't?'

'Won't then. It's ten years ago. I wouldn't write it now. It wasn't very nice.'

'I bet Ros got rid of it before I saw it,' he says. 'I told you once didn't I, she was jealous of you. How many other letters did you send me, that I never got?'

'No more,' she says. 'None after that one. I was that ashamed, I don't know what I was thinking of. If Ros read it she wouldn't have been pleased at all. I'm sorry though. I was sorry as soon as it was too late.'

He finishes his beer; hers has hardly been touched. She wonders, will he get up now and go, now that he has done what his mother must have told him to; he has seen her and offered condolences, which she has more or less dismissed as unnecessary, and thus made him consider that she has no heart, no proper feelings. She has messed things up by bringing Ros into the conversation; he is still bitter, she can see, she has done nothing but make it worse. She wonders, should she buy another round, will that look as if she wants to make an evening of it, or have they each said all they can think of to say to each other?

He shifts in his seat. 'Another?'

'Let me get them,' she says, and stands before he has time to reply.

She comes back from the bar with another pint for him and a glass of red wine for herself, the cost of which, compared to Crete, has made her gasp. She pushes her unfinished half across to him. 'Finish that for me,' she says. 'I'm not really a beer drinker.'

'So I can see,' he says. He is making an effort, she can tell, and they both speak at the same time: 'Tell me about Crete.' 'Tell me about your job.'

So she tells him about the hotel, about her little house, about her peaceful, pleasant life in the sun.

'You don't find it a bit boring?'

'No,' she says. 'Slow, but not boring.'

'Got a boyfriend out there?'

'No.'

Then he tells her about his work in one of the tough schools of the city, where he runs what they call a unit.

'What's a unit?'

'Proper name is Behaviour Modification Unit. BMU. The kids call it the BUM. I get them for sometimes just one lesson that they can't cope with, sometimes a week, full time.'

'So, does it work? Do you, you know: modify them?'

'Some. Some come back week after week, like, you know, some people go back to prison time after time. Maybe they like it better in a small group with me than in a big noisy class. Or maybe they're just born bad and they'll never change.' He looks despondent. 'There's only so much I can do. I can't give them a better start in life when they're already fourteen, can I? I can't give them a different set of parents. I can't bring back the people they've lost – you know, their Nannans, their big brothers – you wouldn't believe how many of them, one way and another, have lost someone they cared about.'

He stops himself. 'Sorry. I forgot, you've lost someone too.'

'Don't worry,' she says, but notices, with astonishment that a tear has dropped into her wine, and that she feels for the first time – *feels* it rather than thinks it – that her father has gone for ever. Gone.

Chapter Twenty-four

Zita's old bedroom remains empty – she sleeps in the attic still. She deals with her father's clothes without a tear in her eye, having first gone through the pockets and found various smallish sums of money, which she has kept. The clothes go in the bin, the work clothes, trousers and shirts that have seen better days, and old overalls; the clean but shabby clothes he changed into when he came home from work. He had what he would have called his 'good clothes' – a couple of newish shirts and a suit of old-fashioned cut which he would wear for the first day of those rare holidays at the seaside. She had considered setting it aside for him to be buried in but found that she could not raise enough certainty to take it to the undertakers. So she drops them into the dustbin with the others, brushing her hands together afterwards as if she has won a fight.

She applies for benefits for her mother; Senga can get upstairs now given enough time, and can creep around the house enough to make a pot of tea. She still needs someone to look after her. Someone being Zita.

March arrives. Zita thinks of Crete – still empty of tourists, still only spring, not summer, but warming up, the sun bright, the sky blue, the houses being given a fresh coat of whitewash. Getting ready for the change in the season. As she is.

For why could she not go back to her home in Crete? Let Dougie do some of the family caring. Dougie has no place of his own to live in. He could move in with his mother. Rent free; Senga would never dream of charging her children for their keep. He could bring the children to visit their grandmother.

'If you were living here,' she says to him, 'would you prefer the attic or my old bedroom?'

'I've never thought about it,' he says, and she says no more.

She lies awake in the attic bedroom. Something – who knows what – has reminded her of the times she and Marion would sneak up into Douglas' bedroom and touch his belongings. They would whisper so that Senga couldn't hear where they were; they would carefully, delicately open the top drawer of the small chest and take out a pair of socks, and pretend to sniff them and make a face. More daring was to take out a pair of his underpants, washed and ironed by his mother and smelling only of Persil; they would hold them up and wiggle their finger through the opening, and giggle till they almost choked. They touched his books but never opened them, and the covers of his records, never playing them because her mother would hear. It was, she thinks now, like archaeology, like piecing together the meagre small clues that might tell them, What is a boy, what is a teenage boy? They were only little girls then – she tries to determine how old. Say Douglas had left school by then, say he was fifteen or sixteen, then she and Marion would have been eight or nine. They were never caught, and by the time Dougie had gone into the army they were in secondary school and had grown out of that kind of researching. Zita, lying awake in Dougie's old bed feels a small sense of shame. Maybe though, she thinks, maybe all I wanted was to know him better; maybe I just wanted to understand who he was.

It must be two in the morning, if not three, she has been lying there so long, changing position, kicking off the blankets, pulling them back on again, counting – how many weeks she has been here, how many weeks since her father's death, how many friends she has (not many), how long till she needs to get a repeat prescription for her mother, how many names can she remember of people she was at school with (not many), how far can she count in Greek. At last she falls asleep and wakes late in the morning, hearing her mother calling her.

'What?' she calls back. She has slept late; her mother is at the foot of the stairs. 'What?' says Zita again.

'Oh, it's all right,' says her mother. 'I only wondered where you were.'

'Where else would I be?' says Zita, nastily, and slams the bathroom door.

Later in the day, having done the shopping, put in a load of washing, and listened to her mother once again wondering if she will ever get to know her grandchildren, she excuses herself from the front room and goes back upstairs. She looks critically at the attic bedroom; it is drab enough to depress anyone. She knows she moved there to put her father in the wrong; she wonders what sort of perversity makes her continue to sleep there, even now he is no longer around to notice. She moves her belongings back to her own room, folds her clothes and puts them into drawers, dusts and vacuums the room, makes her bed and fetches her rucksack out to position it on the floor where she will see it as soon as she wakes every morning, like a promise.

But it isn't yet time to pack the rucksack. This time she has to make sure that her mother's care is secure; she does not want to be summoned home again within weeks of getting back to where she belongs. She goes through the house making lists – things that need fixing, or painting, or throwing out altogether. She cleans the kitchen walls with sugar soap; she calls on Dougie to help and they carry everything that can be moved into the yard so that she can clean in the corners. She paints the walls and the doors though her mother complains that the smell of paint is making her ill. Zita ignores her. She rips up the ancient linoleum and replaces it with a nice bit of vinyl.

The next time she has Dougie to help, she persuades her mother to go to her bedroom for the afternoon and together she and Dougie carry the contents of the living room into the yard so that Zita can clean the room. 'Does it need that much?' says Dougie. 'I thought our mother was a good housekeeper.'

'She's been ill,' points out Zita. 'Anyway, I'm going to bottom this room so she has nothing to complain about when I'm gone.'

'You still think you're going then.'

'I don't think so,' she says. 'I *know* so.'

She takes the curtains down and washes them, along with all the cushion covers; she throws away everything she finds down the recesses of the sofa – handkerchiefs and a pair of tights, sweet wrappers and biscuit crumbs, shopping lists of items that were never fulfilled, scraps of paper that seemed to be letters to sisters that were never finished – Zita feels no urge to try to read them.

'Dougie,' she says. 'If you've got nothing better to do, put the kettle on and take her a cup of tea.'

Another day she turns her attention to the attic bedroom. Strips the old paper off the walls and tears up the ancient piece of carpet; paints the walls white. It still looks bare and uninviting; the bed is ancient and the mattress is lumpy; she cannot imagine Dougie – or anyone – actively wanting to sleep there. She treks downstairs with the nearly empty paint tin and the sticky brushes and in a sudden burst of pessimism chucks the whole lot in the dustbin. What's the point? she says out loud.

'We're none of us as young as we were,' says Betty, and Senga has to agree but when she has said goodbye and put the phone down she thinks to herself that nowadays, sometimes, she feels as if her years, and her cares and worries are dropping away. She feels, sometimes, as if she could carry a bag of shopping up the hill, scrub the kitchen floor on her knees, strip the sheets and blankets off a bed and make it up again without having to sit down a quarter of the way through. It must be the pills, she thinks, and the diet of course, what with Sally-Ann being really strict about it. And of course Sally-Ann has been a godsend, really busy, getting the house into a better state of repair; it's had a thorough turn-out over the last few months, and yes, Senga knows it's because her daughter has been bored and resentful and in need of something to spend her energy on, but the result has been a house free of cobwebs and dust, cupboards turned out and tidied, things that should shine – windows, furniture, the gas cooker, down to the taps and the door knobs – are shining again. If she could only learn to cook properly she'd make someone a fine wife, thinks Senga.

She misses Willie, of course she does. Only a few years off retiring, if he wanted to, they might have been like Doris Ward and her husband: no work to go to, nice little pension, having days out, a coach trip to Scarborough with a fish and chip lunch and a walk along by the sea. Though she knows really that it would never have happened. And if he was not dead – she is gradually more able to think and say the words: death, died, dead, deceased – if he was still alive she would not see even the small amount of Dougie that she currently sees. For Dougie, depending on his shifts, will pop in once a week, or sometimes twice, for a cup of tea. Once he brought his son with him, a tall, silent, wary teenager, although it was maybe too early in Senga's recovery for her to be properly welcoming. The girl refused to come into the house but Senga caught a glimpse of her through the front room window, standing with her back to the house and moving from foot to foot because of the cold. Sally-Ann had gone out and spoken to her; Senga saw her pat Nicole on the arm and come back into the house without her. 'Maybe next time,' said Sally-Ann, but so far there hasn't been a next time.

This divorce business, that all these youngsters seem to be going in for, what good can it do, thinks Senga. Two homes to run instead of one, everybody that much poorer, all those poor kiddies bewildered and not knowing whose side to be on, and all for what? Not that she would say these things to Dougie, but Sally-Ann, when asked her opinion, said something silly about wanting some freedom, she supposed, but she wasn't the right person to ask, having never been married herself. No, Senga wouldn't want to upset Dougie by being nosy, not yet at least, not until he's come to terms with it, as they say, not until he has maybe found someone new. But if, she thinks, if I could put up with Willie for all those years – forty, give or take a few months – if I could do it with him being such an old misery, then why couldn't Dougie and her? Angel. Some angel, I bet, thinks Senga.

Zita has become familiar with Terry's weekly timetable. Two nights a week and alternate weekends, Adam stays over in his Dad's flat. Wednesdays, Terry goes to play five-a-side football; Fridays, he often drops in on his parents. Tuesday evenings, Terry and Zita continue to meet in The Blake.

'Don't you have marking and stuff to do?' says Zita.

'You must be joking,' he says. 'The kids I get don't do enough work to make it worth marking. I just try and calm them down, sort out the immediate problem, get them into a frame of mind where they can go back into lessons.'

'But if they can't? They just sit there doing nothing?'

'Course not. But sometimes a bit of colouring keeps them busy and when they're feeling a bit more like it, then we can have a chat and think about what we can do.'

'Like move to a different teacher?'

'It has happened, when things have really got beyond repair. Quite often I'll put them on report to me, and if they do all right I can give them a reward at the end of the week.'

'Like?'

'Sweets mostly.'

She looks up slyly from her glass. 'What about your boy, your Adam? Does he need rewards at the end of a week?'

'He'd better not,' says Terry. 'He's only six.'

'So…' Zita is nervous about asking this,'…does he cope all right with you and Ros being apart?'

'He's a grand kid,' says Terry. 'I don't think he even remembers us living all together. He was only three when we split.'

'Why?'

'Why what? Why did we split up?'

She nods. She knows she's being impolite but she wants to know. She's his friend, he's said so loads of times, she should be able to ask something like that. Then she thinks, would I tell him something private? Or something I was ashamed of? 'I'm sorry,' she says. 'I should mind my own business.'

'I don't mind telling you,' says Terry. 'I mean, you don't want to know all the gory detail. We were just not happy, that's what it came down to. I wanted us to have another baby, Ros didn't want to. I wanted to do the job I'm doing; she wanted me to be more ambitious. And earn more money. Got so that we couldn't agree on anything. We bought an extra telly so that we didn't have rows about what to watch. I'd do a weekend shop and everything I brought out of the bag would be wrong. Nothing I did was ever right. You know?'

'You must have had some good times,' says Zita.

'Well. When Adam was born of course. Even then, she said I was doing it all wrong. If he cried and I picked him up, that was wrong. If I held him I was doing it wrong. We even argued over his name. I wanted him to have Lawrence as a middle name – you know it's my Dad's name, and it was my Grandad's name, but she wouldn't have it, and I didn't like her choices either, so he's ended up with just the one name. Not that he cares either way.'

'I've seen him,' says Zita. 'One day last year I saw him with your Mum. He looks like a nice boy.'

'The best,' says Terry. 'I have to hold on to that, that we wouldn't have Adam if we hadn't got married. But me and Ros – we just shouldn't have been together.'

'I thought you were in love,' she says. 'What happened to that?'

'What always happens. You get to find out what someone's really like.'

'Do you mean you, or her?'

'Both, I suppose. I was a disappointment to her, and she was a disappointment to me.'

'She was pretty,' says Zita.

'Pretty's not enough,' he says. 'I'd have done better marrying you.'

She can think of no reply, turns her glass round and round.'

'Sorry,' he says. 'I shouldn't have said that.'

'You didn't mean it,' she says, not bitterly; gratefully if anything. 'And anyway, I suppose you wouldn't want to live in Crete.'

'No, I wouldn't,' he says. 'But one day I'll come and see you, if you're still there.'

'I'll be there,' she says. 'It's what I call home anyway.'

'Well then,' he says, and he sounds for once like the old Terry she knew. 'You'll see me one of these days.'

'I'll believe that,' she says, 'when I see you walking up to my front door.'

'I'll bring Adam,' he says. 'When he's older.'

'You do that,' she says. 'I'd better be going now.'

'See you again next week?'

Zita continues to be baffled by their friendship, if that's even what it is. Every week, at the end of their Tuesday evening, well before closing time, they get up to leave.

'You'll be all right?' says Terry, each time. It's his way of saying that if she felt it was necessary he would see her to her door, but that his opinion is that she can look after herself. She is grateful for escaping the awkwardness of having him on her doorstep, wondering whether he wants her to ask him in, and how her mother would take it if she did. Things are maybe more relaxed than they were when her father was alive but she can see that Senga would still be disturbed by a stranger in her house. Or she might go straight to the fantasy that Terry was a proper boyfriend, a romance, a fiancé; she would be dropping hints about weddings as soon as his backside was parked on a chair; or else she would come over all flustered, apologising for the house, for herself, making excuses for there being no cake in the house, pulling at her clothes in some attempt to look less dishevelled, the way she does when Doris Ward taps on the back door once or twice a week, accepts the offer of a cup of tea and sits for twenty minutes with Senga, talking of the weather and the neighbours and Marion's children.

'She's a good woman right enough,' says Senga when Doris has gone. 'But I couldn't be doing with all the make-up, myself. Still, it's good of her to make the time.'

Marion too is an accepted visitor, passing the time of day with Senga, before retreating to the kitchen for a five minute chat with Zita, usually when she has dropped off the baby at her mother's and before she is setting off to the shops, or to give someone a perm in the comfort of their own home.

'Wouldn't your mum like her hair done?' she says to Zita.

'I asked her,' says Zita, 'last time you offered, but she says no thank you. She says she'll go back to Diane's as soon as she's up to it. You know what she's like.'

'I know what that Diane is like,' says Marion. 'Still, it's up to her.'

'And I think she'd like the outing, you know. She hasn't been out of the house for ages, except for appointments at the hospital. But she's a different person now, you know, from what she was before our Dad died. She's talking about going up to Scotland to see her sisters.'

'And while she's away –' Marion digs an elbow in Zita's ribs, like an actor in a bad comedy.

'What?'

'You know. You and Terry. She might stay up there a long time – you and Terry could settle down here.'

Zita sighs and sits down on a kitchen chair. 'Do you know what Maz? Terry's changed. Or maybe it's me. Maybe I've changed, cos I don't fancy him any more. I don't even know if I ever did. I probably just thought I should because he was the only boy who ever took an interest.'

'There was Norman.'

'Well, yes. Some big romance that was.'

'Well,' says Marion, 'it's not too late. Plenty of people get married when they're your age. Older even. You could still do it if you put the effort in.'

'Do you know what I want? I want to go back to Crete and just carry on having a nice time in the sun. Just enough work to get me by, and nobody moaning at me or telling me what I ought to do with my life. That's all.'

'And I tell you what,' says Marion. 'When I can get away from three kids and a husband, not to mention the in-laws – and mum and dad who might be going downhill by then – I'll come and see you and we can sit in the sun together and drink cocktails.'

'Promise?'

'Promise.'

Chapter Twenty-five

'Troubles come in threes, right enough,' says Betty. 'Maggie's Fraser, he's got an ulcer now, they're telling him, from all that worry down at the church. Maggie's run off her feet, trying to get it all done. Father's had another fall, as I told ye, no a bad one, but we live in fear, so we do, waiting for the phone to ring.'

'What's the third?' says Senga.

'Third?'

'The third thing. You said troubles come in threes.'

'Well, your own man,' says Betty. 'Your Willie – I'm sorry, hen, I wouldnae mean to upset you, it just slipped out.'

'Never mind,' says Senga. 'What's done is done.'

'I shouldnae complain,' says Betty, 'for after all we've no trouble in my family, touch wood, fingers crossed, but Maggie wants me to take Father's dinner to him, and bring his washing back and get it all washed and dried, and it's her day for doing it and I've things to do myself –'

Then why are you talking on the phone for half an hour? thinks Senga, but does not say it, because Betty has never been organised anyway, and besides, Senga would rather have her talking on the phone than be peeling potatoes, whether for her father or her husband.

'– so I never be finished before bedtime and it's my day tomorrow again –'

'Sure I wish I could help you,' says Senga.

'I wish as well,' says Betty. 'You were always my favourite sister, so you were.'

Zita arrives home from meeting Terry at the pub to find her mother rolling out pastry on the kitchen table, and a smell of scones coming from the oven.

'What are you doing?'

'Baking,' says Senga and begins to slice apples into a pie dish.

'You know, Mum,' says Zita, taking off her coat and outdoor shoes, 'you won't be allowed to eat all this. Not even some of it.'

'Visitors,' says Senga, covering the apples with pastry and crimping the edge of the pie with the back of a spoon handle.

'What?'

Senga dips her pastry brush into a cup of beaten egg and paints the top of the pie with it. She bends to open the oven and takes out the scones, prodding them with her finger. 'They'll do,' she says, 'though they'll never be as good as mother's.'

She slides the apple pie into the oven and moves the mixing bowl over to the sink.

'What visitors?' says Zita. 'When?'

'Tomorrow,' says Senga. 'My sister Jeannie is coming – she'll need to sleep in your room so you'll need to change the bed –'

'How long for?'

'Just the one night I believe. She said she could take two days off from her work, on account of it owing to her since she did extra hours before Christmas, so one day to get here and the next day to get back.'

'It's a long way to come,' says Zita, 'for the sake of just one night. Why doesn't she wait for a weekend?'

'Oh that's because her lad – that's wee Angus, you've met him that time we went up there – he's coming too, to take a turn at the driving. But he's on shifts you know, and this weekend he has to work.'

'And where's *he* going to sleep?'

'I'm thinking,' says Senga, 'it'll have to be in the attic.'

'And where am I sleeping?'

'Well,' says Senga, 'I thought you could choose. You could sleep on the settee in the front room; it's quite comfy really, though –' she appraises the height of her daughter '– it might be a bit short for you. Or you could come in beside me in the big bed.'

Zita shudders. She has slept in close proximity to several different people in her time, but always fully dressed and usually in the open air. Not at all the same thing as a sagging mattress shared with a large and probably sweating mother; *and* in the bed she used to share with her recently dead husband. Yes, she has changed the sheets several times since he died but still it feels like his bed. Still feels it would be distasteful, if not plain wrong.

'Or maybe,' says Senga, 'maybe Marion could put you up for one night. Her wee boys could bunk in together, could they not? She wouldn't mind if you explained what is the situation.'

Zita cannot believe her mother is saying these things. Whatever happened to keeping our business out of other people's knowledge? Whatever happened to not being beholden to other folk?

'I'll go on the settee,' she says. 'I've slept in worse places.'

'Will we have a scone?' says Senga.

'I thought they were for visitors.'

'Only to try one,' says her mother. 'See if they're all right. Fetch me the butter out of the fridge. Shall we have jam on them?'

'She wants you to come round and say hallo to your cousin,' says Zita to Dougie. 'And your aunt Jeannie.'

'Are they there now? Because I've just got in from work. What I want is something to eat and to get to bed, not coming round being all nicey-nicey to people I don't know.'

'There's plenty food here,' says Zita. 'Come and eat and then you can tell them you're on early tomorrow –'

'That's the truth.'

'And you can go.'

'Right. And you can all talk about me after I've gone.'

Zita laughs. 'They'll talk about you anyway, whether they see you or whether they don't. So you might as well come and take advantage of the cooking. I tell you, she's been like her old self, sending me to the shop every five minutes and using every saucepan we've got. There'll be no shortage of food.'

'So have they arrived?'

'Half an hour ago. They're in the kitchen now, getting stuck into the Victoria sponge.'

Senga has spent the day cooking pies and wondering if she has catered sufficiently for five people. Zita, between trips to the shops for more vegetables, more sugar, more margarine, has made up beds and dusted surfaces that did not need dusting. Her memory of Jeannie from – she counts the years: nine years ago, nearly, is of a business-like and humourless woman, one who would openly look you up and down and turn away as if satisfied that she was better than you would ever be. But, either she was wrong about Jeannie, or else Jeannie, on her best behaviour in her role as visitor, is a different kind of person when greeting her sister: a polite and accommodating one.

Sally-Ann shows her where she will be sleeping, and explains that Angus will be up in the attic. Jeannie puts her overnight bag on the bed and it seems suddenly that the room no longer – maybe never has – properly belonged to Sally-Ann. Certainly doesn't belong to Zita; she has no feeling of ownership towards it at all. They go back down the stairs to the sitting room where the cake and scones are set out, and the pot of tea.

'Unless you'd rather have coffee,' says Senga.

'Tea is fine,' says Jeannie graciously.

There is some talk of the hours and miles covered by the journey; an acknowledgement that Angus did well at the driving, except for being a little inclined to overtake unnecessarily. Angus does not enter into the discussion, but flicks through a magazine that seems to be about aeroplanes.

'So, Sally-Ann,' says Jeannie. 'You've not changed too much since the last time I saw you. Remember?'

'I remember.'

'We're all older, right enough,' says Senga.

'You're not looking too bad yourself,' says Jeannie. 'Considering how ill you were.' There was a pause. 'Weren't you?'

'Yes, she was,' says Sally-Ann firmly. 'She was very poorly and she has to be careful what she eats and how much she does around the house. And she has to remember her pills. And she has to have check-ups every six weeks.'

'Hush,' says Senga, and to her sister she says, 'Don't worry, I'm not a bit as she says. I'm fine, she's just fussing. She doesn't believe how much better I am.'

'Only natural,' says Jeannie, 'to be a little worried. But we'll look after you. Betty will look after you.'

Then, just before it's time to get the dinner on to the table, Douglas arrives. He has taken the trouble to change out of his work uniform and to comb his hair and shave. He and Angus have some sort of masculine conversation about railway engines, and then lapse into silence.

Chapter Twenty-six

Senga travels north in the back of Jeannie's rather luxurious car; wee Angus – who is not at all wee – does all of the driving, his ears apparently closed to the conversation the sisters are having, Senga leaning forward, Jeannie throwing questions over her shoulder.

'So what was it made you run all the way to England?'

'Och,' says Senga. 'I canna remember now after all this time. It wasn't as if we had a plan. We were eighteen, we'd never been out of Scotland, we just found a road and followed it.'

'Maggie always wondered,' says Jeannie, 'whether you were properly married.'

She sounds, thinks Senga, casual, as if she was pretending it didn't really matter – "Maggie wondered" indeed – they all wondered; they all would have had a special expression on their faces when they discussed her, an expression that meant no better than she should be if you take my meaning and Betty might have thought it was funny, or not that important, and Jeannie would have pursed her lips in that way she had when she was wondering; and their parents, Senga was sure, would take no part in the conversation at all, but tell the girls to hold their noise and not go poking into what they wouldn't understand.

'Sure we were properly married,' she says. 'In the Sheriff's office in Hawick. I've got a certificate and everything.'

'Maggie just wondered,' says Jeannie again. 'You know what like she is. And I've seen,' she adds, 'you don't wear a ring.'

'They cut it off me in the hospital,' admits Senga. 'It got that tight they said it would do my finger no good. I just need to get it to the shop to be made right, now I've lost some weight.'

'I see,' says Jeannie.

Senga could have told her that her first wedding ring came from Woolworths and that the gold soon wore off, and that before Willie came back from the war she managed to save up and buy one that was real gold, though second-hand and worn very thin, and that he never noticed what she had done. She always wondered if it really counted as a wedding ring, if you had to buy it yourself. But Jeannie does not seem to be the sort of sister who would hear such a story with any sympathy.

Angus drives straight to Betty's house and there is Betty, on the lookout from the front room window, and hurrying down the front path.

'We'll not stop,' says Jeannie. 'I've things to do before I get a sit-down as it is. You two can have a good blether.'

'Oh, we will,' says Betty, waves to Angus who has not left the car, and ushers Senga inside where there is a smell of newly cooked fruit cake, only slightly burnt.

'So she's gone for how long?' says Marion.

'No idea,' says Zita. 'She's got to stay with Betty, to start with – cos Betty lives nearest to their father – and help Betty look after the old fella, cos Jeannie's at work and Maggie has to look after her husband – although it seems to me that's a bit of an excuse. I never heard that a stomach ulcer needed round the clock care.' This last comment was straight out of Jeannie's mouth.

'So what's your cousin like?'

'Just a kid,' says Zita. 'Studies some sort of engineering. Mad about cars. Not much to say for himself. Can certainly get himself round a lot of cake.'

'And you don't know when she's coming back?' says Marion again.

'Between you and me, Maz – and don't tell your mum I said this – I don't think I'll be here when she comes back. Even *if* she does. She'll be living on cake and suet dumplings up there, believe me, and if she comes back I'll have to start looking after her all over again. So no. It's summer in Crete and that's where I'm going.'

'Good for you,' says Marion. 'I suppose.'

'I know you'd never do something like that,' says Zita. 'You wouldn't go off and leave your mum in this sort of situation. But I'm going to get Dougie to move in here. It'll save him from paying his rent and he can have his kids stay over.'

'He's agreed to it then?'

'Not quite, but he will. Think about the money he'll save. He has to pay money to Angel for the kids so he's never got two pennies to rub together. He says he doesn't want any favours, but I've said to him, it'd be doing Mum a favour by looking after the house while she's away.'

'You've got it all worked out I can see,' says Marion. 'Come and see me before you take off won't you.'

'Course I will.'

Zita puts the phone down and closes the curtains.

*

Betty's husband Johnnie drives lorries, often long-distance so that he is away overnight. Even when he manages to sleep at home he is up early in the morning, in order to get out of the town before the roads become jammed with cars and bikes and schoolchildren. He is pleased that Betty has her sister to stay to keep her company, now that their daughters have grown up and left home.

Each of the daughters, Betty tells her, has children – a boy and a girl apiece, isn't that nice – and she would like to help out more than is possible, what with Father needing so much done for him, and Johnnie's hours being so unpredictable.

'Alison's only up the road,' she says. 'She can leave the weans with me while she gets to the shops, but Annette, she's down at Wemys Bay and I canna drive as you know, so it's a bus or a train and it all takes time, and her wee ones are like to forget me, so they are.'

Senga does not tell her – not yet – that she has spoken to her own grandson only once, and seen her granddaughter, and only the back of her, just the once through a window, and much obscured by a net curtain.

'So tell me then,' says Zita. 'Why did you and Angel split up?'

'I already told you,' says Dougie. 'I couldn't stand the nagging any more.'

'What about?'

'Anything. I couldn't do anything right. Just because she was clever –'

'Was she?'

'Got promoted. More than once. By the time the kids were in comprehensive she was running the show – all the school nurses – she was in charge of the lot.'

'So? How is that a problem?'

'A man,' says Dougie, 'doesn't want his wife earning more than he does. Honestly, she would say – something like – where shall we go on holiday? And I would say, well, Filey's always nice, but no, she'd be thinking of going to Spain or somewhere.'

'I remember you saying that to me years ago. Didn't you ever go?'

'We went. She paid for it. It was all right. I thought, well, that's that, we'll not do it again, and then she started saying she'd like to see

Barbados – where her mum and dad were born – and honestly, there's no way we can pay for four people to go all that way but she started putting money away every month – behind my back, mind – and started telling the kids that she'd take them to Barbados. And even said she'd go without me if I didn't want to go.'

'So you split up just because of that?'

'You've never been married have you? Have you even had a boyfriend? No, not so as anyone knows. So you don't know what it's like, do you?'

'I know how to get along with people though – it sounds like you just want your own way all the time.' She hears herself criticising her older brother whom she hardly knows and fully expects him to get up and walk out of the house for ever. 'I'm sorry Dougie. I don't mean to criticise you –'

'Oh, carry on, everyone else does.' He pulls out a handkerchief – none too clean – and blows his nose.

'I just mean – I mean I'm only asking – you haven't got a new girlfriend have you? And Angel – she hasn't got someone new? Has she?'

He shakes his head.

'So, why don't you try again? You could go to that marriage thing, what do they call it – Guidance?'

'Don't start. That was her idea. As if I'm going to tell some nosey woman all our business, and then – will she be on my side? Not on your life.'

'Sounds like,' says Zita, 'and pardon me if I'm speaking out of turn – but it sounds to me as if you're doing that thing they say – cutting off your nose, whatever, you know, like just hurting yourself and hoping we'll all feel sorry for you.'

'Even our mother,' he says, 'even Mum isn't on my side. You've heard her, "Oh Douglas why ever have you gone and done such a thing? Oh those poor wee children." I just want everyone to get off my back and let me sort my own life out.'

'OK,' says Zita. 'Look, here's the thing. Mum has gone to Betty's, how long for we don't know. I'm going back to Crete –'

'What for? What are you going back there for?'

'I live there,' she says. 'I live there.' That's the truth, she thinks to herself, because being here is not living at all. 'So here's Mum's house,' she says. 'You know it's all clean and nice. I've done every corner of it, you know that.'

'So?'

'What you don't know Dougie, is that this house belongs outright to Mum now – "They bought it?"

'They bought it. They've been paying a mortgage for a while now, and it's been paid off by the insurance when Daddy – you know - died. And when Mum dies it will belong to me.'

He says nothing, taking it in.

'But I thought,' she says, 'I wondered –' Now that it's come to the point she wonders if she can go through with it, this burning of boats. 'I don't want it,' she says firmly, too loudly. 'I'm not going to live in this city ever again. I live in Crete.'

'So you said.'

'So if I make the house over to you – I mean properly, with a solicitor, it would be yours. When Mum dies it will be yours.'

He says nothing.

'On condition,' she says, 'that you take responsibility for Mum.'

'It's a lot to ask,' he says.

'It's a lot to get,' she says. 'A whole house. For nothing.'

'How old is she? Fifty eight – that's no age at all is it. Say she lives to be ninety –'

'I'd be surprised,' says Zita.

'Even so.'

'So,' she tells Terry, next time they meet in the pub, 'I'm waiting for him to come to a decision.'

Terry drinks from his glass, puts it deliberately down on the table, considers. 'You do know,' he says, 'that you sound completely heartless.'

She looks down. Answers run through her mind; she finally settles on, and says, 'One life.'

'What?'

'You only get one life, don't you. I'm trying to get her looked after –'

'Why don't you ask her what she wants?'

'Because I know what she'll say. She wants me to live with her and fetch and carry for her and keep house for her and listen to her saying the same things day after day, and at the end of it she'll die – unless I die from boredom first – and it will be too late for me to do what I want to do, and even if I can go back to Crete nobody will know me any more, and _'

No, she will not cry in front of Terry. She lifts her wine glass and tries to look composed, biting her lower lip to hold the tears back. Terry cannot stand emotional women.

'– and I can't see why he wouldn't do it,' she says. 'He can still go to work, he gets to live rent-free.'

'So you said. But it's not a man's place is it, looking after sick people. All this women's equality, it can only go so far, can't it? And your mum won't want to be looked after by a bloke will she?'

'All he has to do is call the doctor if she's poorly. She's back on her feet now – she can cook for him – he'll be better fed than he's ever been. What if it was your Mum – would you go and live with her?'

'So if – ' he is not going to answer her question '– if she's so well now why does she need anyone to live with her? What's the problem?'

Zita feels the prison door opening. Sees daylight beyond. 'You're right. I can go whenever I like. They can sort it out for themselves without me. None of my business. I can just go.'

'I didn't mean it that way,' says Terry. 'Obviously she's your responsibility, yours and your brother's. You can't just walk away.'

Watch me, she thinks.

Chapter Twenty-seven

She wakes the next morning full of relief and purpose. She pulls her rucksack from under the bed, and fills it with what she needs. She counts her money – not much, not enough for a plane ticket, but she will hitch, she will manage. She writes a letter to Olga explaining that she is on her way.

She puts a set of house keys in an envelope for Dougie, with a note and the phone number of their mother's doctor, and puts the envelope through his letterbox while he is at work. She does not write to her mother, or phone her at Betty's house. It would only upset her and spoil her little holiday. She would find out soon enough, and Zita would send her postcards, when she remembered.

She makes herself some sandwiches for the journey and makes toast with the remains of the loaf and finishes it up. She considers going to say goodbye to Marion's mother but holds back for fear of awkward questions about her decision. She has had enough of that from Terry. And she feels no need to discuss her plans with him any further.

She forms the intention of going to see Marion before setting off, but somehow, when she opens the back door and steps out into the street and hoists her rucksack on to her back, somehow she turns away from the direction of Marion's house and finds her feet taking her downhill, towards the town and the dual carriageway, and the M1, and the rest of her life. At the end of her road she feels she ought to look back at her mother's house, but actually, no, she can't be bothered.

It has been a long slow journey. An aeroplane flight would have taken four hours; she has taken four weeks. It was Easter when she left, without seeing her mother again. Or Marion, or Douglas, or Terry.

Four people, she thinks. In the whole of the United Kingdom, only four people I could have said goodbye to. And two of them are family and I don't even like them, and they probably don't like me. And two of them I might call friends but they won't miss me, I'm not important to them. I can do whatever I like.

She disembarks from the ferry at Rethymnon. It is an evening at the end of May, the air is hot, even by the sea. The town, as she walks through, is busy; the tourist shops are open, the cafes and restaurants have their boards outside, advertising their menus in English and German, their souvlaki and gyros and moussaka; waiters stand outside, ready to persuade customers to enter and eat. Zita smiles at them and bids them kalispera, good evening, but does not stop. She walks through the streets, slowly, breathing in the warmth and the cooking smells and the sight of women watering their flowerpots on the balconies of the apartment blocks, and the chairs on the pavements outside the front doors, there for the evening when it will be cooler and people will sit outside and watch who goes by.

She passes the hotel; she will go first to her little house, leave her rucksack, wash her face and comb her hair, before seeing Olga. She imagines the raised voices of welcome; she thinks how pleased they will be to see her, just in time for the busy season, not just Olga, all the staff, the cooks, cleaners, bar staff, the handyman. She will be back where she belongs. And a few yards past the hotel, there is her house. Not quite as she has remembered it, but of course, Uli has been looking after it, it is Uli who has trimmed the rosemary bush and painted the front door.

She takes out her key, a heavy old-fashioned key, but it does not fit the lock. She looks closer. The lock is no longer an old-fashioned lock but a small shiny one. Maybe the owners, though they live up in the hills away from the tourists, have for some reason changed the lock – or actually – maybe – is the whole door a new one? She goes to the side of the house where there is a small window, but it is covered by a curtain; someone has put it there, she thinks, to stop the room getting too hot; it's a good idea, very thoughtful.

Well, she will just have to go hot and dusty to find Olga and get it sorted out.

The hotel lobby is crowded with new arrivals, newly delivered by the airport bus. They are queuing for their keys, tired from the journey but excited to have arrived, chattering to people they have only just met, looking round at the newly painted walls and the polished brass of the door handles. Zita does not recognise the young woman behind the desk and she knows Olga will probably be in the kitchen or in the dining room, checking that everything is in order. She sits on a chair under the street map of Rethymnon, waiting until the guests have dispersed to their rooms. She knows Olga will come through the lobby sooner or later; there is no hurry, no emergency, she is back where she belongs.

*

Senga puts in a long-distance call to her own house in Sheffield. 'Are you sure it'll show up on your bill how much I owe you,' she says to Betty.

She expects that Sally-Ann will answer and is surprised to hear Dougie's voice. Surprised and pleased.

'She's gone,' says Dougie. 'Went week before last. Haven't heard from her since, don't expect to neither.'

'Gone where?' says Senga.

'Greece. Crete. Where she was before I suppose.'

'I suppose,' says Senga. 'But – how is it that you've answered the phone? Did she leave you a key? Is something wrong?'

'I thought she would have told you,' says Dougie. 'She thought – well, we both thought really – that you'd need someone to keep an eye on things. And since I had nowhere of my own to live – "No, no,' says Senga. 'I'm pleased you're there. I feel better if someone's there. I was just surprised that's all. She never told me all that.'

'So, will you be coming back here any time soon? You know, I'll get some groceries in if you are.'

'Och, I canna tell when I'll be back,' says Senga. 'We're busy here with father – Betty's round there several times a day and it's up to me to cook the meals for him, and for us and for Johnnie.'

'She's lucky to have you then,' says Dougie. 'I could do with some proper meals myself.'

'When I come back,' says Senga. 'When I come back I'll make it up to you. And you can bring your children to see me and see if they like my cooking.'

'Maybe,' says Dougie, and then neither of them can think of a thing to say, unless it's about the weather.

'So, I'll let you get on then,' she says. 'This is Betty's phone bill we're using here.'

'Give my regards to everyone,' says Dougie, formally, and puts his phone gently down in its place.

'See,' says Betty, 'I mind how we hated you after that do at Girvan.'

'As if I didn't know that,' says Senga. 'It was Dada's fault, no mine. He could have sent me home and let you girls have your proper holiday.'

'He wouldn't have trusted you away from himself. And he was hard on all of us after you ran away. It's a wonder any of us found a boy – home for half past nine, always having to leave the pictures before the film was finished – we were a laughing stock. It was put around we had to be in bed by half past seven – not that it was true, but they used to laugh at us when we had to go home early; they'd say: Oh, it must be past your bedtime, time for baby to go to bed. Maggie even slapped some girl who said something – that was another thing – her Da came round and complained and our Da made us all stay in the house for a week, except for going to work or school. He treated us as if we were all going to behave like you did.'

'Well, I couldn't help it,' says Senga. 'I was here while that was going on – remember? Then I decided to leave. I thought he might ease up on the rest of you once I'd gone.'

'Well, he didn't,' says Betty. 'But as luck would have it, I got together with my Johnnie – met him at work you know – and he had to come and listen to Father tell him how strict he was with his girls and what he expected if they started courting serious. And Johnnie pretended he never heard of you and made out to be shocked, and Father eased up on me a bit, and when Maggie found out she got Fraser to come and butter up to the old man, and Fraser – well, he was from a churchgoing family, so that went down all right. But it was more than a year from that time in Girvan – a year at least without any fun and him reminding us all the time to behave us selves, and then it was the war and we had all that. Rationing and bombing and nothing in the shops, and my Johnnie got called up –'

'So did Willie, and wee Dougie only two months old, and there I was, on my own in a strange town. Right enough, he got leave at first, but once he was sent abroad – he was in the desert, so he was, and then Italy – there was no chance of any leave all the way from there and by the time he came home our Dougie was six years old and didn't remember him – "Well, how could he?"

'I know. But Willie – it hurt his feelings. His son wouldn't go to him. He *was* a mummy's boy, of course he was, he'd only ever had me, no one else. And it's my opinion that neither of them ever got over it. I wish they did, but they didn't.'

'Weans are like that,' says Betty. 'Our Alison, now: we could never get her to go near her great granma – that's Johnnie's granma – though she was a really nice woman, but she had these whiskers on her face, you know, and our Alison took against her, and you canna say to an old lady, can you, "she doesn't like your facial hair"?'

'But at least you didn't have to live with her day in and day out. Oh I tell you, it broke my heart, seeing Willie come home after a day's work and his son like sliding out of the room, trying to get out of the way. And never talking to him – "What did you do at school today?" says Willie, and the boy just shrugs his shoulders, doesn't even look at his Da, it was painful to see.'

'But your daughter – your Sally-Ann – did she get on all right with her Da?'

'Oh aye, when she was little. Oh, she'd be waiting for him coming home from work. Oh yes, he'd be the one put her to bed and tuck her in; she was always Daddy's girl. When she was little.'

'See, you're not wrong there, teenagers are another thing altogether, are they no? I mind Johnnie saying to me when the girls hit that stage, "What did we do?" he said. "Someone's took our nice polite girls and left a pair of monsters in their place." But it was just a phase, the mini-skirts and the eye make-up and the stopping out late and the scenes when you told them they'd to stay in, or else when you told them you weren't giving them any more money to waste on buying rubbish and going to dances. But they turned out all right in the end.'

'See,' says Senga, 'our Sally-Ann never went through that, not really. She never had a boyfriend, not that I know of, nor many friends, only Marion from across the road. She was never a trouble to us. Till now.'

'She'll settle herself down one of these days,' says Betty. 'See my friend Rhona, she never married till she was thirty-eight and then she had two weans and you couldn't find a more happy wee family. Everything comes to them that wait. There'll be some man somewhere for your Sally-Ann, just wait and see.'

Chapter Twenty-eight

Zita sits for some time in the hotel lobby, feeling ever more conscious of being dusty and sticky from travelling. Hungry too. She sees Uli coming up from the laundry room with his tool bag, and hurrying up the stairs to the bedrooms and surmises that somewhere someone is having difficulty with the shower in their room. It happens every time. Eventually the crowd of new guests disperses and Zita approaches the girl behind the counter.

'Where is Olga?' She speaks in Greek to show that she is not one of the tourists.

The girl says she doesn't know but Zita suspects that she is suspicious of this scruffy traveller. 'I'm Zita,' she says. 'I work here. Please tell Olga I'm here.'

She sits down again under the street map; watches the girl retreat into the office, hears her voice on the phone. It is not Olga who comes down the stairs, but a younger, bigger woman. It takes a moment to realise who it is and remember her name. Heather.

'It *is* you,' says Heather. She smiles, but only briefly. Zita is suddenly uneasy and fails to smile back.

'Are you working here now?'

'Of course,' says Heather. 'Why not?'

Zita shrugs. She is too tired to ask any more. 'I need Uli really,' she says. 'Or Olga. I can't get into my house – the lock's been changed. I just want a wash and a bit of a rest, then I'll be able to come back to work.'

'I shouldn't think they'd need you,' says Heather. 'Anyway, Olga's busy right now anyway.'

'I'll wait till she's got time,' says Zita. 'I can see it's a busy time. I know what it's like. Do you know where I can get a key to my house though? I've been travelling for weeks, I just want to sleep in my own bed.'

She will remember Heather's expression, or her attempt at hiding her expressions, her eyes looking earnestly at Zita, her mouth twitching a little with the effort to hide her pity, her triumph, her superiority.

184

'They couldn't keep it empty for you,' she says. 'No one knew if you were coming back. Or when. They re-let it.'

'What do you mean?' Zita is still holding what had once been her door key; she holds it up so Heather cannot fail to see it.

'I mean someone else is living there,' says Heather. 'It goes with the job.'

'Who?' says Zita, but she knows before Heather has a chance to tell her.

What can she do but find a room for the night – not difficult – and contemplate her situation. She takes off her shoes and lies down on the hard mattress. She remembers that she had been hungry when she stepped off the ferry on to what she thought would be home ground, but now she has no inclination to eat. Sleep, she thinks, I'll have a sleep and then think about it. It will look better in the morning – that's what Terry used to say when things were not going so well – 'You'll see,' he used to say. 'Get a bit of shut-eye, everything will look better in the morning.'

But sleep does not come. She is tired, her eyes will not stay open but her brain will not lie down, it churns and turns, replaying her arrival at the hotel – a back view of Uli hurrying up the stairs, the milling crowd of guests in the lobby, Heather, Heather's face, trying not to smile. She had even hoped Heather would still be here, another Englishwoman, a friend, or a possible friend, she had imagined sharing their stories, maybe telling her about her father's death, her mother's illness and recovery. Now she imagines going down to the house – Heather's house – and throwing stones at the windows to break them, she imagines breaking in while Heather is working in the hotel and dumping her belongings on to the street outside. She imagines going to the police station, or to the owners of the house, to complain that Heather has stolen her house while her back was turned, but she knows that really she has no claim that would get her home back. She knows she has not paid any rent for the months since November, never thought about it, unless to believe that it wasn't necessary when she wasn't living there.

She turns her face towards the thin pillow and cries a little, 'Give over,' she says out loud. 'What's the point of that?' It's what her father use to say to her, or to her mother, if ever they resorted to tears.

At last she sleeps, in her clothes, lying on top of the blanket, and waking up at the very first faint lightening of the sky, hungry and thirsty and homeless and jobless. And friendless, she thinks.

'Well, what do you expect?' It is her father's voice in her head, or Terry's, or Dougie's or even her mother's or Marion's, and she knows what else they would say. If you were a good daughter you would never have run away – how long ago? Ten years? Twelve years ago. You should never have made your parents worry all that time, sending those stupid careless postcards, and, that, only when you remembered. Not even every week, and not even a loving message on a single one. A good daughter would have stayed in Sheffield, like Marion did, would have got married – though who to? – had a baby or two.

Did you even cry, the voices ask, when your dad died; did you worry when your mother was so ill she had to stay in the hospital? Were you even sympathetic to her aches and pains and disabilities? Would she have behaved like that to you? Would Marion have behaved like that to her mother?

Marion. What did you ever give to the friendship with Marion? You just took up her time and her sympathy, going round there of an evening to complain and moan, when she would have been ready for a quiet sit down in front of the TV once the children were in bed. And bothering her on the phone every time you had a problem – Oh Marion, What am I going to do, my Mum's feeling sick, what shall I do? You took all that support, from her and from Doris, and barely said thank you. Who did you ever offer any support to? Dougie? Terry? Selfish, you are.

Is it any wonder, say the voices, that you've ended up on your own. Serves you right. You didn't even stick around for your grandmother's funeral. Your mum had to do the journey back to Sheffield all on her own and when she got home where were you? Away at the seaside with Marion. And don't tell us you were working. What's that got to do with it?

And that letter you wrote to Terry – what about that? Spiteful, that was, trying to stir up trouble when they'd only just got married. And you think it was lucky that Ros took it and Terry never saw it? Lucky for you maybe, but what about their marriage? Ever thought how she might have read it. She might have brooded over that letter, wondering about you and Terry? And don't tell us that old story about the old Frenchman and his little bit of fumbling as if that's some sort of excuse. You were warned and you thought you knew better. So give over crying.

And you've pushed your brother into caring for your mum, you've manipulated him, you've bribed him with a house. Have you even been to a solicitor to get it properly sorted? No, thought not.

She gets up, she washes herself, she changes her underwear. She pays for her night's lodging, picks up her rucksack and goes out to buy bread for her breakfast.

I'm not that bad, she says to herself. *Didn't I go home for a whole winter? Didn't I look after Mum, didn't I put up with her? What if I didn't cry when Daddy died? Would it have helped if I did? I'm not a bad person, I'm not. Just because I wanted to get away from Sheffield, what's wrong with that? Just because I want a different sort of life. What difference does it make to them?*

She sits eating dry bread looking at the sea. *Anyway*, she says to herself, *anyway, I've got other things to think about. Somewhere to live and a job; a job and somewhere to live.* She cannot go for long, paying tourist prices for a room, and eating in cafes. *Olga*, she thinks, *I never spoke to Olga. She'll help me, one way or another, she'll know somewhere that needs new staff, she'll send me in the right direction.*

She takes her hairbrush out of her rucksack and brushes her hair carefully, that being about the only thing she can do to look more respectable, and walks again towards the hotel. She stands outside, hesitant, hoping to find a way of avoiding Heather. Breakfast is over; two by two, guests are venturing out to look round the town. Inside, she knows, the maids will be working along the corridors, making beds, Olga will be in the kitchen, making sure there is enough of everything for the rest of the day. Once again, she goes inside, warily, approaches the desk and asks for Olga; and once again is told that at the moment Olga is too busy to see her. It is not possible. The girl, polite but knowing, has clearly been told of the situation. *They have plotted against me.*

She goes out of the front door, down the steps, stands looking at the road, and the sea between the few houses on the other side of the road. A dog trots across the road, a cat slinks under a parked car. There are sounds of hammering and men shouting – this end of the town will soon have a new hotel with sea views, that would maybe offer her a job, but she does not have time to wait for it to be finished.

It is Uli who comes out of the door and down the steps, and stands beside her, and after a while, speaks.

'You know Olga,' he says. 'What she is like. She wants not to cry. She wants not for you to cry.'

Zita nods her head without looking at him, without replying.

'Heather too,' he says. He pronounces her name Hetta. 'She will be your friend, if you want, but it is her job now. Also her house.'

Zita shrugs, still looking at the sea between the houses. You don't deserve a friend, says the voice in her head, and aloud she says, expecting no answer, 'What am I supposed to do?'

'I have to go,' says Uli. 'Much to do.' And goes back across the road and up the steps into the hotel.

'Thanks for nothing,' says Zita aloud to the space where he had been.

She spends the morning asking at the hotels, asking for work. She is unsuccessful, although many people are kind and send her on to somewhere else, to someone who might have work for her to do, but, when she asks, they haven't. In this way, by late afternoon, she is on the western suburbs of Rethymnon, where the beach is narrow and stony and the single hotel seems to be not very prosperous. She asks anyway, with no success, and comes back out onto the roadside, knowing that she is at the end of the town and there is nowhere else to go.

She sits on a wall. She is hungry, but she has made a bargain with herself to find a job before she eats anything. She feels now she might have to die of hunger. Would it be so bad? *Stop it*, she says aloud. *Give over*. And she slides to the ground and leans back against the wall, and closes her eyes.

'Zee?' says a voice. A voice accompanied by the erratic putt-putting of a small engine, of Uli's motor scooter in fact. Zita opens her eyes and sees Heather propping it up against the kerb and turning off the engine.

'Go away.'

Heather sits on the ground beside her, not too close. 'I came to say sorry,' she says.

Zita does not reply; she has nothing to say.

'Olga told me off,' says Heather. 'She said I should have let you know about the house, so that you might not come back if you knew. So you didn't have a wasted journey.'

'Oh,' says Zita. 'Why didn't you?'

'I just didn't,' says Heather. 'I never got round to it. And also, I suppose, I wanted you to come back. We got on OK, didn't we, before you went home? I thought we could be friends, maybe.'

'Funny way of being friends,' says Zita.

'I guess I'm not that good at it,' says Heather.

After a long pause Zita says, 'I guess I'm not either.'

'Anyway,' says Heather. 'Olga says I've got to take you to this woman she knows up in a village. She needs help with her little café – *her kafenion* – because she's getting on and it's a bit too much for her.'

'No,' says Zita. 'I've just spent six months looking after an old woman, I've had enough of it.'

'OK,' says Heather. 'You've got a better idea then. Want to tell me?'

It's not so bad. It's not what she wanted but it's not so bad. The old lady – she is called Afrodite – is quite able to look after herself, doesn't need washing for instance, quite independent really, but her eyesight is going – has gone, almost, which has led to minor accidents in the kitchen. She squints at Zita, suspiciously, and then takes her outside to show her the chickens.

'She says it's your job to look after the chickens,' says Heather.

'I know what she said,' says Zita sharply.

They go back inside; Afrodite shows Zita a tiny room with a bed; makes her understand that it is food and board only. No wages. Zita shrugs. What else can she do?

Besides looking after the chickens she will have to be present in the kitchen when Afrodite is cooking, partly to look after her, partly so that she can learn how things are done and be ready to takeover. She will keep the premises clean, go into the town for provisions when necessary, look after the garden under the eye of her employer – if employer is what she is – and generally earn her keep. But it's not so bad. The arrangement reminds her of the café in Arles, except that she's on her own, without Terry. But would I even want him? she asks herself. I manage all right on my own.

At the end of her first week, Olga – who is a distant relation of Afrodite – comes to visit, to see how things are going.

'Not so bad,' says Zita.

'Good?' persists Olga.

'Ok. Good.' She will not say how much she resents the loss of her little house; how isolated she feels out here in a village, away from the town.

'Heather says she will come and see you. If it is all right?'

Zita shrugs. Can she make herself care either way? 'If she wants to.'

'I should also tell you,' says Olga. 'Auntie –' this is how she has greeted Afrodite –'is more than eighty years old. And she is not well. She will get worse.'

Zita nods wearily.

'I'm telling you so that you know,' says Olga. 'If you want to go somewhere else, of course you have the right.'

The words 'somewhere else' land heavily into her brain. 'I'll think about it,' she says, but she knows she is too tired to move on; she knows she will stay, for the time being at least.

'Heather wishes to come and see you,' says Olga. 'She is only young, she needs someone to talk to. She would like to be your friend.'

'I said it was all right. She can come and see me if she wants.'

'I will tell her you will be happy to see her.'

Tell her what you like, thinks Zita.

After Olga has talked to Afrodite and had a cup of coffee, and inspected the chickens and the lemon tree, she gets into her little car and goes back to the hotel, back to Uli, and Heather, and the staff, and the guests and their demands and problems, and their enjoyment and their gratitude for their holidays; and Zita stands in the road watching the car until it disappears at the bend, and then goes to see if any of the hens have laid eggs. And finds three, which will do for herself and Afrodite for their tea.

'So,' says Heather. 'Is it OK here?' They are sitting under the lemon tree and the chickens are scratching around over by the fence.

'It's all right,' says Zita. She could say that it was better than all right, but she is not ready – yet – to admit that to anyone, let alone Heather.

'Olga thinks she won't last much longer. She says all her aunts were like her – on their feet, bossing everyone about, until they just keel over one day and that's that.'

Zita shrugs her shoulders. Keeling over out of the blue is fine by her; a long and dependent illness would see her shouldering her rucksack and heading off to some other town. She is braced for finding Afrodite dead in her bed but she doesn't want to have to nurse her, and she is sure that Afrodite doesn't want it either.

'Olga says I have to say sorry to you,' says Heather. 'About the house, you know.'

'It's all right,' says Zita.

'She says you and I ought to be friends.' She says this hesitantly, as if it's an offer that might be snatched away. 'Actually –' Heather looks into the distance '– I'm not very good at being friends with someone.'

'Neither am I,' says Zita. 'In fact, I'm awful at it, honestly.'

'Even at school –'

'Especially at school –'

'Everyone had a best friend. Except me.'

'I only had one friend. Marion. The other kids called her Shorty – cos she was – and Goofy because she had sticky-out teeth. Even I called her that and I was supposed to be her best friend.'

'So is she still your friend?'

'I suppose she is. Except I don't see anything of her. Even when I was back home, I hardly saw her. Too busy.'

'You or her.'

'Her. Children, housework, working part-time. You know. We don't have much in common these days.'

'Do you write to her?'

'Sometimes,' says Zita, though she knows that the sometimes are far apart. 'Who do you write to?'

'Only my parents. There's not really a lot to say, is there. But I know they appreciate a letter, and they need to know I'm safe. Also, to tell you the truth, they send me money.'

'I'm older than you,' says Zita. 'I should be able to look after myself, money-wise.'

'And are you?'

Zita laughs. 'Skint,' she says. 'Completely. But I've got a bed to sleep in and food to eat. It'll do for now.' The thought crosses her mind that she could tell Heather about her family – her brother's miserable situation; her mother's illness and even her father's death, but no. Too soon, she thinks.

Instead she tells Heather about her first trip abroad with Terry; how daring it seemed at the time, how unprepared they were for being in a country that wasn't England, how foreign everything was, how horrible it was sometimes and what fun it was other times. She tells her about the café in Arles – 'Bigger than this,' she says, waving her hand at Afrodite's little house. 'She did proper cooking, Madame did. I was the skivvy – you know, peeling potatoes, cutting up onions, washing the pots. I wasn't very good at it, but she put up with me.'

'I was an au pair,' says Heather. 'And I'm no good with children, not at all. It was purgatory. I was so relieved when the parents decided they'd be better off sending them back to England to boarding school. Poor little mites.'

'I wouldn't want to have kids,' says Zita. 'My brother's got two, that he hardly ever sees. Marion's got three, Terry wanted to have four, but he got divorced after the first one.'

'I suppose it's different,' says Heather slowly, 'if – you know – you love someone.'

'I wouldn't know,' says Zita.

'No. Nor me.'

Silence fell. After you've said something like that, thinks Zita, there's nowhere the conversation can go. She waves her arms about to get rid of a crow which has landed to get at the chickens' food.

'Getting late,' says Heather. 'I should be getting back.'

'Tell Uli,' says Zita, 'that if he needs a helper on one of his walks – you know – I can probably get away for a morning.'

'He's stopped doing them,' says Heather. 'I offered to help but he says he hasn't got time. He says he has more dental work these days.'

'Pity,' says Zita. 'I used to like that bit of the job.'

'I think I would like it,' says Heather. 'But –'

'What?'

'We could do it. You and me.'

'I suppose.'

'Think about it,' says Heather, and stands up and walks across to where Uli's scooter is waiting for her. Then stops, turns and comes back to Zita.

'I have to say something,' she says. 'I sort of nearly said it but not properly. I want to say sorry to you, not because I took your job –'

'And my house.'

'– but because I should have let you know. I should have written you a letter so that you didn't have to come back –'

'I would have come back, anyway.'

'But you would have been prepared. I'm sorry, really. Writing a letter – not such a big deal is it. You wouldn't have been so upset, maybe. So – sorry. I mean it.'

'It's OK, honestly,' says Zita. 'It's done. It's all right.'

'Good,' says Heather, and this time she kicks the scooter into life and sets off down the road.

'Dear Cicely – I hope you are well. I got your letters and I always meant to write to you but I never got round to it. I am back in Crete and I often think of you whenever I see the sea, because of our time living on that little beach. I'm not near the beach here but I don't mind too much. I have a roof over my head which is the main thing and I help this old lady who has a little café but she's not really up to doing all the work herself. You would laugh if you saw me looking after the hens like you used to do in Corfu.'

There's not that much that needs saying to Cicely, except for the failure to reply to her letters, no real wrong has been done to her. But

Zita has decided to make some apologies of her own, and Cicely is the easiest to start with.

'Last time I saw you I wasn't in a good mood. Things weren't going very well. So I'm sorry if I seemed a bit grumpy. Things are better now.

I don't think I will ever have enough money to come to New Zealand but whenever you are in Greece come and see me.'

It's not satisfactory as a letter, she knows, but it's a first attempt. It will have to do. She has written it in the evening, sitting on an old chair at an old table in the garden. She can hear the clunk of goat bells from further up the hill. *I should have put that in*, she thinks, *to remind her of Greece*. But it's too late, she has stuck down the envelope and the next time she goes to the town she will buy stamps. Plural.

'You would laugh, Maz, if you saw me feeding the chickens and planting the vegetables with the old lady standing watching me to make sure I'm doing it right.

You were always a good friend to me. We had a lot of laughs didn't we.

I never said thank you to you for all the phone calls - I'm sorry if I bothered you. In fact I should say thank you to you for all the times you helped me, and your mum too. I shouldn't have taken you for granted like I did and I would like to make it up to you one day. I'm sorry I never came to say goodbye too.

Don't forget you are going to come and see me here one day.'

She seals the letter without reading it through; she knows it is not satisfactory. It's too short, but if she were to write more it would come out all wrong and she would have to start all over again. She seals the envelope – that's enough for today

On the day that Afrodite fails to get herself out of bed in the morning, Zita wastes no time in standing around wondering what to do. She pulls out the big old black bicycle from the outhouse and cycles down to the main road to telephone to Olga. Who arrives shortly after, with one of her cousins, and takes charge.

'What should I do?' says Zita, hovering uselessly, half in and half out of the kitchen.

There will be another cousin coming soon, Olga tells her, and possibly another aunt. Zita will not be needed, so as soon as she has dealt with the chickens, she must cycle along to the hotel and do what she can to help there. Which she willingly does, full of relief.

'Dear Douglas, I hope things are going well. I'm sending this to you at Mum's

house because I think you might be living there by now. I will be writing a letter to her too, just to tell her where I am, because I'm not at the hotel any more, though I still see the people from there sometimes.

I hope your children are OK and that you and Angel are getting on better.'

She really cannot think of anything else to say to her brother; she cannot even believe that it will matter to him whether he hears from her or not. She knows he will never reply.

Chapter Twenty-nine

'Letter for you,' says Betty. 'Looks like it must be from your Sally-Ann. Been forwarded from Sheffield by the look of it.'

Senga takes the letter. She would never have known what Douglas' handwriting looks like, but it must be him who has sent it on.

Dear Mum, I hope you are well and taking all your medication.

I am fine here now. The old lady I worked for has died but Olga says I can stay here for the time being, and do up the café and see if I can make it pay. Also, me and Heather have a plan to set up a little business taking tourists for walks in the country.

I haven't any plans to come back to Sheffield just yet but I will let you know if I ever do. I hope Dougie is looking after you properly.

Love from Zita.

P.S. Please say hello to Mrs Ward from me.

'What does she say?'

'Not much,' says Senga. 'But then she never has said much. The odd postcard – you know – Hope you are well I am fine. She's not one for a long letter, our Sally-Ann. Looks like she thinks I'm back in Sheffield.'

'I surmised as much,' says Betty. 'But I hope you're not thinking of going back just yet. I don't know what I would do without you, right enough. But you'll want to be seeing your Douglas, and your grandchildren.'

'Aye,' says Senga, doubtfully. 'But – I don't want to say this – but they are strangers to me. Our Dougie, well, he's a help if you ask him to do something for you but he's no company, never tells you a wee story, or a funny thing that happened. Even Willie was better at that sort of thing. And the children - well, they are teenagers now. It's too late for me to know them. I'm just some fat old white woman to them. I never even knew when their birthdays were. Nobody told me. I used to send them presents at Christmas but missing all those birthdays – I could cry when I think of it.'

'Och, hen,' says Betty. 'So you can stay with me for a bit longer.'

'I need to get back to Sheffield for my hospital appointment,' says Senga. 'Week after next. But –'

'But you'll come back,' says Betty. 'That's the best thing you could say. Go home and have a wee rest from me, and then, as soon as you feel like it, come back and help me again with Father, and the cooking and everything. I've told you, I feel a new woman since you've been here.'

'Thank you,' says Senga. She wipes a tear from each eye. No one has ever appreciated her like Betty does.

'And if you should be here with us when your Sally-Ann comes home, well, she can always come up here to see you. Sheffield to Dumbarton is nothing to what travelling she's done.'

But as it turns out, Senga will never again see her daughter. She will live for another decade, mostly with Betty, with occasional visits back down south – not too often, once or twice a year, to find Douglas occupying Sally-Ann's old bedroom and keeping the house as well as can be expected, for a man.

And Zita – Sally-Ann that was – will never again see her mother, or her brother. She will hear about her mother's death: she had a stroke, while on the MegaBus, on her way back to Scotland – but the funeral was over and done before the letter arrived, and there will never be another reason for Zita to go back. She does not think of Sheffield as home, although there are nights when she has bad dreams of being there, hanging on by her fingernails as if someone is wrenching her away from her old house, or else struggling to open a door which has been locked and the key lost. And a voice saying it's all her fault. She wakes up, on these occasions and looks round at her tiny, barely furnished bedroom with relief and joy.

It is a year or two after her mother's death that she is surprised by a letter from Terry. She shows it to Heather. 'What do you think? They can't both sleep here, him and his son. Should I book him into the hotel? Suppose he's already booked somewhere?'

'Hotel would be better,' advises Heather. 'You know my brother stayed there a year or so back. It was fine.'

'But you were right next door. I don't want him thinking I don't want to see him.'

'Look,' says Heather. 'He says they want to walk in the mountains. He'll be wanting taxis – or a bus at least. He won't find that out here, will he.'

'He could rent a car.'

'That's up to him,' says Heather briskly. 'Look, I'll book him a twin room, half board. You write and tell him. If it's wrong I'll change it and no one ever needs to know.'

These days, Heather is Olga's right-hand person, practically running the show as Olga gets older and more dithery, and Uli gets more grumpy. Zita thinks to herself that she would have done just as good a job, but finds that, mostly, she doesn't care. They still have the Tourist Walks business, but Heather now is too busy to do more than check the books and join the occasional walk on her day off.

So Terry and Adam arrive with their rucksacks and boots and maps of the White Mountains, and Zita closes the café for the length of their stay so that she can be available to accompany them. If they want me that is, she thinks, ready to be disappointed.

She meets Adam in the hotel lobby, while Terry is still in the shower after their journey.

'You must be Adam?' she says, tentatively. Though he has Ros' blond hair and blue eyes, his whole being says he is part of the Brown family; he has the smile, the ease, the eagerness.

'You must be Zita,' he says.

Then Terry appears, and hugs her. 'How long is it?' he says. 'I've been trying to work it out – how long?'

'Fifteen years,' she says.

'You haven't changed,' he says. 'I would have known you anywhere.'

Then Olga appears, and Heather, and there are handshakes and explanations, and they go to the bar, and then walk around the town, and come back to the hotel to eat, and go back to the bar, and although Zita is careful about how much she has to drink, she finds herself, riding her little moped back to her cottage, feeling quite giggly, and a bit wobbly, and full of plans for the week ahead.

When she looks back on it, it was a good week, a week of walking. Once or twice Adam decided to stay beside the pool, and Zita and Terry walked together, talking of old times, of his parents and his brothers, of his promotion to Deputy Head, of Adam's degree and the job he was hoping to be interviewed for when they arrived back home. On two of the days Zita had walks booked in anyway, and her visitors joined in on one of them, and went off together to the mountains on the other day.

She meets them in the evening for dinner in town. 'How was it?'

'Hot.' But they had completed what they set out to do, seen vultures and snakes, and views of the sea to all sides. 'Something a bit less taxing tomorrow.'

'I haven't swum in the sea yet,' says Adam. 'Beach day tomorrow, and then it's our last day. Already. What should we do for a last day?'

Zita has no doubt. 'Samaria Gorge.'

'But,' says Terry, 'isn't it just a tourist trap? And we've been down a gorge already, with you.'

'That was a little one,' says Zita. 'Still, you don't have to do it if you don't want to, but this might be the only time you come to Crete – well, you might find you've missed out.'

'I'm up for it,' says Adam. 'Go on Dad.'

'Early start,' says Zita. 'Bus station eight o'clock. Sandwiches, water, swimming trunks on under your shorts.'

'When did you get to be so bossy?' says Terry. 'Hey, that was a joke, I'm not having a go at you. Just – you've changed a bit since I first knew you.'

Zita shrugs. 'Just grown up a bit I suppose. It happens.'

'Not to dad it doesn't,' says Adam. 'I tell you, my Nan and Grandad are so proud of him, and at the same time they can't believe it – "Our Terry? Him that never took anything seriously? In charge of something? Give over?"'

Zita laughs. 'I know what they mean. This is the man who lost his wallet in the south of France, and nearly had to have his foot amputated in India.'

'And would do it all again if I was still twenty-one. Wouldn't you?'

Zita thinks for a long time before she smiles and says, 'Yes.'

The bus drives away to the airport; Zita stands in the road – it's six-thirty in the morning – and waves until it turns the corner. It will be another fifteen years before she sees him again.

'Come in and get some breakfast,' says Heather.

*

'Believe it or not,' writes Marion, 'Hubby and I have been married forty years, and we think it's time to celebrate. Do you think you could wangle us a discount at that hotel?'

Well, no, not really but seeing as it is for Marion, Zita is prepared to subsidise her without her knowing. She reads the rest of the letter. 'All the kids are coming, and the grandkids, but don't worry – they are staying in a villa. They said me and Brian could stay in it with them but some of the babies aren't even sleeping through the night yet, so we fancy a quiet time in a nice hotel.'

It is May when they came, a little out of season for swimming, but Marion says that's fine, her swimming costume days are over, if in fact she ever had any.

Zita still, in some of her moods, could cry when she remembers how she looked forward to it, and what a disappointment it turned out to be. All her plans for walks and outings, all her expectations of long evenings of talking about their lives, past and present – all wasted and what – spurned; yes spurned. Marion and Brian did not want to walk anywhere, they hired a car and drove to a beach. Any beach would do, as long as it had a café or a bar. There they surrounded themselves with Faye and Ryan and Mark, and the spouses and small children of Faye and Ryan and Mark, and although they invited Zita to join them, and she tried to every day, she did not feel – wanted. They did not want her. She failed to be properly interested in the five small children of various sizes, and the five small children seemed to know this, for they shrank away from this tall old woman who wasn't like their own dear Nannan.

And that was all Marion and Brian wanted to do, sit on a beach and be surrounded by buckets and spades and damp towels and bottles of baby food, and to talk to Faye and to the two daughters-in-law about the coming through of back teeth, and MMR vaccinations and whether boys were easier than girls, or the other way round, while Brian and the young men talked about cars and football, as far as Zita could understand. And food. Zita tried to hold on to her plan for what she hoped Marion and Brian would do with their holiday, but she failed. They did not want to see anything archaeological, either in a museum or on the ground; they were not impressed or charmed by Zita's little home; they did not take to Heather. Brian said outright that he preferred Spain, and Zita caught Marion nodding in agreement. And Marion did not talk of old times but only of her children and grandchildren and their achievements and prospects, while Zita, having no children, had nothing to offer for conversation.

At the end of the ten days, Zita again gets up early to go and see them onto the bus to the airport.

'I shall be glad to get home,' says Marion loudly to Ryan, and he, seeing that Zita was within hearing distance, assures his mother that it has been a good holiday, nice beaches, plenty of food, only some of the babies were a bit too young to appreciate it all.

Zita says – because she feels she has to try one more time – 'Maybe you can come again next year, just you and Brian. I could show you round properly.'

Marion does not answer.

*

'I have an email for you,' says Heather.

Heather still works at the hotel, days and weeks and years of confirming bookings, counting groceries, training maids, advising guests about taxis and buses and places to eat. Uli has died in the hospital in Heraklion, and Olga has sold the hotel to new owners who have changed it completely – new furnishings, new pool, 'all up to date' they said, and up-to-date includes office computers and the innovation called email, but Heather is still there. Zita has had her own days and weeks and years of selling eggs and cups of coffee, of looking after the hens and tending the garden and the lemon tree, and sometimes helping out in the hotel too.

The email is from Terry, with the suggestion that he should come and see her again.

'Show me how to reply,' she says to Heather.

'What do you want to say?'

What does she want to say? To ask why it has been so long? To tell him that she doesn't want him if he's going to be like Marion was? To say, Sorry but she doesn't like visitors?

'He says to book him a room, single if we have one, half board,' says Heather. 'Shall I do it?'

Zita looks around the office – she'd only popped in to the hotel to bring some eggs and say hello to Heather.

'What do you think?'

'I'll book him in,' says Heather. 'When he's here you can avoid him completely if you want.'

'I suppose,' says Zita.

The Terry who arrives, on his own, in the last week of August – 'just having a break before the new school year' – seems like a weary man, without his usual bounce. He has put on weight and now wears glasses – Zita at first does not recognise him as he steps off the airport bus along with twenty or so other people. But he seems to recognise her straightaway, though he turns away to collect his luggage – only a medium sized rucksack – from the compartment.

Then he seems to gather himself, find a bit of a smile from somewhere and come towards her. There is no hugging this time.

'Hello Zee,' he says and even Zita can feel what an effort it is for him. Then he stands and looks up at the hotel, and shrugs his shoulders as if to say, Well, I'm here – just have to get on with it.

Zita says, 'You look tired. Why don't you go and get your room, and have a bit of sleep, and I'll come over this evening and we can have a drink.'

'My Mum died,' he says.

'Oh,' she says. 'When?' And then, remembering what people say – 'I'm so sorry.'

He shrugs, and picks up his rucksack and turns to the steps.

'See you later,' says Zita, but so quietly that she does not know if he heard.

She is hesitant about going back to the hotel in the evening – she even phones Heather at the hotel to ask her advice.

'What do I know?' says Heather. 'He's your friend, not mine. Why don't you just come on over and wait in the bar, see if he joins you.'

'What do I say about his Mum though? What do people say?'

'*I* don't know, do I? Ask him he wants to talk about it I suppose. Just be nice to him. *I* don't know.' And she put the phone down smartly to let Zita know that she is too busy to even pretend to be helpful.

She should have known – there is no need to ask Terry anything. As soon as he sits down in front of his glass of wine, he begins to tell her – what hospital she was in, how his dad broke the news to the boys, how Darren came all the way from Poland but too late, what the doctors said, how Peggy managed to keep smiling, how he, Terry, had been run off his feet at work, even while he could think of nothing beyond her operation, her treatment, his latest visit to her, his next visit, how he would break it to Adam – 'It's like having half a dozen radio stations all playing at once,' he says. 'And I know school's been closed for the holiday but I was so behind with everything, I've been in there every day, and then evenings I've been to my dad, poor bloke, *he* doesn't know how to cope – but our Barry's there now, and his girls.' He looks at his glass of wine as if he had forgotten it was there, and lifts it and chinks it against hers. 'I just needed to get away and I thought, Crete, and Zita, that's the most peaceful place for me. I hope you don't mind.'

'I'm sorry I –' says Zita. She was going to say 'can't cry' when she finds her eyes full of tears, and wipes them hurriedly away, for fear that he thinks she is pretending.

'She'd be glad I've come to see you,' says Terry. 'She always liked you.'

'She was always lovely to me,' says Zita. 'I wish I'd kept in touch better.'

They have a week together – it's like being back in the south of France all those years ago, except that Zita knows where they are so there is no getting lost, and they stay mostly away from other people, so there are no new acquaintances advising them and telling their stories and trying to borrow money. And they are not poor any longer so they have proper meals, and can take a taxi if they want to.

And – though Terry, understandably, talks mostly about his Mum, his dad and brothers, and Adam – Zita, though she never expected it to happen, has become the authority here. She knows the paths, the gates, the taxi drivers. She knows the weather and the quietest places to eat, and she knows – somehow without knowing how she knows – how to fall in with Terry's changing moods, when to suggest they move on, when to check what he wants and when just to tell him where they will go next. They spend time just sitting in her garden, watching the chickens peck and hearing the sound of the goat bells in the late afternoon.

'So peaceful,' he says. 'This is what you should do Zee, make it like a B & B for people who need a break from their lives. You know, need a bit of peace and quiet.'

'No,' she says. 'I like it the way it is. *You* can come here whenever you like, and so can Heather, and Olga, but if it was strangers – *here* – it wouldn't be peaceful anymore.'

'Going home tomorrow,' he says. 'Even if I don't come back soon, I'll always see you in your little hut–'

'–house.'

'Hut–'

'Home.'

'All right, home.'

She is still there, in Afrodite's little house, which she bought from Olga's family when she and Heather sold the walks business for what seemed to them a handsome sum. You can still get a cup of coffee or a soft drink from her little café, if you are lucky enough to find it open. She has electricity now, though it can be intermittent.

She does not write letters any more; she sees hardly anyone. Olga and Uli are dead; for all she knows so Dougie might be. Heather went back home in England, to look after her own mother, thinking it would not be long before she could return. I could have told her, thinks Zita – her mother will live to be a hundred and I'll never see Heather again, so what's the point of writing, especially when there's no news to put in a letter.

Zita no longer takes people to Samaria; she no longer even goes there by herself. She is seventy-six now; she has lived longer than her mother did, or her father. She is still as tall and even more gaunt. Her hair, white, is long again, has been for years now, wisps of it escaping from the rubber band that is supposed to keep it out of her eyes. Often her café is closed, because she likes to walk, through the olive groves, on her own, just looking about her, feeling the sun on her shoulders, looking inland to the mountains, or northward to the sea. She greets people and they greet her. She is known, she is invited to weddings and christenings, and she knows how much money she is expected to give on those occasions.

She is an old woman, who was once a young woman who was puzzled by the nature of love. And is still. Did my parents love each other, she still wonders? And if they did, why was it different to what was between Terry's parents, Peggy and Lawrence? And if Terry grew up seeing that, between his parents, that calm and sober cheerfulness, why could he not find the same with Ros? How come Marion and Brian could seem to have something like it? What is it, she wonders, that keeps people together, that makes people believe they will be happy with this or that person.

And as she walks past the farms where the dogs bark at her from their chains, and past the olive groves and the tiny churches and the places where people believe there are Minoan graves, she thinks of these things, and wonders, and when she gets back to her little house, and lets the hens out and looks to see if there are eggs, to eat or to sell, she finds herself smiling a little, because her life has been her own, and is still her own, and is the one – she believes now – is the one that she wanted all along.

Dear Reader

If you enjoyed reading this it would be great if you could do a quick review on Amazon, Goodreads or whatever book review sites you use: a line or two would be great. Reviews and personal recommendations are really appreciated by authors and small publishers and help us to keep doing what we do.

Please also have a look at the other books by Susan Day:

Who your Friends are

Back in the 1950s Pat and Rita are childhood best friends, but their lives diverge. Rita is ambitious and determined and becomes successful in a way neither her family nor Pat would ever have imagined. Pat's life is of marriage, children, a job as a carer – she follows Rita's career with interest but without envy, always believing in the enduring quality of their friendship. When Pat finds herself without a job, with her children all grown up and time on her hands, he past history with Rita is due for a reassessment.

Hollin Clough

Jen admires her father and Frank believes that his daughters are happy, but no one in any family knows the whole story. This family has fractured before, and been patched up by secrets and evasions. Now things are about to change.

The Roads they Travelled

A moving saga about the lives of four young women who live through the precariousness of the Second World War, telling how the events that unfold in the following fifty years shape them and their children.

Watershed

Pamela, is a teacher at the end of her career. The death of her twin sister and the fall-out from that has an impact on her and the wider family. Her own coming to terms with it is slow and difficult as she reflects on and is intertwined with flood events from 1953, with the Great Sheffield Flood, and the more recent flooding in 2007.

Back

Everyone in this novel would like to go back in one way or another: recently widowed Bill's search for Joan, a lost love from his student days. Then there's Viv, Joan's friend who gets entangled in Bill's search. The adventures of all three are woven into a comedy of errors.

Lostlings

Nothing is more important to Lynn and Dave Wilde than family: two married daughters and a newly married son, Jamie. Jamie's wife, Niecey, is an enigma – she appears to have no family, no friends and no past. Jamie discovers, by accident, two birth certificates and consults his parents and sisters about what this might mean: are they Niecey's children? Does this explain her constant wandering around the city, her hovering outside school gates? The secret gradually comes out...

Milton Keynes UK
Ingram Content Group UK Ltd.
UKHW040943130923
428595UK00001B/4